The Primrose Pursuit

By Suzette A. Hill

A Little Murder
The Venetian Venture
A Southwold Mystery

The Primrose Pursuit

a&b

The Primrose Pursuit

SUZETTE A. HILL

Allison & Busby Limited
12 Fitzroy Mews
London W1T 6DW
allisonandbusby.com

First published in Great Britain by Allison & Busby in 2016.

Copyright © 2016 by Suzette A. Hill

A CIP catalogue record for this book is available from
the British Library.

First Edition

ISBN 978-0-7490-1967-9

Typeset in 11/15.75 pt Sabon by
Allison & Busby Ltd.

The paper used for this Allison & Busby publication
has been produced from trees that have been legally sourced
from well-managed and credibly certified forests.

Printed and bound by
CPI Group (UK) Ltd, Croydon, CR0 4YY

To the memory of Alexander Wedderspoon,
who had a soft spot for Primrose

AUTHOR'S PREFACE

The events of this tale are set in the Lewes area of Sussex towards the close of the 1950s. Primrose Oughterard is the assertive sister of the late Revd Francis Oughterard who, when living in Molehill, Surrey, had the misfortune of inadvertently slaying one of his parishioners, the cloying Elizabeth Fotherington. This caused the amiable vicar some consternation, and severely intruded upon his hitherto quiet and blameless life. Thus for several years he lived in constant fear of the hangman's noose – and the officious attentions of his episcopal superior, Horace Clinker. His fumbling efforts to elude both are recounted in *A Load of Old Bones* and in his four subsequent diaries, the final being *A Bedlam of Bones*. Following his death (not on the scaffold but in an equally distinctive context), Primrose commandeered his dog and cat – the intrepid Bouncer and fiendish Maurice – and has taken them to live with her in her Sussex home. Meanwhile, her brother sleeps securely in the Molehill churchyard, his misdemeanour undetected by the police and his reputation intact.

CHAPTER ONE

My dear Agnes,
Of course I am awfully fond of Primrose, she's such
a brick. But there are times when she is what you
might call 'overpowering' . . . well she overpowers
me at any rate! As I think she did that brother
of hers: the vicar Francis Oughterard – he who
died falling from the church tower rescuing that
tiresome Briggs woman from being impaled on a
gargoyle. Naturally, poor Primrose was terribly
cut up at the time, but as you might expect she
has coped bravely with the event and has actually
taken custody of those slightly disturbing pets her
brother would insist on keeping – Maurice, the cat
is called, and that distinctly dubious mongrel dog
Bilious or Bouncer or some such; begins with a 'B'
at any rate.
Still, the point is not so much the animals as
their new custodian, our dear friend Primrose. She

9

is behaving a little oddly – odder than usual I mean. Or at least it is not so much her behaviour that is odd as her words: she has been saying some rather strange things about the school's new Latin master, Hubert Topping. You may remember my telling you about him: arrived in mid-term to replace old Appleyard who went gaga and had to be put away. Topping's application was a godsend – there was nobody else – and the headmaster, Mr Winchbrooke, appointed him immediately. We were all very relieved, as grappling with Latin verbs has a most constructive effect on the third-formers. At that stage – when they know they are about to transfer to the big school – they become so bumptious, and a dose of classical rigour cuts them down to size. Topping has been doing that most successfully and we are all extremely grateful.

So I was somewhat taken aback when Primrose announced to me across the tea-table that she proposed keeping her eye on him. When I asked why on earth she should want to do that, she replied that it was not a case of her wanting to but that it formed part of her civic duty.

Well, as you can imagine, I had no idea what she meant! I don't know about you, Agnes, but personally I have never associated civic duty with Primrose Oughterard . . . You will recall for example that awful fracas with the council over the town clerk's allocated parking space: declared she had parked there all her life – since living in Sussex anyway – and had no intention of yielding her rights to 'pettifogging public functionaries and that he must take his chances with the rest of us'.

She got her way too! As she did in the matter of the proposed rates rise to fund the aldermanic robes: refused point blank to cough up, saying she didn't toil away all day at her easel just to subsidise the mayor and his penchant for dressing up in a garb which made him look like a demented mushroom. Personally, I think that was fair comment – though had he looked less like a mushroom, demented or otherwise, and more like Errol Flynn I wonder if her views would have been the same?

Well one thing is for sure, nobody could mistake Hubert Topping for Errol Flynn; a less swashbuckling man it would be hard to find. However, the boys seem to like him – which is why I cannot understand Primrose's current concern. It has, I gather, something to do with the tone of his voice and the fact that he reads the Manchester Guardian: *the first is too soft and the second too pink. But when I said, 'My dear Primrose, you can hardly hold pink reading matter and a quiet voice against him,' she said, 'Oh yes, I can,' and added darkly that there were other things too.*

What other things I failed to learn, as at that moment the new dog shambled into the room and all attention was directed to its bone, its basket, the type of dog food it should be supplied with, the state of its toenails and my views on whether it would look best in a blue or a red collar. As its facial features were largely obscured by fronds of matted fur and a cascading fringe, I thought the question immaterial. However, wishing to be tactful I said that since she was the artist I would leave such aesthetic choices to her, but whatever she selected it was bound to add to the creature's undoubted charm. (NB My father used to say that if one were going to tell a lie it should be an absolute whopper – no point in sinning by halves.)

Anyway, rather frustratingly the dog palaver diverted us from the school's most recent appointee; though doubtless the topic will be resumed. As you know, unlike her late brother, Primrose has an impressive faith in her own judgement, and once she has a bee in her bonnet few things will dislodge it. Such a bee is evidently mild Mr Topping and her conviction that his surveillance is to form part of her social responsibility. I shall be rather glad when you and Charles return from Tobago. Charles has a firm hand which on the whole I think Primrose rather respects. She defers to few people but your husband is one of them.

How nice it will be to see you both back here in May with the first call of the cuckoo and the boys at the nets. I am already planning my new series of nature walks – those South Down rambles are such an education for the London boarders and even our local boys seem to enjoy them, or so they tell me (though in my experience a measure of sharp scepticism rarely comes amiss when dealing with the young). I wonder if I can get Mr Topping to join our jaunts – a means of escape from P's vigilance perhaps? . . . Heigh-ho, bring on the summer I say. Won't be long now!

Your good friend,
Emily

CHAPTER TWO

The Primrose Version

Curbing the dog may be a problem. I do not mean quelling the racket he makes in the garden or indeed persuading him to remove his bones from the conservatory . . . No, it is simply that he will keep on *staring*: occasionally at the cat, but principally at me. Not being used to others in the house I find such scrutiny unsettling and wonder whether he did the same with my brother. I daresay. But then Francis may not have noticed, his mind usually being otherwise engaged – largely with the matter of Elizabeth Fotherington, his tiresome victim (or at any rate with the police and how to foil their intrusive curiosity). Well thank goodness one has seen the back of that palaver! Death does have its compensations, and dear Francis has gone to his grave without a stain besmirching the family name. One must be thankful for such mercies. Indeed that is largely why I have seen fit to adopt his companions Maurice and Bouncer. Under the circumstances it was the least I could do. I think Francis would have approved, and it is a way of giving thanks that Ma and Pa continue to rest easy in their own graves, reputations untainted by one of their son's more unfortunate gaffes . . .

I wonder if the dog stares because it is expecting me to sit down and play the piano as its master used to. I gather it rather enjoyed the ritual. Well I am afraid there is no piano in this house – though I suppose the creature could come and watch me paint if it wanted to. However, a musical ear is no guarantee of a discerning eye – least of all with that fringe! – and it might feel short-changed. Perhaps I could persuade the prep school band to come in once a month and give a little display. Would that suit it? I can hardly ask. And what about Maurice? Does he have preferences? Francis would recite long catalogues of the cat's phobias but it was never made clear what it actually *liked*. Not much I suspect, except for haddock and making mischief . . . Though I must say that so far it has been strangely civil – too civil really. In fact like the dog's, its behaviour is slightly unnerving. Just now, for instance, after I had come down from the studio, there it was sprawled in the middle of the hall rug mewling like a kitten and waving one of its paws in the air (the one with the white glove). 'Hello,' I said, 'what's up with you?' Whereupon it leapt up, twirled round in circles and then slowly approached me doing what I can only describe as a feline version of a rumba. Then with a sort of falsetto purr it parked itself on my foot and wouldn't budge until I had ruffled its ears. I am not used to such mateyness from Maurice. During my visits to the vicarage the cat would spend most of its time on the top stair looking poisonous; and on the few occasions that Francis brought the pair of

14

them down here to Lewes it stalked about in calculated disdain. I find the current warmth slightly sinister.

And talking of sinister, I am not enamoured of the new Latin master at Erasmus House: Topping by name but not topping by nature – not in my book anyhow. There's something about him that I *know* to be pure fake. Pa was awfully good at spotting fakes, human ones at any rate – couldn't tell a Landseer from a Lautrec, of course – and it is something I have inherited. I mentioned my doubts to Emily and she seemed bemused. She often is I have noticed. Now I am fond of Emily, but I have to say that while she may be a very sharp school secretary (the headmaster would be lost without her) I sometimes feel she is not entirely on my wavelength . . . though that may be said of a number of people. Curious really. Ah well, it takes all sorts. And it must be admitted that Francis and I were not always at one; but we did share a kind of stumbling empathy and now that he is gone I feel oddly naked.

Still, it's no use looking backwards as Pa would say: not that his forward looking was especially clear. The great thing is to grasp the nettle, *carpe* the *diem*, gather the rosebuds and stride ahead . . . Which takes me back to Hubert Topping. A man who makes a fetish of wearing a rose in his buttonhole every day is immediately suspect, particularly as the colour is invariably the same: pink. Goes with the shade of his newspaper presumably. Besides, where does he get such things at this time of year? Flown in from Madeira? Especially cultivated at Kew? If so, he must have a great deal of money to afford such daily indulgence – and in that case what is he doing teaching Latin declensions in a minor prep school on the south coast? Perhaps he is a shopwalker manqué, or a stockbroker gone bust and spending his final shillings on frippery, or a retired actor keen to retain the thespian mode (was that the flash of a crêpe sole I saw in church the other day?). Well whatever he is, a bona fide schoolmaster he is not. Apart from anything else the voice is too quiet – you need strong lungs to deal with those little Turks, as I know to my cost when I go there periodically to judge their questionable daubings. I arrive home so hoarse I can barely swallow the gin. So I doubt that his dulcet mumbling of '*amo, amas, amat*' can do much for their education.

Emily asked me recently whether I was being a mite pernickety. 'Certainly not,' I replied, 'you need your wits about you in this life.' And I reminded her that had I been less pernickety with the town clerk his dastardly requisition of that parking space would have gone unnoticed. Fortunately with my intervention he lost it within the week. It also occurred to me – though naturally I didn't say this to Emily – that had poor Francis been a little *more* pernickety about his choice of woodland walks he might never have encountered Elizabeth that fatal day, and thus been spared the distasteful consequences . . .

However, as said, it doesn't do to dwell on the past; one must look forward, such as to an aperitif and then a downland ramble with the dog. I just hope he doesn't alarm our Sussex sheep as he did the goats in the Auvergne . . . but they were French, of course, and couldn't cope.

CHAPTER THREE

The Cat's View

Being of a sensitive nature I have found these last few days somewhat trying. Our master's untimely, and characteristically careless, demise was an unsettling experience for all of us, and the period following his spectacular plunge from the church tower was not only vexing to the spirit but also bad for my digestion. One gets used to certain humans – even one as insane as the vicar – and naturally his sudden loss occasioned some dismay. But being deprived of our customary victuals for at least two days was, I consider, the height of ill-manners: a disgraceful oversight which only goes to show how thoughtless the human species becomes when faced with the unexpected.

Oh I do not mean that they left us to starve exactly, but their idea of a suitable diet was far from satisfactory. Would you believe it – they resorted to *tins*. Even F.O. in his wildest moments would have baulked at that. However, all is not lost, for today the vicar's sister, Primrose, arrived to take us to live with her near Lewes in Sussex. Naturally, I reserve my optimism as it doesn't do to anticipate things. Nevertheless during our previous visits here I had found the territory not uncongenial and so like to think that there is an even chance of things being acceptable. We shall see . . .

In my kittenhood I was regularly reminded by my illustrious great-uncle that circumstances alter cases. He was a fund of sage observations and I clearly benefited from his tutelage. It has made me the cat I am: shrewd, practical and well versed in the inanities of human psychology. However, I have to say that in this particular instance Great-Uncle Marmaduke's dictum may have been a trifle flawed. You see, while our circumstances are undoubtedly *changed* following our master's loss, as far as I can make out the *case* of Bouncer remains resolutely static. Since our arrival, I have watched the dog closely in the vain hope of seeing some improvement; but alas, as yet there is not one sign of alteration. Brazen, loud and barbarous, the dog and its manners remain much the same in the sister's domain as they had been in the brother's. There is a faint chance that the Sussex air and coastal winds may have some ameliorative effect but on the whole I suspect the odds are against. No, I have to admit that contrary to Marmaduke's pronouncement, cases do not always alter – however shifting the circumstances.

Take today, for example. He had made his first visit to the rabbit hutch in the garden, or at least his first since our arrival – there had been an unfortunate previous encounter with these creatures as noted in my past memoir – and the result was disastrous. For the inmates, of course. You would think that our transfer from Surrey to Sussex being

18

permanent the dog would be on its best behaviour and ready to bury old hatchets (or bones). Not one bit! He came racing back to the house whooping and roaring, and telling me what a fine fellow he was for having 'buggered up' the chinchillas' morning. Apparently Karloff had collapsed in dazed stupor and Boris had flown into a rage of gothic frenzy, a fact that afforded Bouncer much merriment. I was less amused – indeed, I remonstrated with him fiercely.

'Really, Bouncer,' I protested, 'has it not occurred to you that we are no longer mere guests in Primrose's household but *residents*? It doesn't do to antagonise the natives, there could be unfortunate repercussions.'

For a moment he looked puzzled, and then said, 'You mean if I badger them enough the bunnies might go even more bananas?'

'Exactly,' I said, glad that he had grasped the point.

'Whah-ho!' was the response. And with tail flailing like a manic windmill he floundered off into the kitchen in search of food.

I closed my eyes in despair; but opened them quickly for at that moment P.O. had appeared draped in one of her paint-spattered smocks (not unlike F.O.'s surplice, though the defacements on his had tended to be cigarette burns). She carried a brush in one hand and a turpentine bottle in the other and was evidently on her way to or from the studio.

I dislike the smell of turpentine, ranking it little better than the odour of incense for which her brother had such a penchant, but nevertheless emitted a winsome miaow and made gestures of approval. She looked startled but I persisted, going so far as to make a couple of playful pirouettes and to show interest in her left shoe. You may wonder at such antics, but again I am in debt to the wisdom of Uncle Marmaduke. '*Never* compromise with humans,' he had warned, 'unless it be to your advantage.' The advice has been invaluable and I have followed it faithfully. Thus in view of Bouncer's crass goading of the chinchillas I thought it politic to affect an air of silken deference – a temporary device naturally, but necessary to secure our acceptance in the new ménage.

This ménage I may say is not without its merits, having a large, ill-kempt garden, a warm stone wall and no immediate neighbours. Admittedly the shrubbery does harbour two hedgehogs but so far they have been suitably respectful – though what will happen once the dog gets wind of them I am uncertain. And while our late master's cabaret of blunders had been a source of painful amusement it is reassuring to think that life in the *artist*'s household will be less ruffled than that of the vicarage. It will certainly be more regular for I am glad to note that our new mistress is timely in serving my meals, a courtesy her brother could never quite grasp – but then efficiency never was his strong point. Ah well, *nil nisi bonum* . . . And to give him his due, as human beings go, he was a kindly creature. Just absurd.

Mind you, absurdity is not the prerogative of vicars, for in my experience many are so afflicted: tabby cats, field mice, writers, gravediggers, schoolmasters, pedigree dogs, mongrel dogs, policemen, vets, squirrels, most dog owners, all speckled hens, elderly bicyclists, youthful bicyclists, beards (male or female), bell ringers and bishops . . . The list is endless but its repetition a useful way of inducing sleep on the rare occasions when such aid is needed. Not that I expect insomnia in our new environment – unless, of course, P.O. were so foolish as to follow F.O.'s example and eliminate one of the locals. (A merry jest and one that I must remember to tell Bouncer!) Yes, I think I can confidently predict that my days here will be passed in leisured sanity, untrammelled by the disruptive practices at Molehill and of our previous associates. There is one problem that remains, of course: the dog. If I can curb him all will be well.

CHAPTER FOUR

The Dog's View

I am getting the hang of this place now and it's better than I thought, much better in fact. True, we don't have the vicar's graveyard to race around in and I do miss him pounding the old ivories; but the swirls of fag smoke are much the same, and his sister, Primrose, has given me a brand-new basket and a really fancy rug to go with it. Mind you, I was a bit miffed about that at first and didn't go near either of them. I mean it's quite a shock for a fellow to have his special hairy bedding taken away and to be told to kip in something all fresh and *foreign*. For a start it smelt different . . . No, that's not right, it didn't smell at all! What do you think of that? Not nice, I can tell you. In fact I took a leaf out of the cat's book and went into a SULK. You didn't think Bouncer could do that, did you? Well yes, it did seem a bit strange at first, but I've seen Maurice doing it often enough and thought I would have a go too. So I crawled under her kitchen table, made god-awful panting noises and didn't touch my grub for a

22

WHOLE DAY! Maurice told me I was in a trormer (or some such word) due to loss of basket. I told him I didn't care what I was in but that I jolly well wasn't going to have my kit interfered with!

Anyway, unlike F.O., P.O. seems to notice things and she soon twigged that I was out of sorts. And do you know what she did? Went to the dustbin, fished out my old rug and put it on top of the new. I thought that was quite sporting and so made it clear that I could manage a little food after all. Don't suppose F.O. would have done that: just effed and blinded and crunched his humbugs.

But you know, it still feels a bit off without him; though I'm not too sad as Maurice says he has gone to where all good dogs and vicars go: to the wondrous kennel in the sky, full of gin and bones and really good smells like rotting rabbit and that smoky stuff he used to spray the church with which made me sneeze. Oh yes, he'll be fine up there all right. In fact I expect I'll join him one day; you never know, it could be pretty good fun. But *meanwhile* there are important things to do down here, i.e. get the lie of the land and the measure of our new owner.

You see it's all right for Maurice (so far as anything ever *is* right for the cat) because he has already had one lady owner – the Fotherington woman who the vicar did in. So I suppose he knows a bit about mistresses. But I've only had masters, so having the Prim to deal with may be tricky. Maurice says the thing to do is to watch closely and keep quiet. He says it's all about making the right . . . uhm . . . *assment* or some such, and then acting accordingly. I'm not too good at keeping quiet myself – never seen the point of it – but I think I can make an ass-whatsit all right, it just needs concentration. The great thing is to keep a guard on your rear. F.O. was always having to guard his, so I expect I've learnt a bit from him. Besides, I've got what the cat hasn't: sixth sense. Maurice doesn't like me talking about that, says he doesn't believe in it and it's all *non*-sense. But I know what I know, and it comes in pretty handy, I can tell you. So I'll use some of it to get P.O.'s number . . . A bit of the old dog-nous beats cat-craft any day!

And talking of getting numbers, I went to inspect the chinchillas this morning, the same ones that were here when we came before – Boris and Karloff. They got a shock all right. I was just strolling casually up to their cage door (well, not strolling exactly – sort of charging), when I heard Boris say, 'Oh my arse and whiskers, there's that's blithering dog again!' 'Which one?' its mate asked. 'The bouncing bugger,' roared Boris, 'take cover!' And that's what they did: scuttled into the back of their hutch and stayed there like stuck hedgehogs. All I could see were those pink mad eyes glowing in the dark.

Ho! Ho! I thought, three can play at that game! So I sat down on my haunches and waited patiently, pretending to be Maurice. In fact I even tried doing one of the cat's special miaows (you know the sort, those awful rump-freezing ones), but somehow I couldn't quite get the hang of it and it came out sounding a bit odd – odder even than when Maurice lets fly. Still, it seemed to do the trick as the next moment there was a great thumping and squeaking from inside and I knew it was Karloff having the vapours. And then Boris broke cover and hurled himself against the mesh shouting 'Swine!' Personally I thought that was what the cat would call 'common' and told him to calm down otherwise he might trip over one of his stupid lugholes. (I mean what self-respecting rabbit has ears that sweep

24

the ground? Plain daft I call it.) I could see he didn't like that as he started tearing chunks out of his soppy carrot and spitting them on the ground. A right old mess he was making, and I pointed out that if *I* made that sort of mess in the kitchen I'd get the slipper. He squeaked back that he had every right to make a sodding mess if he wanted and that if he were my human owner it wasn't a slipper I'd get but a socking great boot. I thought that was RUDE.

Just goes to show, anyone can see that these chinchillas are 'not used to polite society' as Maurice would say. Still, they are better sport than that Mavis Briggs person who used to plague the vicar; so all in all I think I could get to like it here. As the cat says, it's just a question of waiting upon events . . . or as I would say, cocking your ears (or leg for that matter) and sniffing the wind. NO FLEAS ON BOUNCER!

CHAPTER FIVE

My dear Agnes,

Delighted to hear how well things have been going in Tobago and that Charles's horticultural researches are a success. What fun it will be to see Podmore Place quite transformed with the new plantings once you are back. How brave to tackle its total restoration!

Meanwhile, life here jogs along in its customary way: hacking coughs among the juniors – I often think they put it on just to get into the san; Erskine Minor's parents being difficult as usual; the penance of the Spring Fair (why will Miss Twigg insist on a gym display? It's not as if anyone enjoys it, least of all the participants); the termly tests with the usual rows over cheating – not my domain fortunately; and young Mr Cheesman, who, having attended a half-day course on child therapy, has come up with the scintillating idea of each boy being assigned a pet rat to look after. I ask you! He says it would be good for their psyches (the children's not the rats'). It certainly won't help my psyche to find one of those little beasts leering at me from the office filing cabinet! Thus I told Mr Cheesman that while it was a most inventive plan I rather doubted if the headmaster would sanction the cost – pointing out that rats were noted for their voracious appetite. He looked most crestfallen and murmured something to the effect that money was of small account compared with the nurture of a child's soul . . . You know, I rather suspect that he doesn't intend staying with us much longer: better suited to being a Jesuit or a zoo administrator perhaps.

So, my dear, nothing of great moment to report – unless you count Primrose's growing antipathy to our new arrival Mr Topping. She is absolutely convinced that he is not what he seems – a perfectly inoffensive little Latin master with a pleasing smile and polite manners. He also plays bridge rather well, so when you get home you might find him useful for making up an occasional four. Though just remember not to include Primrose as his partner.

Incidentally, she rang me last night in high dudgeon, complaining she had just bumped into Topping taking an evening stroll, and that he had invited her to a little 'in-house' soirée he is giving, and that as such a notable local artist and one of the judges for the school's annual painting competition, her presence would be most agreeable. Being Primrose, she seemed to see his overture as some sort of insult – 'presumptuous' she kept muttering. So is she going? Of course she is, if only to have her prejudices confirmed!

Anyway, I must fly – we have a visitation from the auditors tomorrow and you know how that affects the headmaster. (Must remember to ask Matron about the aspirin supplies.) Will resume this on Wednesday and regale you with news of the Topping event.

Wednesday Night

Unusually good weather for early April – really warm in fact. Indeed so warm that it rather went to Mr Topping's head and he had let it be known that should we be graced with a mild evening he might hold his soirée in the garden. Rather thoughtlessly I mentioned this to Primrose who practically had an apoplectic fit. 'Outside?' she fumed, 'he must be mad.' I was slightly startled by the vigour of her response, and said vaguely that after the trials of winter a little cocktail en plein air might be rather nice . . . Not a good idea. She gave me one of those withering looks and said that drinking ropey sherry in the teeth of midges and a howling gale was bad enough in summer, but to attempt it in a spring dusk was sheer lunacy and that only one as questionable as Hubert Topping would suggest such a thing. I was a trifle bemused by this and said that I couldn't recall having encountered midges in howling gales, least of all in spring, and in any case how could she be sure the sherry would be ropey. She replied that regarding the latter she wasn't sure but wouldn't mind taking bets; and as to the former, it was clear that her experience of al fresco gatherings was considerably wider than mine. Well I thought it best not to argue, and as things turned out the matter never arose: it rained. Heavily.

Thus huddled in Topping's flat – the one in that cottage Miss Dunhill lets out at those outrageous prices – we smiled politely and sipped amontillado and warm Piesporter. Primrose sampled both, made the most awful I-told-you-so faces and continued to imbibe at the rate of knots. She was wearing that rouched taffeta frock, which I have to admit rather suits her, plus the dangling jet earrings inherited from her mother and those stilt-like heels her brother gave her (goodness knows why: I don't think Francis knew anything about clothes – or women). The effect, as you might guess, was quite striking; and being tall, even without the shoes, she towered over Topping, making him look like a benevolent gnome.

Less gnome-like, but equally benevolent, was the headmaster. We had passed the auditing test with flying colours and I rather suspect that his consumption of the Piesporter was a mere stomach-liner for something more abrasive when he got home. Anyway, he was certainly on good form and was heard to murmur to Hutchins (Geography) that the school was fortunate in having such a generous member of staff. Hutchins, not noted for his prodigality, observed that the next time the new member chose to put his hand in his pocket he might consider atlases rather than alcohol . . . There is something rather Stygian about Hutchins (a common trait with geographers perhaps?) but Mr Winchbrooke affected not to hear and just smiled. He has Not Hearing down to a fine art – surely an invaluable asset in a headmaster, particularly at Erasmus House.

Thus things were progressing fairly well – the theme of juvenile imbecility getting its usual airing and glasses being quaffed with genteel abandon: rather unwisely guests had been invited to help themselves from the sideboard. But then I noticed the absence of our host. Nothing odd in that you might think, probably popped to the kitchen for some more crisps. But neither was there any sign of Primrose, seen only moments previously being condescending to the German art mistress. As you know, Primrose does not exactly melt into the shadows of a room and she was definitely no longer amongst us. Intrigued by the coincidence of the double displacement and bored with Mr Neasden's lugubrious banter, I slipped from the room ostensibly en route for the lavatory, where in any case I might have found Primrose and we could have had a little pow-wow.

I had just moved a few feet along the passage when I was brought up short by seeing her pressed squarely against the study door in what can only be described as 'listening mode'. 'Primrose,' I gasped, 'what are you doing?' There was no answer except the furious mouthing of, 'Shut up!' Then re-applying her ear to the panel she signalled me to go away – which I did in some haste. Back in the drawing room I avoided Neasden, sought out the peanuts and thought the more.

A minute later Primrose reappeared, scowled at me, beamed at everyone else and engaged in animated conversation with Hutchins. Actually that is not quite accurate as animation is not Hutchins' forte. It was, you might say, a unilateral engagement. Then two minutes after that Topping returned; and also beaming, including at me, bustled about replenishing drinks and being generally obliging. The noise waxed, the drink waned and little Milly Hopkins got one of her migraines and had to be taken home . . . .

Yes, on the whole it was a successful evening and one which certainly enabled the new member of staff to win nodding approval from amongst his colleagues: a sort of self-baptism by grape I suppose . . . But approval, nodding or otherwise, was hardly Primrose's view; or at least, judging by her extraordinary behaviour at that door it wasn't. I cannot think what she was doing there, and am unlikely to learn until I have returned from the Isle of Wight. Yes, my periodic pilgrimage to mother is nigh, and Mr W. is sanguine in his assumption that things will run smoothly in my absence. They won't.

So, my dear Agnes, it seems we have a little mystery on our hands; and I just hope that on my return it will not be to hear that our dear friend has been ferried away by the white-coated ones for 'tests' – as I believe incarceration is termed.

Your good friend,
Emily

CHAPTER SIX

The Dog's View

On the whole, she's not bad: quicker than F.O. – more on the *ball* you might say; and when we were out on the downs just now she walked along at a good old lick which meant that I didn't have to keep turning round to see where the hell she had got to. (You have to keep an eye on them because so long as you are in their sights they *think* they are in control. They're not, of course, but it stops them bawling your name all over the place and getting ratty.) Mind you, she got a bit edgy when we passed some sheep – obviously thought I was going to duff them up. Nah, not worth it: sitting ducks! They stare at you blankly, then bleat their soppy heads off and fall on their rumps running away. It was fun when I was a puppy but now that I'm a big dog I've got better things to do like stalking the rabbits, for instance. Now *they* can be a challenge. Some are easy, of course, but there are others that are real buggers. Cocky with it. And from what I can make out there's an awful lot of 'em down here – much more than in our other place, and that's saying something. Yes, Bouncer's going to have his work cut out keeping them in order! Still, this afternoon with the Prim I was as good as gold and hardly moved a muscle, just sniffed the wind and made a crafty recky. But once I'm really dug in here I'm going to sneak out one evening and make an ONSLORT and then they'll know it!

I tell you what though, when we were coming home we met someone just outside the house, a smart little geezer with a sort of pink plant stuck in his jacket. When he got level with us he raised his hat and started muttering. I'm not too good at understanding what humans say: I mean there are some things that are easy enough – like 'who's a good dog then?' or 'get out of the way, you little blighter' – but for the most part they gabble and you really have to strain your ears. But it's specially tricky grasping what they're spluttering about when they lower their voices. And this chap's voice was pretty low – *pi-haa-no* as the cat would say.

Anyway, the man went burbling on and P.O. had the sort of look that the vicar often had, especially if he was with Mavis Briggs; the look that says, 'For Christ's sake, get to the point because I want my gin!' Well, I think he did get to the point because she started to smile and said something like, 'How very kind of you Mr Top-Ho. Yes, I would love to come. A little party, how charming!' Can't say that she looked very charmed – leastways not when we had got back inside, because the first thing she did was to kick off her shoes, light a gasper and say to Maurice, 'Well really, that's all one needs!' No response, of course: the cat was in one of his po-faced moods, knackered by the soft-soaping earlier, he can only keep it up for so long. Then she started to shove her face in the newspaper and made awful crackling and rustling noises. I have noticed that human beings often do this when they are feeling ratty (which is quite often); they don't seem to *read* anything, just make a rumpus turning the pages.

Then with another blast of crackle she threw the paper down and went to the blower in the hall. I didn't know who she was phoning but someone was getting an earful all right, and this time it wasn't F.O. More's the pity? Dunno. Let sleeping dogs and vicars lie. That's what the cat says, and I expect he's right. After all, the master always did like lolling about so he's probably having a fine old time. A good long kip: just up his street!

As it happens, by that time I felt like having a kip myself and started to stretch out on the floor, but I could see that Maurice was fidgeting and had begun to twitch his right ear, a sure sign of something in the wind. 'Ay, ay,' I thought, 'he's on the prowl.' And he was too – nipped off the pouffe and slunk after her into the hall. He likes doing that: listening to them when they're bawling down the blower, says it's a challenge to his wits (very keen on his wits is Maurice). Not too good at it myself. It's all that sitting still; makes me lose the thread and I get muddled – and besides it's not as if they talk about anything useful like grub or bones. BORING! Still, if the cat has anything to report he's bound to tell me . . . unless, of course, he gets one of his sulks. Then he'll shut up for hours: give us all a bit of peasanquart as F.O. used to say.

CHAPTER SEVEN

The Primrose Version

Personally, I found it all very peculiar. Topping threw this party at his lodgings and for some strange reason wanted to include me. Well naturally I was far from inclined, but not one to be churlish, graciously accepted. I suppose he wanted to establish himself with his colleagues and presumably felt the local artist would add kudos to the event. A little presumptuous I thought, but there we are . . . Emily seemed full of enthusiasm and told me he was thinking of holding it in the garden – an absurd notion at this time of year. Fortunately it rained incessantly so one was spared that particular penance.

Anyway, for the most part things proceeded as anticipated; with poor drink and indifferent conversation. At one point I felt like suggesting that we all play charades, but knowing the headmaster's aversion to theatricals (including the annual school play), doubted if the idea would be well received. However, in the event there was enough drama as it was, or at least so I judged. A drama based on the most remarkable coincidence.

You see two days prior to the party, I happened to be in Lewes High Street when who do you think I bumped into? *Ingaza.* Yes, Nicholas Ingaza, the Brighton art dealer, last seen at my brother's funeral tearfully hogging the sandwiches and guzzling brandy from a furtive hip flask. In the past Francis and I had had a certain amount to do with Ingaza, including a rather trying trip with him to the Auvergne[1], but since the funeral I had heard nothing. The silence was not uncongenial, for, and as Francis would often lament, Ingaza is somebody of whom one is never quite *sure*, although I have to admit that my own dealings with him had been less fraught than Francis's. He needs a firm hand, which alas, Francis did not have.

If anything he looked thinner than when last seen, but observing an even bigger diamond glinting in his tie pin I assumed business was brisk.

'Well, what do you know? Primrose Oughterard!' he exclaimed. 'Wonderful to see an old face, dear girl.'

'Enough of the old face,' I snapped. 'What are you doing here, Nicholas? I cannot imagine that the ancient stones of Lewes have much to offer you.'

'No,' he leered, 'but something else has. All rather productive really . . .'

'You've made a killing,' I said.

'Oh not a killing as *such*. Shall we say that certain things have rather played into my hands and—'

'And now you are on the way to the bank to deposit the

1. To read more about these previous shenanigans, please refer to *Bones in High Places*.

36

spondulicks before your client gets cold feet or asks too many questions.'

He contrived to look pained. 'You know, Primrose, you are just like poor Francis, *so* cynical!'

'He had some cause,' I retorted dryly.

He gave a wide but wistful smile. 'Perhaps, perhaps . . .' and slicking the brilliantined hair added quietly, 'one misses him you know.'

I did know and for once took his words at their face value. However, I had no intention of swapping personal nostalgia with Ingaza, least of all in the middle of Lewes's Kasbah, so instead enquired after his execrable Aunt Lil.

'Huh! No change there. Says she's bored and wants a fancy man. I ask you!'

'Well,' I said brightly, 'most enterprising at eighty-six, shows she's still alive.'

'Too bloody alive,' was the grim response.

'Ah,' I said, 'but just think, with a fancy man in tow it would let you off the hook from your weekly jaunt to the Eastbourne bandstand. It's an ill wind that—'

'Like hell. That would make two of the beggars to cart around!'

I sighed. 'Oh well, Nicholas, we all have our crosses to bear. My current one is to be charming at a party given by one of the prep school masters. A man called Topping. He's new and apparently thinks it a good idea to ingratiate himself with the headmaster and the locals, or at least one particular local, me.'

At those last words Ingaza sucked in his breath. 'Hmm,' he said, 'he'll have a task on his hands there, like clawing at granite.' And he gave one of those maddening slow winks.

I ignored that and was about to make my excuses and move off, when he said, 'I knew a Topping once, a year below me at Merton; a quiet little chap and a first-rate Greek scholar. Good at ingratiation too – used to hang on to Professor Gilbert Murray's coat tails like grim death.'

'Really? Well I doubt if this man is first-rate, and it's Latin he does, not Greek.'

He shrugged. 'They tend to go together. Still, despite its illustrious name, it's unlikely that Erasmus House would interest my chap. He went far.'

'How far?'

'Became a croupier at Christoff's.'

'Became a *croupier*? At Christoff's! You mean that frightful place in Malta, the one the Messina brothers are rumoured to have run?'

He nodded. 'That's it. I gather he did rather well. Chemmy was his thing, though I think he had a hand in various other of the Messina specialities – the girls and such. It's amazing what a classical education can do for you.' He gave another slow wink, made an absurd flourishing bow and slithered off in the direction of the bank.

Yes, I thought acidly, Ingaza's own classical education had resulted in his being ejected from the theological college once attended by my brother, and into clink for conduct unbecoming in a Turkish bath. However, such misfortune had done little to inhibit his rise through the less scrupulous echelons of Brighton's art world, or indeed to acquire the dubious reputation of being the south coast's prime 'fixer'. From Hastings to Hayling Island the name of Nicholas Ingaza was synonymous with slick acquisition and quiet discretion. I gazed after the spare figure with the tango hips and natty chalkstripe suit . . . and then thought of Francis, gangling in his baggy flannels and ill-fitting clerical collar. They had been an incongruous pair and not just sartorially. The sharper had survived; my brother lay prematurely to rest, safe from snares.

Turning on my heel, I marched smartly to the butcher's to harangue the girl for muddling my order.

Harangue over and chops retrieved, I returned to the car – conveniently parked in the space liberated from the town clerk – and drove home. On the way I thought of Hubert Topping and his soirée and debated what I should wear. I also thought of Ingaza's tale of the other Topping, consorting with the sordid Messina brothers and fleecing gullible punters in Malta. Not pretty. But a curious coincidence both being classicists . . . And then another thought struck me and I crashed the gears. *How* had Ingaza described him? 'A quiet little chap,' those had been his words. How quiet? How little? I tried to fix the new master's age. Yes, presumably about the same as Ingaza's, fifty give or take, which could indeed make him a contemporary. The broad similarities certainly increased the coincidence but I am not fool enough to mistake similar for same. Oh no. After all, Primrose Oughterard is not like the Mavis Briggses of this world: vacant.

Nevertheless it doesn't do to be slack in such matters, so the moment I had got home and fed the cat I picked up the phone and called Brighton. At first I feared I should be greeted by the raucous Eric, Nicholas's ebullient companion, but luckily was spared the grating bonhomie . . . No doubt out playing darts or frightening the horses.

'Nicholas,' I said, 'this Topping person you were telling me about, how tall was he?'

'Tall? Oh I don't know, not very; about five foot six – a bit less perhaps. Why?'

'And what was his voice like?' I asked, ignoring the question.

'Softish. One couldn't always catch what he said; he had a habit of dropping the last word at the end of a sentence. Some people do that; damned irritating I always think.'

'I see . . . I don't suppose he also had the habit of wearing a pink rose in his buttonhole?'

'No, not at all. Now, my dear Primrose, if you don't mind, would you kindly get off the line. I am expecting a call from a client and, with the greatest respect, his enquiry is likely to be somewhat more useful than yours.'

'So he didn't wear a pink rose?'

'What? No, of course not. Didn't I say? It was yellow, always yellow. Now do go away dear girl!'

I replaced the receiver and gazed out at the ridges of the downs, absorbing Ingaza's words. I knew it! Clearly in the intervening years Topping's aesthetic taste had softened and pink had replaced yellow as the preferred shade . . . Short, *sotto voce*, with a penchant for ancient languages and floral buttonholes, the two Toppings were obviously one and the same; and from what Nicholas had said about the Maltese activity, clearly not to be trusted a single inch. Vindicated! I knew he had to be watched and watch him I would!

The dog wandered in. 'Well, Bouncer,' I said, 'you are very lucky to have such an astute mistress. It's not many owners who can spot a fake at 500 yards.' He looked a bit vacant at first and then beamed – at least I suppose it was a beam: the tail wagged and the face took on a kind of furry smirk. I addressed him again. 'And now as a little celebration I shall have a sherry and you a biscuit, and then we'll go for a nice walk and inspect the cows.' He likes doing that. There was an explosive woof which startled the cat, and the dog rushed into the hall, returning immediately with lead in mouth. I had never seen that happen before and was slightly taken aback. However, I rewarded him with two biscuits in place of the promised one, and sherry finished we set off at a brisk rate. I had much to think about.

The following day was Topping's soirée. I had arranged to collect Emily en route and picked her up at six o'clock. She was clearly in festive spirit and kept twittering on about the food and drink. I told her it was bound to be awful – which, of course, it was. Emily is one of those kindly but mistaken people who see good in most things. I have tried to break her of the habit but to no avail. Thus she laughingly said I was an incorrigible pessimist and that she was sure everything would be 'topping' – and then collapsed into paroxysms of mirth. Having a passenger heaving about uncontrollably in the front seat does not aid concentration and I nearly had us in the ditch. However, we got there in one piece and were greeted by the headmaster who had arrived a little ahead of us. Like Emily, he too was in genial mood (having, I later learnt, contrived yet again to fox the auditors) and hustled us up the stairs to join the others.

On the landing we were greeted by our host – a sort of Peter Lorre figure wearing, if you please, a pair of two-toned, co-respondent shoes and a cream 'tuxedo' (as I believe the Americans style it) *with*, of course, the inevitable pink buttonhole. Not the sort of attire our little town is accustomed to, and even the headmaster looked startled. The usual courtesies were exchanged and Topping welcomed me as if I were some long lost soulmate and enthused about my pictures. Naturally, I was suitably responsive but asked him rather pointedly if he had seen any good American films recently. He said that he hadn't. I nearly added that my own favourite was *The Maltese Falcon*; however, not wishing to get a knife in my back, thought better of it. It also occurred to me that in the course of polite chit-chat I might mention my recent painting expedition to Sicily via the Straits of Messina, but in view of what Ingaza had said about the gangster connection, feared that that too might prove hazardous. Thus I accepted his putrid sherry and went to mingle with the other guests.

I was glad to see John Rivers there, the music master being one of the brighter of Winchbrooke's staff. We generally find something to talk about, mainly I suppose because we share so-called artistic talents – though I am not sure that artistry has much of a chance at Erasmus House, rugger and nature walks seeming the preferred activities. The gym mistress does her best to bring diversion but that doesn't take us very far. Anyway, seeing Rivers reminded me of Bouncer. I think the dog finds my rural water colours small beer in comparison to listening to Francis belting out Liszt and boogie-woogie on his ancient upright. In fact judging from its response when last invited into the studio – a sniff at the easel and tentative lift of the hind leg – I should say the hound has no visual sensitivity at all. Still, I *am* its guardian and I owe it to Francis to see to its interests. Thus I asked Rivers if he would mind if I occasionally brought Bouncer over to sit in on his piano practice, explaining that the dog has a keen ear and would be an attentive listener. Rivers looked curiously blank and then turned the conversation in another direction.

Well, if he imagined he could slip out of it as easily as that he had another think coming. I said nothing but resolved to use a more subtle approach next time, i.e. arriving on his doorstep unannounced bearing flowers *plus* dog, and suggest he give us a tune. That would fix it.

My second glass of sherry was worse than the first. Strange really, one usually gets inured to the base. So I moved on swiftly to the German wine: dreadful. Our host must have bought it in flagons from the off-licence; but since cold mint tea was the only alternative I had to stick with it . . . And talking of things German, at that moment *Fräulein* Hockheimer sidled up looking smug as usual and prattling on about 've artists'. Other than teaching the boys how to distinguish the colours in their Winsor & Newton paint boxes, I cannot see that she contributes one jot to the cause of art. However, one tries to be gracious, especially to foreigners. So I enquired kindly if she had succeeded yet in getting anything accepted for the Royal Academy's Summer Exhibition. She looked rueful and said alas she hadn't. Thus I gave her a few useful tips and murmured something to the effect of 'onward and upward' as Bismarck could have said – or indeed a more recent German chancellor whom she might possibly recall. Either way I don't think the exhortation was understood for she continued to hover with a fixed smile and perplexed Teutonic brows.

I was just wondering how I could extricate myself from the *Fräulein* when there was the faint sound of a telephone ringing somewhere along the passage. At the same time I happened to notice Topping in the act of decanting sherry into a jug. He dropped the jug, turned dead white and rushed from the room. Well, jostled really but he would have rushed if he could. The unctuous smile worn since our arrival was replaced by a glazed grimness. I have seen a similar expression on the face of the cat when baulked of some treat or purpose, so knew that something was amiss. Thus curiosity stirred and more than bored by Hockheimer, I decided to trail our host and see what was cooking. (Francis once accused me of nosiness – bossiness too I recall – but as I told him, enlightened interest in the affairs of others can save a deal of trouble. And as to bossiness, well *someone* has to take a hand!)

So I followed Topping into the passage and watched as he scuttled into the room where the phone was ringing. Despite his haste he was careful to close the door, which in itself I thought curious: after all it wasn't as if anyone was near – apart from me shrouded behind the landing curtain. Clearly the phone call was of some concern.

Emerging from the cretonne folds I took up my position at the door and applied an ear. That house is appallingly built and the walls are like plywood so I had little difficulty in catching his words, especially since the usually low tone was more than a little raised.

'I told you not to call this evening,' he cried, 'the house is full of sods: I am entertaining. Can't it wait?'

It evidently couldn't for there followed a long silence, and then he suddenly burst out: 'But I checked it myself, there was at least fifty grand's worth, and besides—' There was another pause, and then he said more evenly, 'Are you sure of that? Because if so I think a little action is required, don't you? We can't allow that, there's far too much at stake. Now listen carefully. What I suggest is . . .'

But I failed to learn what was suggested, or indeed what was at stake, for at that moment *dear* Emily appeared looking shocked and spluttering my name. I gestured her to go away which after some dithering she did. But it was too late, and all I caught were the words, 'Yes, yes, the usual method, of course,' and then the sound of the receiver being put down. I immediately leapt into the adjacent loo and began powdering my nose vigorously.

Frankly, I was none too pleased with Emily and rather cold-shouldered her for the rest of the evening. She evidently took the hint and tactfully hitched a lift home from the headmaster instead of with me. Fortunately her Isle of Wight visit started the next day and when she returned a week later cordiality was resumed.

The excitement of my frustrating vigil at our host's study door, plus a glass too many of his painful drink had made me rather tired, and with the party over I was glad to get back to the comfort of my bed and reflect soberly, or so it seemed, on what Pa would have termed 'the evolutions of the day'. The reflections were short-lived and I woke at five in the morning with a splitting headache and no aspirin. Thus pallid on pillows I tried to divert myself with further thoughts about Topping and his telephone conversation; but the effort was too much and I returned to fitful sleep until roused by the querulous call of Maurice demanding his breakfast.

CHAPTER EIGHT

The Cat's Views

I have a nagging feeling that my earlier assumption of life being smoother here than in the vicarage may have been precipitate. The sister too is beginning to show signs of paranoia. One might charitably argue that given the circumstances of the Fotherington mess our master had some cause for anxiety. In P.O.'s case I as yet see none. Perhaps it is merely a passing phase. One certainly hopes so. I have become nicely attuned to the surfaces of the garden wall and find the lemon thyme under the dining-room window much to my taste. It would be too bad to have such pleasures compromised by further human folly.

Possibly I am being overly sensitive – an affliction of the more intelligent – but I can't help noticing that our mistress is exhibiting a peculiar fondness for the word *topping* which she mutters to herself and occasionally to others such as that Emily person or as just now down the telephone to Ingaza the Brighton Type. It is a term that seems to induce in her both satisfaction and annoyance – simultaneously and in equal proportion. I must reflect upon it and speak with Bouncer . . . not that the dog will illuminate matters; but occasionally he can make an observation that will spur my own train of thought.

Pursuing my intention I have thus spoken to the dog. 'Does the word "topping" mean anything to you?' I asked.

He looked characteristically bemused and stared at his grub bowl, and then said slowly, 'You mean like topping a rabbit?'

'Well,' I began doubtfully, 'I suppose one could—'

'Because if that's what you mean, Maurice, I can tell you it's not all that easy. In fact if you really want to know it's quite—'

'No,' I said firmly, 'I don't think it has anything to do with rabbits, more with people actually. It's something P.O. keeps muttering.'

'Oh *that* Topping.' He took his eye off the bowl and started to sniff at his blanket.

I looked at him sharply. 'What do you mean exactly?'

'Well, she's always on about him, isn't she.'

'On about whom?'

'*Topping*, of course.' He looked perplexed. 'Who'd you think I meant?'

I cleared my throat. 'Ye-es, yes, of course . . .'

'I mean that's the geezer she's got her knife into. Wouldn't you say so, Maurice?'

I shifted my position, wafted my tail and replied quietly, 'Oh indubitably.'

'What?' He looked vacant and then gave a cavernous yawn. 'Cor, it's been a heavy day; what with a new bone and a new ball, I'm knackered!' And with that he flopped into his basket and promptly fell asleep.

I sat for some minutes studying the heaving flanks and twitching nose, piqued and nonplussed. So what was it that Bouncer knew and I didn't? And why were canines so impossible? There being no ready answer to either query I repaired to my own bed in some annoyance. It was a bit much!

Fortunately today has brought enlightenment. I do not mean about canines, who I fear will always remain opaque, but about the Topping enigma. As Bouncer had implied, he is indeed of the human species: one of those pedagogues at the boys' school across the fields into which P.O. occasionally disappears, wielding a paint brush.

My source of information was the grey Persian who sits just inside its entrance gates. On the whole she is fairly couth and we have got into the habit of passing the time of day – briefly, of course. She told me that Topping is newly employed at the school to teach the rudiments of the Roman tongue and that the headmaster is much relieved, as the previous incumbent had become too old and peculiar and left under a cloud in a van. Considering the collective insanity of humans I often wonder how they distinguish one case of derangement from the many: randomly, I suspect.

Anyway, Eleanor – a reassuring name for a Persian – said she had not as yet made an assessment of Topping but was working on it. I enquired if she assessed all those who entered the premises at that spot. 'Most certainly,' she exclaimed, 'one should never underestimate the value of vigilance.' Evidently a cat after my own heart and one whom I may cultivate further. Indeed on closer acquaintance

I might go so far as to invite her to a night on the tiles. Since coming here I have not had many of those, the roofs of Lewes being less proximate than those of Molehill. It would be pleasant to trip the light fandango beneath the moon and the chimney pots with one as shrewd as Eleanor. She would be useful too in introducing me to the better class of mouse colony – one has to be in the know about such places and a sponsor is generally required. Yes, pursue the Persian, that's what I must do.

In the meantime, and with Persians and chimney pots aside, the more pressing task is to get to the bottom of this Topping character and P.O.'s seeming obsession. One just trusts that nothing unsettling will emerge. The antics of our late master were quite enough.

CHAPTER NINE

My dear Agnes,
So glad that Charles is coming home any moment,
but rather selfishly I am sorry to hear you have
chosen to stay a little longer in Tobago. Though
if that were me I suspect I should want to be a
permanent fixture there. Lucky you! It will be
lovely to see Charles again and hear all your news
and his plans for the manor. But I have to say it
will be good for another reason: Primrose. She
really is behaving very peculiarly regarding this
Topping master; the dear girl has a bee in her
bonnet that he is shady, as Edgar Wallace might
say. I am not quite sure what she means by that
but gather he is likely to be an international arms
dealer, gangland boss, white slaver or something
equally murky . . . My dear, as mentioned in my
last letter, you cannot imagine a more inoffensive
little man. He has charming manners and a racing

bike! Yes, one of those drop handlebar things, just like your nephew's. Well not quite so dropped but almost; anyway, it has pale blue mudguards and looks very dashing. He zooms about on it exploring Roman sites such as Fishbourne and running useful errands for the headmaster. Primrose, of course, likes neither the bicycle nor its rider.

I am now safely returned from my sojourn with mother and am relieved and mildly surprised that other than Mr Winchbrooke having his licence endorsed for an unusual manoeuvre on the Eastbourne road, nothing untoward has occurred at Erasmus House . . . Or at least nothing that is verifiable, by which I mean that Mr T's hoodlum activities as envisaged by Primrose continue to go unrecognised by the authorities.

I think I mentioned in my last letter that I had come upon Primrose leeched to Mr Topping's study door when we were guests at his little party. Thus when I got back from the Isle of Wight and she was once more in a welcoming vein I plucked up the courage to enquire what it was she had managed to hear. Her response was what your Charles would term 'opaque' – though I was made to understand that had I not appeared at that specific moment she would now be in possession of damning facts. I said that I was sorry to have impeded her enquiries and would she care to be my guest at the local fleapit. They were doing a revival of The Petrified Forest *with Leslie Howard, and since Primrose has always had a craze for that actor I thought it might be a useful move. It was. And I am now returned to favour. But more importantly it has taken her mind off poor Mr Topping . . . temporarily at least.*

The dog too has its uses in that respect. Since it was once her brother's, she feels duty-bound not only to minister to its welfare, but as far as I can make out, pander to its every whim. It is an amiable enough creature but I do rather draw the line at being expected to stand in the garden endlessly throwing filthy bones for it to retrieve. It's not as if it actually does; instead it seizes the things and bears them off to some lair in the shrubbery whence it returns empty-jawed and bellowing for more. There must be a veritable ossuary in there! Primrose says it's all part of his training, though training for what I cannot imagine. She also assures me it has musical tastes (apparently it used to sit regularly by the piano while her brother pounded the keys) and she feels these are not being properly catered for. John Rivers is distinctly worried as he has an aversion to all household pets and has been approached by Primrose suggesting she bring the dog to listen to his arpeggios. He comforts himself by saying she will forget about it. But she won't you know! Ah well, doubtless the novelty will wear off. And, as said, at least Bouncer can deflect some of the Topping interest.

Tuesday

Great excitement today – well, moderate I suppose – as Bertha Twigg, the gym mistress, had organised an expedition for the third-formers to visit the Long Man of Wilmington on the downs near Eastbourne. They were all very keen – except for Harris, of course, who complained he had seen it too flipping often and couldn't he just stay behind and read the new Mickey Spillane sent by his uncle. (Personally I think that uncle has a lot to answer for, but naturally being merely the school secretary who am I to comment?) Mr Rivers sensibly told him that he could certainly stay behind if he chose although his pastime would not be the reading of unsuitable thrillers but writing . . . 500 lines. That brought him to heel all right and we set off in the charabanc in merry mood.

Being a keen walker as well as cyclist, Hubert Topping had been persuaded to join us, and I have to say that his presence was really most instructive. He is a fund of knowledge about local hill forts and native butterflies. In fact he put me right about one of the latter – very firmly! I had pointed out one of those charming little grey-blue types seen so often around here, and said I thought it was exclusive to Sussex. 'Oh no,' he said, 'we used to see a lot of those in Malta though I am surprised they are found so far north.' He seemed very sure about it and I asked how well he knew the island. Apparently he had been there at the end of the war in some capacity and had stayed on for a while afterwards. He didn't enlarge, and in any case at that moment we were diverted by Harris relieving himself in the foot of the Long

Man. I think he was piqued at being baulked of his Mickey Spillane. It's amazing what children will do to make a point.

The rest of the afternoon passed most agreeably and even cook's sandwiches seemed a little fresher than usual. Mr Rivers actually produced a small guitar from his rucksack and started strumming 'con brio' as they say. It was a valiant effort but didn't last as a sharp east wind got up and stifled the sound; besides, apart from a couple of the politer boys most seemed to prefer rolling down the steep turf or playing at being Dan Dare. However, all in all it was a successful outing and clearly Bertha Twigg was much relieved – her ideas are not always so fruitful. The only slight mishap was Mr Hutchins' ankle: he sprained it climbing over a stile and then looked woebegone for some hours; but then he often looks like that.

On the way back I asked the coach driver to drop me off in the High Street as I wanted to pick up some provisions at the grocer's, and I was just coming out when I bumped into Primrose. She was striding up the hill at the rate of knots – the only person I know who can do that without succumbing to exhaustion; she has her brother's long legs. Seeing me she stopped and remarked tactfully: 'Well it's obvious that you haven't just come from the hairdresser's, more like from the proverbial hedge I should say!' She put on that superior face (you know the one) and patted her own disciplined coiffure.

I explained that I had just had a bracing

experience on the downs; at which she roared with laughter and said one could never have too many of those and was he nice . . . Well really! From what I recall the Oughterard family was never noted for its humour, ribald or otherwise, and as such she is a-typical. I suspect her days at the Courtauld have much to do with it: art students being notoriously 'broad' in their outlook. Anyway, I ignored the sally and went on to tell her how much the boys had enjoyed themselves and how good, relatively speaking, they had been, one or two even showing sympathy for Mr Hutchins and his ankle. And then, perhaps foolishly, I alluded to Hubert Topping and his knowledge of butterflies. The instant I mentioned Malta and his having been there, she cried, 'My God, I knew it!' And then in a tone which seemed to mingle shock with triumph, added, 'Nicholas was so right. It's disgraceful!'

I was startled by the reaction and said mildly, 'But Primrose, I cannot see what is so disgraceful about Mr Topping's interest in the butterfly life of Malta.'

'It wasn't the butterflies that interested him,' she replied darkly. 'That man must be stopped.'

'Stopped from what?' I asked.

'From whatever he is doing, of course!'

'Yes, I see,' I said mystified. 'And, er, what exactly is he doing?'

There was a pause, and then she replied, 'Hmm. That's the problem. I'm not sure yet; but something is afoot all right and I fully intend to

55

find out.' She looked very fierce. And then just before taking off she hesitated and staring at my hair said, 'You know Emily, I think it might be an idea if you made an appointment with the hairdresser, they've got a new girl there now and she's fearfully good.'

As you can imagine, I walked home in a puzzled mood. What on earth had she been talking about? And was my hair really as bad as she implied? And who for goodness' sake was Nicholas? I brooded. And then, of course, it came to me – or at least the answer to the last question did: Nicholas Ingaza, that rather oblique Brighton art dealer. I had met him once at an exhibition she had taken me to and was not impressed. In fact, frankly Agnes, he is not one I would normally choose to have dealings with – too clever by half and with smarm as long as your arm! I think she had met him through her brother – though what one as correct as the vicar had to do with that type I could never quite fathom. But at one time I believe Primrose and he had some sort of business arrangement – though its exact nature was never defined and since she volunteered no information, I never liked to enquire. I got the impression it ended rather abruptly, but I suppose there might still be a link. But personally, Agnes, if it is the Ingaza man whom she thinks is 'so right', then in my opinion that is all the more reason to doubt her judgement regarding nice Mr Topping!

As said, I look forward to Charles's return and

trust he may be able to inject a modicum of common sense into things . . . In the meanwhile I think perhaps it is time I had a fresh perm – but naturally I shall go to my own hairdresser and certainly not the one counselled by Primrose.

Your good friend,
Emily

CHAPTER TEN

The Cat's Views

Alas, my fears of a ruffled future are proving well founded. Remarkable how accurate a cat's instinct is, far superior to a dog's so-called sixth sense. One had hoped that P.O.'s odd behaviour was merely a passing phase and that fundamentally she was more balanced than her brother. This is not the case. The Topping business is clearly preoccupying her and she returned the other night in a state of some volatility, pacing the kitchen and muttering about 'that ghastly man' and 'asinine Emily'. Having apprised the kitchen of her feelings she retired to bed, and then *omitted to rise in time to give me my breakfast.* I was forced to express sharp words which luckily remedied matters.

Nevertheless I just trust this is not the prelude to further lacunae in my feeding schedule; there were quite enough of those with F.O. Still, one must be charitable and assume it was an aberration. Let us hope so as it will save the onset of a sulk. Though on reflection, I haven't had one of those for a while so perhaps it is time.

I am also a little anxious about her renewed contact with the Brighton Type. Our experiences in Molehill with the vicar have taught me to question anything which may involve the Ingaza specimen. She would do well to steer clear; but humans being contrary creatures I doubt if she will. And talking of contrary, Bouncer has been unusually quiet of late. Not that I am complaining, of course, but if by chance he is sickening for something then there will be all the drama of the new vet. I must make enquiries.

Enquiries made, it transpires that there is nothing wrong with Bouncer – that is to say no more than usual – but he has, I gather, 'been thinking'. This is not entirely reassuring for I am never quite sure which is worse – when the dog does not think or when he does. Either way it can be a troubling experience. When I enquired what he had been thinking about he looked smug and said I must be patient as he needed to prepare a mental list. 'Oh really?' I replied, 'surely there are only three things on your mental list: bones, more bones and bunnies.'

'Balls,' he said.

'What!'

'Balls, Maurice. You forgot to mention those two rubber balls she bought me from the pet shop. So that makes five things.' He beamed, looking even smugger. It has taken the dog a long time to count up to five so he flaunts the ability whenever the chance arises.

I said nothing and settled down to observe the sparrows. But peace was not to be, for at the next moment he bellowed, 'But there's something ELSE, Maurice, something pretty rum!' With a frenzied flurry of wings the sparrows scattered to be replaced by the dog standing four-square in front of me panting.

I sighed. 'What is it?' I asked wearily.

'You know last night, when the Prim came back and went to bed?'

I nodded.

'Well *I* didn't.'

'Yes, you did, you were snoring your head off; making an awful racket!'

He grinned. 'Ah, that may have been *then*, but I wasn't later. Do you want to know what I was doing later?'

'Not really.'

'I'll tell you then. I was out.'

'Outside? In the night?' I was surprised by this as normally the dog sleeps heavily till dawn and unlike myself has no inclination for nocturnal strolls. 'Whatever for?' I asked.

He explained that he had thought it was time to get the lie of the land just in case he had the sudden urge to make a midnight raid on the local rabbits, and thus he had wanted to test out the hidden escape route. I asked him what route he meant.

'Oh, don't you know, Maurice? The one in the cellar, of course, that door with the broken bit she hasn't bothered to nail down, the one that leads up the steps to the kitchen garden. I thought you would have known all about it.'

As it happened I wasn't even aware the house had a cellar but I certainly wasn't going to tell the dog that. 'Oh yes?' I replied indifferently, 'and then what?'

'Then I scrambled out under the gap, sneaked into the lane and saw *what I saw*.'

There was a pause, presumably for dramatic effect, as

60

he nonchalantly began to cock his leg against a flower pot, but I wasn't playing that game. 'That's enough, Bouncer, tell me immediately!' I hissed.

He lowered the leg. 'Top-Ho on his bicycle.'

'In the middle of the night and in the rain?' I exclaimed.

He nodded eagerly. 'Yes, I thought that was odd too which is why I followed him. He was moving at a good old lick so it was quite difficult keeping up.'

'Don't tell me you were going full pelt behind him on the open road. Ridiculous!'

''Course not. Wasn't born yesterday, you know. I was running along on the *other* side of the hedge. That's something O'Shaughnessy and me used to practise back in Molehill, trailing people without being seen . . .' A wistful look came into his eye, and I wondered if the dog was missing his old cronies such as the dreadful Irish setter. (I winced at the memory.) Naturally he is fortunate to have my guidance, but dogs as a species are gregarious creatures and enjoy their own kind. I will make enquiries of Eleanor; perhaps she can suggest a canine companion for him – though *not* one as raucous as O'Shaughnessy and certainly not a poodle . . . the last thing one needs is another Pierre the Ponce and his Gallic whims.

'So where was he going?' I asked.

'To one of those things we had on the pavement outside the vicarage.'

'You mean a telephone box?'

'Yes, that's it, one of those. He went in there, gabbled away for a few minutes and then came out, got on his bike and scooted back home again.' The dog gazed at me quizzically, head cocked on one side. 'Like I said, a bit rum, isn't it?'

I agreed that it was indeed rum. Why should Top-Ho leave his house in the dead of night in the pouring rain, and peddle off to make a call from a public telephone box when presumably he had a perfectly good instrument at home? Peculiar really; but then, of course, humans are apt to do things like that. Still, as all cats know, curiosity is an invaluable tool in divining, or frustrating, human intention, so I instructed Bouncer to keep on the *qui vive*.

'On what?' he grunted gormlessly.

I flicked my tail impatiently. 'Prick up your ears!'

He leered. 'Your language, Maurice!'

CHAPTER ELEVEN

Charles Penlow's Journal

Six weeks of non-stop sun and rum is certainly to be recommended. But after a time you begin to experience a sense of unreality and an itch to return to something more abrasive. Not that one can call Lewes abrasive, unless you count the internecine furies of the Plantswomen's Guild and the rivalries enjoyed by the town's countless historical societies, but it has a parochial busyness, a sort of brisk, needling vitality, which after weeks of lolling in the lavish arms of the Caribbean I begin to hanker for. And a Sussex sea is different from a Tobago sea; and beautiful though that island is, it has nothing on Mount Caburn in the moonlight or Chanctonbury Ring at dawn. Agnes being less of a sentimentalist and more of a sybarite than myself is only too happy to cling to Tobago for another month before facing the harsher realities of Podmore Place and our project for its retrieval from ruin.

It is, I fear, a ridiculously rash undertaking – though some have kindly called it bold – for the scale of restoration is huge, the work immense and the cost appalling. My younger brother, Jack, has advised me to stick to draughts and jigsaw puzzles, but since on principle one never listens to a younger brother I push on regardless. Why? Because to quote George Mallory, 'Because it's there'; but perhaps more pertinently because it has belonged to a branch of our family for generations. Its previous owner was an ancient cousin, and being the last of his line and with no one better to hand it on to, he left it to me. 'White elephant,' Agnes had protested.

But, as it happens, I am rather partial to elephants, and as a boy living in India, had once rescued a baby jumbo from a swamp. So I suppose I thought I could do the same again. However, this is no Indian jumbo: British, white, and certainly no baby! But then that's the problem with sentimentality: it lands you with things, e.g. marriage and collapsing houses.

So I am back now, having rented out our house at Firle and installed myself at Podmore in the small east wing which we have made moderately habitable while the renovation progresses . . . or not, as the case may be. At least the grounds are taking shape and I have dreams for a small orangery, though God knows where. Meanwhile, I must make a date to see our friend Primrose Oughterard: Agnes has been receiving some rather strange reports from Emily Bartlett (why that woman chose to be secretary at the boys' school after the dreary husband died beats me. She should have gone round the world and had a good time . . . well, as good a time as Emily is ever likely to have. Still, she seems to enjoy it which is the main thing. Horses for courses I suppose).

Anyway, according to Emily's reports, I gather Primrose

has recently taken possession of her late brother's dog and cat, but is also pursuing some sort of grudge against one of the school's masters. Emily says she is becoming quite unhinged over it. I have to say that being pursued by Primrose, with or without a grudge, is not something one would take lightly! But I rather like the woman: she is refreshingly frank and, despite certain oddities, no fool. She keeps a good class of whisky too – which cannot be said of the sherry: dry as a bone in the desert. I remember the brother sipping it dutifully with closed eyes and crinkled brow. Primrose doesn't talk much about feelings, a good thing in my opinion, but I think she misses him. I shall go and cheer her up and inspect the new acquisitions. I could take Duster but don't know if the new residents would look kindly upon him, you can't be too pushy with animals. Best leave it for a while, we don't want a godawful skirmish on Primrose's terrace; it might unsettle the cows in the neighbouring field.

<u>Saturday</u>

Well that was certainly an agreeable nightcap. Primrose on typical robust form, dishing out copious Scotch and regaling me with her student capers at the Courtauld all those years ago. Though from what she described I imagine some of those ageing mentors are still reeling from the experience. But the animals were intriguing as well. The dog, Bouncer, a shaggy brute, seemed to take a shine to me and kept sniffing my trousers and making sheep's eyes. For an uneasy moment I thought it was gearing up to perform a baptism, but luckily one was spared the honour. And then having 'cased' my turn-ups it began giving my knee a series of head buffets. Primrose was delighted and said it just went to show what a really sweet boy he was. I am not sure that sweet is quite the word I would use but the creature does have a certain rustic affability. The cat, on the other hand, is neither rustic nor affable: thin, aloof and unnervingly watchful. I don't think it took its eyes off me the whole time I was there. It is entirely black except for one white paw which now and again it wafted imperiously. Primrose assured me I should be flattered as generally when visitors call it stalks from the room in dudgeon; the fact that it remained was apparently an accolade. Well I suppose one should be grateful for such honours, however subtle.

Subtlety, of course, is not Primrose's style. And over the whisky and Bath Olivers she held forth fulsomely on the subject of this new Latin master at Erasmus House. She is convinced that not only is he a charlatan but also some sort of shady mobster. I gather he looks and sounds not unlike the actor Peter Lorre, yet also rides a racing bicycle. Not noted for my imagination, except perhaps where grandiose building schemes are concerned, I have difficulty in connecting those features. However, I didn't like to question Primrose's description and listened instead to the more relevant details. These involved a series of coincidences which she was convinced pointed to the fellow having once worked in the infamous Christoff's (now closed down), reputed to be run by the Messina gang. I asked how she made these deductions and she said she had got much of her information from Nicholas Ingaza.

Given his reputation as the slickest spiv south of London, some might think such a source dubious. But I happen to know Ingaza, or did once upon a time – though *these days our few encounters are marked by a mere nod and a wink – and I can say he is no idiot. Far from it – you don't get an Oxford first, or indeed the Fitzer Memorial Prize for Greek prosody, for nothing. Slippery as butter, of course, always was; nevertheless there's a kind of bastard integrity there . . . otherwise they would never have used him at Bletchley. One of our best operators he was, sharp as an East End ferret! Well those days are long gone, but even now it's all hush-hush and we're still bound by the OSA on pain of some dire penalty or other. Of course his subsequent life is hardly to my taste, pretty scandalous really by all accounts. But old comrades and camaraderies die hard and in a way I can't help liking him.*

But that's beside the point: the point being that if he thinks this Topping is the same cove that was on Malta with the Messinas then there is a fair chance that he is. However, as I pointed out to Primrose, just because a chap has had a seedy past doesn't mean that he is still at the same game. For all one knows he may have undergone a spectacular moral conversion, and the drilling of small boys in the basics of Latin grammar is all part of the penitential process. I don't think Primrose thought much of that as she remarked dryly that sometimes talking to me was not unlike talking to her deceased brother.

She also insisted it was obvious that no such conversion had occurred as quite by chance she had overheard Topping engaged in a highly suspect telephone conversation with some unknown. 'Ah,' I said, 'and I suppose you just happened to have been passing and by chance had stooped to tie your shoelace?' She said it was exactly that and how shrewd of me to have guessed. The few fragments she cited – 'far too much at stake', 'we can't let that go on' and something about 'fifty grand' didn't really amount to much – though I suppose the last might be an unusual term from a quiet schoolmaster – but clearly Primrose sets great store by such 'evidence'. And since it had not been my ear clamped to the keyhole, possibly I am in no position to judge . . . Thus I said that she had better watch out she doesn't get a knife in her back, and in the meantime was it too much to ask if I might be allowed a drop more whisky. She said it certainly was too much and promptly filled my glass to the brim.

Yes, a most amicable evening; and on reflection I really quite like that dog of hers. With luck he and Duster might get on – though one will need to beware the cat.

CHAPTER TWELVE

The Dog's View

'You see, Maurice,' I told him, 'she said I was sweet. Now that's something, isn't it!'

'Dilooded,' the cat replied, 'just like our master was. It's amazing how blinkered human beings can be.'

Maurice has a thing about 'dilooshun' and says the word a lot: he likes it. I think it means you don't know what you are talking about. Well you can't say that about Bouncer because I *know*, you see. And *I* know that although P.O. is the sister of F.O. she is *not* dilooded. She is like me: got a sixth sense. So if she thinks I'm SWEET you bet she's right – and if she thinks Top-Ho is BAD then most likely he is!

Mind you, I thought that Charles person we saw this evening was NOT bad, especially as he's got that really good whiff about him. It reminds me of a Jack Russell I used to know . . . Cor! He was a good mouser if ever there was one. Put old Maurice in the shade all right. Anyway, I made sure I was on my best behaviour as I quite liked that Charles – a bit like F.O. really (though the vicar was dafter, of course).

69

And I also like a good trouser leg. Ladies' stockings aren't nearly as good: sort of thin and cold and they don't pick up spoor in the same way . . . Hmm I wonder whose spoor that was? I'll have to do a bit more sniffing around and find out. Just like P.O. with that Topping person: we've both got to keep our muzzles to the ground. As a matter of fact, the Prim has got quite a long muzzle but I bet I get there first.

Maurice says he did not *dis*like that Charles person . . . So crikey that's a turn up for the bones. If the cat didn't dislike the visitor then he must be all right! Perhaps we'll see more of him. I hope so because I'd like to discover more about that nice niffy trouser leg, it had a really matey smell.

Later

Do you know what? There *is* a cairn in the neighbourhood and it's called Duster. Maurice has been quite useful and made some enquiries of that Persian friend of his, the cat with a face like a grey mop – Eleanor I think her name is. Anyway, Mop Face says that Duster belongs to a tall man who lives in a big house just outside the town. Now being what you might call a sharp sort of dog I've put one and one together and made TWO. (Maurice says I'm getting jolly good at my numbers these days.) So number one is that the man here last night was tall; and the next number one is that his trouser leg smelt of *cairn*. So putting those together you get two: which means that the tall man owns a cairn; and I bet you the tall man is Charles and his dog is the Duster that the Persian was talking about . . . See? No fleas on this one's coat and that's for sure. I'll go and tell the cat what I think.

* * *

70

His nibs was kipping under the dining-room table. (It's where he goes when he thinks he won't be seen; but I could see him all right because he'd forgotten to fold that white paw under his chest so it stuck out like a sore whatsit.) I was going to wake him up but thought better of it; there's still a scratch on my nose from the last time. Besides, I want to do a bit more thinking about that Top-Ho chap. There's a funny smell there you know, and smells just happen to be Bouncer's *for-tea*, as Maurice would say. But before I start thinking I'll just trot off to take a dekko at those daft chinless wonders in their hutch. If they're having a kip like the cat I'll soon wake 'em up . . . Wah-ho, Bunnnies! Here I come!

CHAPTER THIRTEEN

The Primrose Version

I had spent a long day at the easel, 'rusticating' the church tower and trying to give the features of the cropping sheep a semblance of expression. Why go against nature one might ask? Because that is what the punters want. They have a sentimental view of the countryside, and ancient churches and personalised sheep are what sell my pictures. *You mean you attended the Courtauld simply to churn out bogus rural idylls for the urban and undiscerning?* an inner voice asks. 'Certainly,' I reply, 'since that is precisely what delivers maximum dosh for minimum effort.' It also happens to keep me in gin, pays for this comfortable house and allows me periodically to indulge the occasional aesthetic urge in trips to foreign meccas – Paris, Vienna, Venice. Stuck in a garret grappling with serious stuff might enhance one's artistic integrity but hardly one's bank balance. I tried to explain this to Francis on a number of occasions but he never quite grasped it . . . unlike Ingaza who grasps it wholeheartedly. That said, commercial empathy is no guarantee of close amity, and our relationship rests on a mutual wariness – a condition also of mutual approval.

Anyway, having at last supplied the sheep with a trace of animation and contrived a gothic aura for the church, I was about to call it a day and lose myself in the soothing scandals of the *Daily Telegraph*, when I was rung up by Melinda Balfour.

'That wretched girl has ratted,' she cried.

'Which of the many?' I enquired.

'Blanche, of course. Swanned off to London at the last moment and left me in the lurch without a partner, and I've got everything arranged!' she wailed. 'You couldn't *possibly* substitute, could you? I mean I know it's fearfully short notice but I do have the most marvellous supper laid on. You wouldn't starve.'

Melinda's bridge suppers are renowned, and participating invariably means a convivial evening, especially if her husband is otherwise engaged; that awful pipe and grating laugh – features surely the cause of many a missed trick. Thus despite the rigours of the day I said I would be delighted to fill the gap but would she mind if I brought Bouncer as he and Maurice had had a little spat earlier on and it was best to leave the cat to its own devices for a while. 'Of course, of course, anything you like,' she trilled. Such was her relief that doubtless she would have welcomed a pack of staghounds had I requested. Thus swapping my painting pinny for a vampish black sheath dress – a mite tight I fear – and dousing myself in some indiscreet scent, I seized the dog and sallied forth to slay them at the bridge tables.

Negotiating the tortuous lanes leading up to Firle Beacon, I contemplated the evening ahead. Undoubtedly the food would be good, some of the guests amusing, the stakes interestingly high – and providing Freddie Balfour was out being worthy at a Rotary dinner, my own performance might proceed with customary luck. The real question mark was the dog: would it behave itself? I glanced sideways at the passenger seat. 'You have got to be very good, Bouncer,' I warned him, 'one false move and I'll never take you anywhere again.' The words were met with silence followed by a mild burp.

As things turned out, the dog was obligingly well behaved – sickeningly so in fact. He made sheep's eyes at all and sundry, rolled gaily on his back, and at the advent of the cocktail sausages even performed some creditable begging tricks. Consequently he was stuffed with food and cooed over unceasingly. Gross.

The evening developed well. As hoped, Freddie Balfour was mercifully absent, the cards lively and my own efforts sound. We left just after midnight, dog sated and owner pleased . . . Yes, I mused, Melinda Balfour had been lucky to have me as a partner and she would notice the difference when Blanche Swithin returned next week ('Oh what a falling-off there'll be!' – Shakespeare, more or less, I think). I patted my handbag containing the proceeds and addressed my companion. 'Well, Bouncer, that'll get me a new bottle of Chanel and you a fresh bone – perhaps even a toy rabbit if you are very good.' He remained silent, being engrossed in the moving shapes of the gorse bushes as we trundled along the rutted track to the road that winds across the downs and into the valley.

As I drove still amused by my lucrative bridge skill – a legacy from Pa – I was put in mind of Hubert Topping suavely bankrupting the martini set at Christoff's . . . Yes, one could just see him in the role of croupier: dapper in dinner jacket, raking the counters while purring words of cheer and consolation to gullible punters. And afterwards? Doubtless slipping with cronies into some curtained recess to split and toast the evening's spoils. And in the dawn light did he perhaps retire with a cup of delicate Lapsang and a volume of Horace . . . or with volumes of vodka and a sultry showgirl? I contemplated the possibilities. But not for long as my reverie was halted by the dog: it wanted to get out.

'Oh really, Bouncer,' I protested, 'can't you wait? Lie down and be a good boy.' He didn't lie down but squirmed in the seat emitting reproachful grunts. Reluctantly I stopped the car and shoved him out. The night was clear with bright stars and a waxing moon, and I was persuaded to take the air with a cigarette and imbibe the silence. Far off, the lights of Lewes twinkled. But up on the ridge, apart from the dog shuffling in the gorse, all was still and tranquil.

I drew on my cigarette, and glancing to the right realised I had parked by the old dew pond, a favourite spot with children and local ramblers. Indeed as children ourselves – and although denizens of the eastern Weald – we had come up periodically to sail toy boats and splash in its shallows. On one occasion Francis (typically) had fallen in, and there was an awful hullaballoo because he had refused to come out. I smiled at the memory, savouring my cigarette and gazing at the gleaming waters and the abandoned years . . . And then I stopped gazing and instead stared hard. There was something floating there, long and solid; a distinct blot on the smooth surface. A discarded bundle of rubbish? A couple of logs or— 'Christ almighty!' I yelped, and leapt back in appalled disbelief . . . Legs, not logs. It was a body: a body on its front, half in and half out of the water; but worse than that, a body minus something. Its head.

For a few dazed seconds I convinced myself the thing was a battered shop mannequin discarded by a disgruntled floor walker; or perhaps the girl guides had been up there with a stuffed dummy practising their first aid and in an access of experimental zeal had been too free with the scissors. When one's own body is struck with horror it is remarkable how active the brain becomes in seeking palliatives. But the images of invention dissolve and there remains the raw reality. Thus I stood transfixed in the clawing silence, numbed by that reality, my hands stiff and feet riveted to the turf.

Then suddenly from the depths of lost years I heard the shrill voice of my brother: 'Let's play cops and robbers! I'll lie down and pretend to be dead and *you've* got to come and examine my corpse with the magnifying glass. Hurry up, Prim, do!'

Thus mechanically but minus magnifying glass, I dutifully edged towards the pond and craned forward to get a closer look; and despite the dark and revulsion registered certain features. The form was fairly slight and short but seemed to be male and was clad in what looked like a brown-checked sports jacket with patches on the elbows; a pallid hand flung sideways from the water displayed a signet ring on the little finger . . . Then, scrutiny over and now thoroughly yanked back to the present, I was about to dash to the car when two further details confronted me. One was the rosebud floating primly on the lucent waters; and the other was an additional accoutrement – the severed head. It lay a few feet from the pond's edge, propped against a piece of flint, battered and balding . . . This time I closed my eyes and refrained from inspection.

I have to say that the whole experience was exceedingly monstrous and disgusting, and I felt far from well. The dog, of course, was in its element, prancing around in slavering delight emitting the most sordid noises and with tail wagging non-stop. Typical. I was neither prancing nor slavering (being sick in a gorse bush actually). And on reflection I can definitely say that it was not something my brother would have approved, his own dispatch of Mrs Fotherington having been the essence of discretion. I mean, this was so *messy*!

It was perishing cold up on those downs and if Bouncer thought I was going to hang about just to indulge his morbid appetite he had another think coming. So I clipped the lead onto his collar, hauled him back to the car and took off pretty damn quick. By the time we gained the main road the dog had ceased its clamour and sat meekly on the front seat presumably lost in its own thoughts. As I was in mine. Who was it for the good Lord's sake? Could it *really* be him?

It was not pleasant reviewing the evidence, particularly of one so truncated; but such things tend to stick in the mind and it required no effort to recall the details. They were there already assaulting my eyes, rearing and jostling in the driving mirror: brown-checked jacket, short, smallish frame, receding hair (I winced), signet ring on right hand, and above all the confounded rose. There was little doubt: the corpse must surely be that of the recently appointed Latin master to Erasmus House, the county's most favoured prep school. Singular to say the least . . .

What a relief to get back to the outskirts of Lewes and see the beckoning lights of my house. I felt better immediately, and once inside mixed a more than liberal pick-me-up. Despite the warmth of the drawing room I was chilled to the bone – shock, I suppose. So I put on all three bars of the electric fire and stood in front of it, throwing down the drink and seeing that awful head. Fortunately by the third glass the head started to diminish, but my attention was caught by Bouncer and the cat. They seemed to be behaving rather oddly: standing facing each other with muzzles almost touching and just staring. The dog's ears were cocked, the cat's flattened and each was slowly waving its tail. They must have sensed that I was watching for in the next moment, amid yowls and growls, there was a flurried exodus to the kitchen and I heard no more . . . I don't really understand animals but Mrs Fobbs from the sweetshop swears blind that they use a form of private speech. It's amazing what people will believe.

Anyway, to return to the head – and the torso for that matter: clearly Topping had not engineered his own decapitation, so someone else must have had a hand. *Not*, I thought, the headmaster because despite what Emily had said regarding their dispute over the timetable clashes, Winchbrooke is one who will do anything for a quiet life, or so Emily assures me, and going so far as to murder one of his own staff would surely defeat the object. Such urges can backfire – as my poor brother once found to his cost. No, surely someone else was the culprit.

I reflected upon the rose. For a bloom that had been

in the pond for some time you would expect bedraggled petals or none at all. But from what I recalled the thing had looked perkily pristine, which rather suggested that Topping's committal to water had taken place shortly before my arrival. Whether the gory *coup de grâce* had been struck in situ or at an earlier stage, or indeed whether it had been delivered pre- or post-mortem, were not aspects I cared to pursue: the fact that the committal, in whatever mode, was likely to have occurred just minutes prior to my being there was more than enough. Just think, it could have been happening at the very time I was scooping that fourth trick from under Daisy Wingate's nose!

I downed further fortification and after which began to feel distinctly queasy – though whether the effects of squeamishness or overindulgence I couldn't be sure. Possibly the brandy itself: our wine merchant's stock is notoriously poor. (Must remember to order from Berry Bros in future.) But nausea apart, it was now past two o'clock and time for bed. On my way up I looked in on the kitchen where to my surprise I saw both animals curled up in Bouncer's basket. I had never seen that before and Francis used to tell me they couldn't abide each other's sleeping quarters. Strange . . . but then so was Topping and his lost head. I had always said he spelt trouble. Bloody man!

As I undressed, it crossed my mind I should apprise the police of my startling find; a quick call to the station should have them up and running all right. I pictured Sergeant Wilding at the duty desk bellowing his cohorts into action with truncheons primed and walkie-talkies jabbering – and somehow the scene plunged me into even greater weariness. I paused irresolute, envisaging the pandemonium; and with stocking in one hand and pyjama top in the other, weighed the pros and cons. Police or sleep? The latter was the more enticing. And thus with dawn only four hours hence I decided to shelve the matter. After all, it was not as if the body had been found in a river and thus liable to float away: one cannot proceed far in a dew pond. And even in these urban times, here in Sussex there still lurks a random shepherd or two, and doubtless such a one would make the same discovery. A hue and cry would ensue while I could remain at a safe distance, i.e. in bed, and thus be spared the tedium of a nocturnal visit from the investigating authorities.

Yes, I told myself, when in doubt wait and see – one of Pa's more practical dicta. Luckily the condition of doubtfulness rarely afflicts me, unlike it did Francis, but when such moments do befall, staying one's hand is no bad thing.

The hand, however, was not stayed for long as curiosity got the better of me. Thus with the first note of the blackbird I flung back the bedclothes wildly agog to learn more of Topping's misadventure and the cause of such malice – for malice there had most certainly been. Naturally, the man must have done something pretty dire to inflame such an attack. My earlier suspicions were entirely justified, spot on surely; though I have to say that I had not foreseen him as a *victim*, rather the reverse. Nevertheless it just went to show that he had been far from kosher, however good his Latin. I mean if he had been above board he wouldn't have got murdered, would he? (Admittedly no one could have accused Mrs Fotherington of not being above board, but then she had been a special case . . . as was her assailant.)

I dressed hurriedly but dallied over breakfast, filling up

on jam and black coffee while devising a pretext for visiting the school to see exactly what was going on. I sat and brooded, idly scanning the spines of the cookery books. And then suddenly a title caught my eye: *Pen Scratches from Mongolia: An Artist's Vision*. I was perplexed. What an uninspiring title and whatever was it doing there? It certainly wasn't one of mine for I had no desire to visit Mongolia, still less have a vision of it . . . And then, of course, I remembered: the book had been thrust upon me by Winchbrooke on my return from the Auvergne a couple of years previously. He had seemed to think the two regions held some similarity, though what I can't imagine, and had presented it to me on a 'long loan'. Well, long or short, I certainly didn't want it cluttering up my bulging shelves: it should be returned to its owner forthwith. A splendid excuse. I leapt from the table, grabbed the book and my coat, and with mind ablaze with questions, set off for Erasmus House.

Halfway there I bumped into Charles Penlow and his cairn terrier ambling towards me on the path leading from the school. 'I say, Charles,' I demanded, 'have you just come from Erasmus and did you hear anything?'

'What?' he said, looking blank.

'The *school*. Have you been there, and if so what's going on?'

'Er, well no actually – we've just been to the vet's. Duster's got something in his paw, a thorn I think. Roberts has mixed some stuff for it and I have to give the little blighter hot poultices until it starts to—'

'Oh dear, poor dog,' I said impatiently. 'So you haven't heard anything then?'

'Heard what?'

I started to relate my ghastly discovery but stopped abruptly. It doesn't do to be precipitate in such matters; far better to stick to my original plan of simply making a casual appearance at the place and subtly absorbing what intelligence I could. Thus I gave dog and owner a ravishing smile and said I hoped they would both be better soon. I thought Charles looked a little puzzled but I hadn't time to hang about and took off smartly.

Entering the school gates, I crossed what they ambitiously call the quadrangle – a sort of flag-stoned yard with pots of ferns festering in dank corners. At the main door a miniscule child accosted me whom I recognised as Sicky Dicky – Richard Ickington, grandson of the high court judge of the same soubriquet. Dicky had been the proud recipient of a prize I had recently presented for the best junior painter of wildlife – newts principally – and he took his Fine Art studies very seriously.

'I say,' he piped excitedly, 'you will never guess what we've seen up at the dew pond!'

'Really?' I enquired blandly, heart lurching.

'*Yes*, it's super-duper! Gave us quite a shock I can tell you. You ought to go up there and take a look, Miss Oughterard. You'll get a big surprise.'

Like hell I would! . . . I gazed benignly at the little boy, trying to project an air of unruffled interest. Friends with children tell me one should never evince alarm or undue agitation with the young, it unsettles them. 'And what would that be?' I murmured.

'Masses of them, the thing's simply crawling. All over it they are!'

'What *thing*?' I said sharply, revolted by his words.

'The pond! All those tadpoles – hundreds of them and baby newts too. It's chockers! We were there yesterday morning and Mr Cheesman says it's the sudden warm weather, makes them hatch and grow you know.' He beamed rapturously, and then plucking my arm added, 'And what's more I'm going to paint them – all in different sizes and in different patterns. Perhaps I'll get a prize again. Grandpa would like that; he says I'm a right little Picasso. Do you think it's a good idea, Miss Oughterard?'

'Wonderful,' I said faintly. He capered off, warbling Colonel Bogey, while I sat down heavily on the porch bench and drew a deep breath.

Collecting my thoughts I considered my next move: obviously a direct approach to Winchbrooke's study flourishing book and gushing its praises . . . Foiled again. *Fräulein* Hockheimer clattered towards me garbed in a voluminous smock which she clearly thought had something to do with Renoir. I put my head down and scrabbled in my handbag, vainly hoping she would pass by.

'Ach, Madame Hooterayde,' she exclaimed, 'what honour to zee you hi-er. I was just telling ze boys vat interesting talks ve hef hed at the party of Hoobat!'

'Of who?' I said.

'Herr Topping. You remember ve spoke of—'

'Ah . . . yes, indeed. And, er, tell me *Fräulein*, how *is* Mr Topping?'

She looked a trifle downcast. 'Alas, he ist gone.' Too right he's gone, I thought. 'A big shame because he vas going to help me viz my picture framing but suddenly he disappear!' I was about to enquire how suddenly when she

83

added brightly, 'But he certainly come beck tomorrow.'
Her faith was almost touching.

'Well that's nice,' I said kindly. 'Now tell me, have you
seen the headmaster because I really need to speak—'

'He is gone too.'

'Where? To the police station?'

'Oh no, they cancelled ze fine.'

I regarded her with mild irritation. 'I am not referring
to Mr Winchbrooke's misdemeanour on the A27, but his
going to the police to report a crime.'

'But he is not with ze police; he is in London with Herr
Topping. Hoobat is going to present there a special paper,
"*Vax Lyrical Viz Latin Syntax*".' She beamed. 'He is *very*
clever, you know. Now if you will excuse me I must go and
"zound ze brass"!' She pounded off, smock billowing; and
the next moment my ears were rent by the crashing of the
school bell. It was, I felt, time to leave.

CHAPTER FOURTEEN

The Primrose Version

I walked home in a semi-daze stunned by Hockheimer's words. Could the woman be right? Was Topping really in London with Winchbrooke 'vaxing lyrical' with his Latin syntax? If so, what was he also doing up at the dew pond minus his head? Clearly the two conditions were incompatible. Assuming the art mistress was not totally addled (questionable), there were two possibilities: either the headmaster had slain his companion – or the thing I had seen the previous night had not been Topping at all but some other corpse.

I reflected on this, bringing to mind the hastily noted details of build, jacket, signet ring, receding hair and, of course, the floating rose. Rather reluctantly I had to admit that the first four features were not necessarily the monopoly of Topping – a lot of men were below average height, wore brown-checked jackets with elbow patches, were growing thin on top and, albeit more rarely, wore signet rings. Thus I conceded that the victim could perhaps be A. N. Other. But then what about the rosebud for God's sake? Surely A. N. Other hadn't been given to sporting one of those as well.

I was just musing upon these matters and deciding that I should ring Emily immediately to verify if Winchbrooke and Topping were indeed in London, when I was startled (bludgeoned) by the blaring of a klaxon. Its provenance was a black vintage Citroën of Gestapo mien parked by the bridge. One sees few of such models these days, and indeed the only one that I know hails from Brighton and belongs to Nicholas Ingaza. I glared at the vehicle and was acknowledged by a languid wave from the driver's window.

Crossing the road I was torn between remonstrating about the noise and divulging my astonishing news. The latter seemed the more interesting. 'I say, Nicholas,' I said, manoeuvring myself into the passenger seat, 'I've had the most ghastly experience, you've simply no idea.'

'Oh yes?' was the response, 'the town clerk asked you to elope, has he?'

'No, a different sort of ghastliness. I have encountered a headless corpse at the Chalk Hill dew pond; yesterday just after midnight. It was dreadful!'

Ingaza raised an eyebrow and observed mildly that if I insisted on roaming the Sussex downs in the middle of the night then I must expect such horrors.

'Don't be facetious,' I retorted, 'I was returning from a bridge supper and stopped to let the dog out.'

'Ah, I see: half-cut, I suppose.'

'Certainly not!' I snapped. 'Kindly be sensible and just *listen*.' And I proceeded to apprise him of the gory details and my perplexity over the victim's identity.

When I had finished he said thoughtfully, 'I must say, you Oughterards seem to have an appetite for trouble, or do I mean aptitude? Either way, you manage to get embroiled easily enough. I wonder if it's to do with—'

I was incensed. 'Aptitude for trouble?' I cried, 'that's rich coming from you, Nicholas! If Francis hadn't found himself in your clutches his life might have been considerably smoother. As it is—'

'As it is it was largely through my solicitous direction that the dear boy escaped the scaffold. Why, without my guiding gaiety to keep him sane he wouldn't have stood a chance. Fair dos, Primrose.' He had the nerve to grin.

'Fair dos, my arse! What about your abortive scheme flogging my paintings to the Ontario art market under false pretences? I could have lost my reputation over that.'

'But you didn't. And you also made a nice little packet, initially at any rate.'

'Less lucrative than yours,' I reminded him sharply.

He sighed. 'Yes, I fear that's the way with business, the middleman takes the biggest cut. Now have one of these and let us give thought to your current situation; rather more pressing I should say.' He whipped out the Sobranies, and in a fog of swirling fumes we assessed the matter and discussed my next move.

In fact my next move amounted to nothing; for we agreed that the best thing was for me to return home as originally planned and wait for 'intelligence to filter through', as filter it surely would.

'So you don't think I should report anything to the police?' I had asked.

'If they don't know yet, they soon will,' was the

dry reply. Having once been caught in a delicate position (indelicate really) involving a Turkish bath, Ingaza regards the police with a wariness bordering on paranoia. It was a wariness that my brother, for another reason, came to share. Personally, I had no particular reason for wariness other than the knowledge that reporting a crime does not automatically exclude one from the list of suspects. 'Speak when necessary,' Pa had always counselled, 'and *never* before.' Had he taken his own advice, life at home would have been infinitely quieter . . . However, the principle was sound enough.

I was about to get out of the car when Ingaza asked if I had told anyone else.

'Haven't seen anyone except for Charles Penlow. I thought he might have heard something but he obviously hasn't; kept rambling on about that po-faced cairn terrier of his, so I said nothing and went on up to the school.'

He looked surprised. 'Penlow? I thought he was playing the *flâneur* in the Caribbean.'

'Well he's back now playing the master-builder in Sussex, though I can't think why. That Podmore Place of his should be bulldozed and replaced by a set of smart town houses. He could make a lot of money that way.'

'But it's not in the town,' Ingaza objected.

'Irrelevant. It's the concept that counts.'

He looked at me thoughtfully and said something to the effect that for an artist my outlook was refreshingly materialistic.

'Well, that makes two of us,' I replied briskly. 'Now what about this corpse? Do you think it's Topping? I bet you it is.'

'Evens?'

'Certainly not. Ten to one on.'

He nodded. 'Cash, of course.'

'Of course.'

CHAPTER FIFTEEN

The Cat's Views

Alas, I have been proved right. Peace here in Sussex is as illusory as it was in the vicarage. Our mistress has taken it into her head to pursue the Top-Ho character, and from what I can make out has resumed her contact with the Brighton Type. It seems he has given her information which has turned her suspicions into certainties and we all suffer accordingly. That is not quite correct: *I* suffer, the dog rejoices. Bouncer has a puerile lust for excitement, hence his goading of the chinchillas, and is more than intrigued by Top-Ho and whatever shenanigans P.O. imagines he is engaged in.

Rather reluctantly, however, I have to admit that there may be some substance to her views. In my few idle moments I have passed a discerning eye over the man and am not entirely taken with what I see. Homo sapiens with small feet and glib tongues are generally suspect, and he undoubtedly belongs to that category. Besides, he rides a bicycle, a machine that I have never found appealing. I recall my mother once having a contretemps with such a contraption – or rather its rider; and while she survived with ease – clinging to the spokes and dislodging the incumbent – the incident did little to endear me to the things. Bouncer's tale of seeing Top-Ho peddling furiously to the telephone box that night was intriguing and I still haven't fathomed the purpose. But I shall get to the bottom of it without a doubt . . . I might enquire of Eleanor. She is a sound sentinel and may well have some views on the matter.

And talking of Eleanor, she has been most useful in introducing me to the better type of local feline. I am not by nature a gregarious cat but it is nevertheless reassuring to know there are others in the area who share the same cultural bent as myself. I think too that I have already established myself as a cat worthy of regard, and one not averse to waving a gracious paw when occasion requires – providing, of course, the recipient is not a tabby or a Manx; naturally a line has to be drawn somewhere. For the moment, however, such social niceties must yield to more pressing matters – the sampling of the pilchards P.O. has prepared. And after that I think a little snooze is in order . . .

Great Cod! What a to-do. Bouncer has found a dead head if you please! Yes, up on the downs in a pond – or at least the body was, its head being on the grass. P.O. had gone on some card-sharping jaunt and taken the dog with her, and apparently on the way back he had let it be known that he wanted to stretch his legs (or squirt the bunnies as he so crudely put it). Apparently our mistress got out with him, lit a cigarette and wandered around gazing at the stars, something humans like to do. He said that ten minutes later he heard her making a sort of gagging noise, and when he went to take a look, noted she had her nose shoved in a gorse bush. Thinking that was a bit odd even for the Prim, he started to move closer and came face-to-face with a circular apparition on the edge of the pond. 'A bloody great bonce with staring eyes' were his exact words. Now Bouncer, of course, is given to melodrama so one cannot vouch for the eyes, but the rest of his description has the mark of veracity. He said it was a cracking adventure because there was also 'a thing' sprawled in the water wearing a brown-checked jacket, but that P.O. did not seem to share his interest as she insisted on dragging him back to the car which she then drove home 'at one hell of a lick'.

As it happens, I could see something was amiss the moment they came through the front door. Instead of going up to bed in the usual way, our mistress rushed to switch on the fire in the drawing room and then made a headlong dive for the drinks cabinet. I had seen her brother do that often enough and recognised the symptoms: blind panic. Bouncer too was in a turbulent state and once we were in the kitchen I had to speak to him very firmly. Rather to my surprise, after he had exhausted his energies with the usual theatricals he went totally silent and just lay there gnawing his paw and gazing into space. I was about to retire for the night to my usual spot in the laundry room, when he suddenly said, 'I say Maurice, I don't suppose you would like to share my basket, would you?'

In normal circumstances nothing would induce me to get into the dog's basket (you never know what you might find – all manner of grisly items: bones, bits of chewed rubber, hairy biscuits and other unsavouries), but it struck me that he might be in the grip of delayed shock. Now, my grandfather had always insisted that we were a family noted for our nobility and skills of self-preservation. The latter I have in abundance but as yet have had little cause to exercise the former; but here perhaps was an opportunity. Thus gritting my teeth I said, 'By all means, Bouncer, I should be honoured'; and without more ado leapt into his basket and began to purr. I think the dog was a little surprised for his jaw hung open for at least twenty seconds. But we settled down easily enough and spent a warm and surprisingly amicable night.

With the first shaft of dawn I dug him in the ribs and urged him to reveal further details of his escapade. 'So apart from the staring eyes, what was the head like?' I enquired.

'Pretty good,' he growled.

I sighed. 'No, Bouncer, it is not the calibre but the character that interests me. Being a cat of forensic interests I should like to know a little of its physicality, such as dimensions, density, colour, texture, amount of hair and colour of eyes etc. – all that sort of thing.'

'Cor,' he grumbled, 'you don't want much, do you?'

'The usual aspects,' I replied carelessly. 'After all, if you come and tell me that you have encountered a human head resting on the brink of Chalk Hill dew pond, I think you could assume I might want the full picture.' I flicked a morsel of chewed Chum off my left paw. 'Reasonable enough I should have thought,' I added.

The dog looked doubtful but then said briskly: 'Well, as dead heads go, I should say it was definitely about average – sort of football size.'

'Really? And how many dead heads have you seen?'

'Hundreds,' he said.

Lies, naturally. But I could see a mulish glint in his eye and conceded hastily that there had indeed been a couple in the past – although from what I could recall, those had been of the attached variety. However, it doesn't do to be pedantic, least of all with Bouncer.

He picked up his bone, dropped it and then licked his chops. 'And,' he grinned, 'not much hair, blue batty eyes and a bit white around the old gills and gullet.'

'Ah,' I said, 'so there was a gullet?'

He cogitated and started to frown. 'No not much, just a bit. What, Maurice, you would call a . . . a . . .' I could see he was groping for the right word but fortunately found it before I had to prompt him.

'A *remnant*,' he shouted triumphantly. 'That's it – the bonce had a remnant of gullet!' He paused, and added brightly, 'though I suppose it might have been his wind funnel.'

I closed my eyes: partly to muffle the noise, partly to blot out the image and partly to decide whether I should congratulate him on his improved vocabulary or rebuke him for the reversion to slang. Teaching the dog the Queen's English is a taxing task – every step forward entailing at least another backward. But I feel it my bounden duty and thus I press on . . .

CHAPTER SIXTEEN

The Primrose Version

I lost my bet. And, needless to say, Nicholas was scrupulous in exacting payment. However, such pedantry irritated me far less than learning that the headless ghoul in the pond was definitely not Topping. It was in fact one Dr Alan Carstairs whom the local newspaper assured us was 'a much loved member of the Mathematics Department at Erasmus House'.

Personally I had never heard of Dr Carstairs and he certainly wasn't in evidence at Topping's little soirée; and neither was I aware that the school ran to a *department* – in maths or anything else. The term implied a scholastic grandeur which I couldn't help feeling was not entirely commensurate with the institution's status. However, this was a minor puzzlement compared with the identity of Carstairs.

My first line of enquiry was naturally Emily, who assured me that he did exist (or had) and that, as suspected, there was no such department but simply the arithmetical teaching of Dr Carstairs – who as far as she was aware had not been especially loved anyway. I found that a trifle sad. I mean not to be much loved *and* to lose one's head does seem a bit of a raw deal. Clearly Emily thought the same for she kept repeating, 'So sad! So sad!' . . . until I have to admit it rather set my teeth on edge. Lamentation is all very well but there comes a point when enough is enough. That point had long been reached and I told Emily so in no uncertain terms. She regarded me reproachfully and said that clearly I had no conception of the vileness of Dr Carstairs' fate and that lacking an imaginative sensibility I was incapable of visualising his awful end. Feeling denial might be injudicious I refrained from telling her that I recalled every grotesque detail.

As previously explained, on the night of my discovery I was so exhausted by the experience that the prospect of raising the alarm had been too daunting. However, some might wonder why, as an upright member of our community and not one for shirking her civic duty, I did not march straight down to our local police station the following morning and furnish them with the essential data. The answer is simple: wisdom. Having had a murderer for a brother (and he a vicar), I do have some small insight into such matters. And part of that insight is the recognition that silence is golden, or at least moderately useful. Francis's part in the Fotherington episode and its embarrassing aftermath might have turned catastrophic had he not exercised considerable verbal restraint. There is no point in thrusting oneself into the limelight unless such thrusting is to one's immediate benefit. And given the circumstances I felt that my personal knowledge of Carstairs' fate was unlikely to confer much of that. Indeed quite possibly the reverse . . . It is amazing how quickly police and press jump to erroneous conclusions; and when all is said and done one does not care to be compromised by a severed head. Thus following parental advice I concluded that the less said the better.

However, it was not simply unease concerning the questionable acumen of the authorities that checked my tongue, but also unease concerning the perpetrators. Who knew what they might think – or more to the point *do* – were it to become known that Primrose Oughterard had been at the dew pond only minutes after the victim had hit the waters? I mean to say, they could have wondered what exactly it was that I had seen or heard. Luckily I had heard nothing other than my own retching into the gorse bush but they weren't to know that. Thus to avoid any wrong assumptions on their part I deemed silence the best course.

Alas, it was a discretion I was unable to sustain. I had overlooked the fact of Nicholas Ingaza, and that in my initial anxiety I had been so foolish as to inform him of my experience. At the time it had rather piqued me that he had not accorded my account the respect it deserved; but *now* I fervently hoped he would forget about it altogether. A vain hope, naturally. Ingaza forgets nothing – particularly anything that might place him in a position superior to that of his confidant; something my poor brother learnt to his cost.

Thus just as I was deciding that silence was by far the best policy and that at least no one else should hear of my nightmare, the telephone rang and it was Nicholas himself enquiring whether I would care to accompany him to one of the Brighton Pavilion's periodic *thé dansants*. Now, I was under no illusion that it was the pleasure of my company that he sought, but rather an appreciative audience for the finer points of his tango routine. This routine is invariably slick, convoluted and subtly spectacular; and in the course of time I have developed a grudging admiration for the skill of its exponent. What Nicholas Ingaza may lack in prettiness of character is made up for (nearly) by prettiness on the dance floor.

My own skill being the ordered predictability of the foxtrot, it is not I who partners him in such movements but some leaden-faced girl called Mona. Other than the articulation of 'cor' and 'that was a nifty one, Nick', I have never heard Mona speak. In fact I rather doubt if Ingaza has either, their relationship *off-piste* being as frigidly distant as it is closely intimate *on*. The gulf between professional and private worlds can be wide, something which my brother's troublesome victim had failed to grasp. Had she done so we might all have been saved a heap of vexation. Still, that was then. And *now* my immediate concern was what to wear when listening to tango rhythms at five in the afternoon and applauding the Ingaza gyrations.

But inevitably the sartorial question gave way to cynical suspicion. Was it sheer coincidence that Nicholas had issued his invitation on exactly the same day as the newspapers were at their most fulsome regarding 'the butchered schoolmaster'? The item was front page and double-spread, and had even merited a reference on the six o'clock news. At the time of telling, Nicholas had received my bombshell with scepticism, not to say a bantering levity. But with the press luridly confirming my tale, his interest could have been spurred into wanting to re-hear the details – as confirmed from the horse's mouth.

Well, I decided, the horse might just turn mulish and demand several cocktails plus dinner at the Grand before she re-spilt the beans. So with that settled I returned to the question of frock and earrings.

As things turned out my accoutrements were a great success. 'My dear,' Ingaza murmured, his sallow cheeks a little flushed after a rousing fandango with Mona, 'I *love* the ensemble – so chic. And how those danglers match the colour of the formidable peepers!'

I narrowed the peepers. 'This won't get you anywhere, Nicholas,' I said. 'Pretty compliments butter no parsnips.'

'It's not parsnips I'm after, dear girl, merely information. Here have one of these.' And he thrust an inevitable Sobranie my way. I took it and said nothing. He in turn shrugged, flicked the snake hips and, gesturing imperiously to Mona, resumed the floor.

I had to admit it was a masterly display; and the other couples, able though they were, seemed bland in comparison. I watched with pleasure and irritation. Francis had once dubbed Ingaza an adroit bastard. Both terms were apt. But mesmerised by those mercurial twists and flips, and despite agreeing with my departed brother, I couldn't help recalling the bastard's tears at the latter's funeral . . . I sighed. Yes, I acknowledged, I'll tell him every detail – and be glad of it. After all, the only other witness had been the dog and I could hardly discuss it with him.

Thus over supper, *not* dinner at the Grand, but nevertheless a fair menu and cocktails at the Old Schooner, we chewed the cud and assessed the situation.

'I take your point,' Nicholas said cheerfully, 'your own

position is a trifle slippery. Some people would go straight to the authorities and demand police protection. But in my experience that is of dubious value. If they really want to get you they will.' He smiled, and set about filleting his plaice with deft precision.

'Always such a comfort, Nicholas,' I said coldly. 'And naturally you have knowledge of such matters.'

'Oh not *personally*, of course, but I do know those who have.' The left eyelid came down like a shutter.

'Doubtless,' I said tartly. 'But honestly, Nicholas, who ever are these fiends? And what on earth had that faceless little maths teacher done to warrant their attention?'

'Ah well,' he replied darkly, 'you can never tell with assassins. Take Francis for instance—'

'Certainly not,' I snapped. 'Any such comparison is vulgar.'

He ignored that, and laying down his knife and fork said, 'And have you got a story ready for the police?'

'No idea,' I began, and then stopped. 'The police? What have they to do with it? I have just *told* you, I haven't reported a thing.'

'No but that doesn't necessarily preclude their interest. They will probably want to interview everyone connected with the school, even visiting artists however worthy. Besides, you might have left a clue.'

'Don't be ridiculous. What sort of clue? A splodge of sick, I suppose. Really Nicholas you are being absurd.'

'No, not the contents of your stomach but a set of tyre marks, for instance. You did say that you had revved up like hell in your haste to get away. A fine night admittedly, but it had rained heavily the previous day and the ground would have been quite soft – ideal terrain for leaving tyre prints. Actually, now I come to think of it I seem to remember your dear brother having a little problem with tread patterns, quite a palaver, wasn't it? But he foiled them in the end . . . with our help I fancy.' He gave a dry smile, and then, scanning the room, gestured to the bar in the corner. 'Do you know, if memory also serves me right, it was from that very stool that I suddenly saw him after a ten-year gap. He hadn't changed, of course, just as awkward. Poor old Francis. Mind you, at that point there was something for him to be feeling awkward about, wasn't there?' He gave a sly wink.

'Enough of this nostalgia,' I said impatiently. 'And, as it happens, I had parked on the road, not the grass; so kindly stop spreading alarm and despondency about tyre marks. You only do it to annoy.'

He shrugged. 'Only partly; it's mainly a friendly warning. Be prepared for a visit from the heavies, that's all.'

Friendly or not, the warning had unsettled me, but I remained cool and replied that I was sure I could deal with the attentions of the police *were* it to become necessary.

Ingaza replied that he was sure I could but was I equally confident regarding the perpetrators? 'After all,' he said, 'you have no proof that they still weren't there when you stopped the car to walk the dog. It's not inconceivable. Perhaps Chummy the Axeman was in the middle of sluicing down his weapon when you and Bouncer came blundering on the scene and he hid behind a tree and tracked your every movement.'

'There are no trees on that part of the downs,' I replied icily. 'I certainly do *not* blunder, and you are making me sick. What's for pudding?'

We scrutinised the menu, opted jointly for treacle

101

sponge and turned to the question of Carstairs alive.

'Emily tells me he was very pleasant,' I said, 'but then Emily says that about a lot of people; it doesn't mean a thing – merely that they haven't caused her offence. An unreliable witness you might say.'

'Pleasant or not, he had evidently caused offence to someone. Something that necessitated his disposal; though I have to say that the head-hacking does seem a trifle otiose: a whimsical afterthought perhaps.'

I shuddered. 'Disgusting!'

'Of course it may have been some form of further punishment, the product of vindictive pique.'

'Some pique,' I exclaimed, 'they must have been mad.'

'Dangerous certainly but not necessarily mad. According to the press reports the beheading was posthumous; which, if one discounts crude humour, suggests an act of calculated intent.'

'What intent? Hardly to veil the victim's identity; the head was left *there*, all primed for public exposure. It was propped against a stone.'

'Exactly. So it was to make a point perhaps.'

'Do you mean a sort of example, a warning?'

He nodded. 'A kind of *memento mori* to deter others from intended transgression.'

'Intended transgression? Gosh, you sound just like Francis after he had had one too many. Must have been that seminary you were both at: clearly the idiom gets into the bones. Anyway, what have you in mind – some Vatican revenge on one of its stool pigeons?' I laughed loudly – not because I was in jocular mood but rather to deflect my mind from what Ingaza had said about the danger of my own situation. It was too bad: I had been seeking reassurance!

How naïve; one should have known better. Ingaza has the talent to perturb honed to a fine art.

It is an art that Maurice shares; for when I returned home it was to find the cat curled up in the open hat-box left on my bed. The hat had been delivered from Swan & Edgar only that afternoon and I hadn't even had time to try it on. And now it was crushed and covered in cat hairs with Maurice snoring gently on top. Had Ingaza been a cat, it was exactly the sort of cavalier indifference he too would have shown.

CHAPTER SEVENTEEN

The Cat's View

'You know,' Bouncer said, 'I'm not too sure about that Duster fellow, a bit cranky if you ask me.' He gave a shove to his grub bowl, a gesture invariably indicative of smug assurance. It's the clatter: I think he feels it clinches the point.

'Actually,' I replied, 'I was not intending to ask; but since you raise the subject I should say he is pleasantly quiet and—'

'That's just it,' the dog bellowed, 'too blooming quiet! And he's got this funny face, it always looks the same.'

'If you mean he is restrained and not given to making gross and vulgar grimaces, then I would agree. He strikes me as being couth, Bouncer, *couth*.'

He looked puzzled. 'What's couth?'

'It is what you are not; and the opposite of your erstwhile accomplice O'Shaughnessy.' The Irish setter had been Bouncer's bosom pal in Molehill; a creature of intemperate habits whose main aims in life had been to rev up 'the craic' and irritate *me*.

A wistful look entered the dog's eyes and for a moment I regretted my words. Not for long, of course. It doesn't do to be overly indulgent.

'Well,' I said briskly, 'I am sure when you get to know each other a little better you will find Duster a most congenial playfellow. There's probably more to him than meets the eye.'

'Hmm,' he grunted sceptically, 'let's hope so.'

'Come now,' I said, 'it's not like you to be so negative. Why this sudden wariness of the cairn?'

'I met him the other day on his lead with the tall man. I was on my lead too with the Prim, and they hung about jabbering for ages. So while they were doing that I took a good look at the cairn. And do you know, he just stood there staring into space – well, into the hedge as a matter of fact. Personally, I don't think it's a very interesting hedge, not as hedges go that is. I mean there are some hedges which are just the job but—'

'Job for what?' I enquired with interest.

'Most things,' he replied vaguely.

'And this one wasn't?'

He shook his head. 'Not that I could see but the cairn seemed to think so.'

I cleared my throat. 'Uhm, you don't think by any chance that he was trying to avoid your eye, and hence the fixation with the hedge?'

'Avoid my eye, my arse!' the dog barked. 'Why should he want to do that? There's nothing wrong with Bouncer's eye!'

'Nothing at all,' I agreed hastily. 'It's a very fine eye, as is the other one.' I was about to add *when* it can be seen through that mountainous fringe – but thought better of it.

'But bear in mind that Duster being a cairn is quite small; and you as a woolly mongrel are quite large. You may have intimidated him.'

'Done what?' he said.

'Perhaps you put the frighteners on him. He is probably shy.'

There was a silence while the dog digested this. And then a slow leer spread over his face and he said, 'You mean, Maurice, that the cairn was SHIT-SCARED!' The tail, which until then had been hanging loosely, began to wag rhythmically.

'Well, I wouldn't put it quite like that,' I began, 'but—'

He emitted a low chortle. 'But that's what you mean I bet.' The wagging accelerated.

Picking my words carefully I replied, 'What I mean is that Duster may not possess your confidence and robust temperament. He may not share your – how shall I put it? – your *élan de guerre*.'

The dog frowned, evidently puzzled. And then after giving his bowl a few thoughtful shoves, looked up and said, 'What you are saying is that I am tough and he is weedy.'

'A slight simplification. Do not mistake silence and short legs for weediness. You may well find that he has remarkable qualities.' I was slightly doubtful of this but it doesn't do to encourage the dog's prejudice. 'Remember,' I continued, 'we are still new to the neighbourhood and it is rash to pre-judge or annoy the natives. Take my advice: cultivate the cairn. Ask him what he finds so fascinating about the hedge; enquire what type of bones he prefers. You may be pleasantly surprised by his response.' I added one or two other helpful tips, and smiled encouragingly, rather pleased with my little homily.

The dog scratched and then yawned. 'Well I'm for a good kip. See you in the morning, Maurice.' And seizing a couple of his hairy toys he settled into his basket and went to sleep . . . As a coda to my words of wisdom, this struck me as rather limp. I gave an indifferent shrug and prepared for my nightly prowl.

In fact it turned out to be a most productive prowl – longer than anticipated but very absorbing. I was just gliding quietly along the lane in the direction of Podmore Place when who should I meet coming from the opposite direction but the Persian, Eleanor. Since last cavorting with her amid the chimney stacks of the town brewery, I had been practising my steps for the Kit-Kat Trot – a caper much in vogue among the more fashionable of the Sussex *catarati*. And thus I was just about to enquire whether she might like to accompany me to the next rooftop gathering, when she said she had something rather intriguing to show me and would I like to follow her back to the Big House. 'We shall be just in time,' she said.

'By all means,' I replied, 'but in time for what exactly?'

She gave a discreet miaow and said she couldn't be sure *exactly* but there was definitely something afoot and that doubtless my probing mind would solve the mystery.

Modesty prevented me from agreeing about that, but I eagerly followed her to Podmore Place where she led me round to the old stables at the rear. '*He* lives over there,' she said, gesturing with her paw to a far wing, 'but he can't see anything from that angle.' She obviously meant the owner, the tall man whose cairn terrier had so exercised Bouncer.

Judging from their dilapidated state, these stables had obviously not been used for years. Nevertheless my sensitive nostrils quickly picked up the whiff of ancient horse. I have an aversion to these ungainly beasts, as I have to many things, and thus was not especially drawn to loitering within their habitat, however long deserted. But Eleanor seemed very keen that we should; and so despite my distaste I settled down beside her in the lee of a rotting wheelbarrow.

I was just about to ask her what on earth we were supposed to be doing when she gave a soft mew and lightly touched my tail with her claw.

I looked up. And in the far distance, coming down the disused drive, I saw the faintest glimmer of a light getting gradually nearer. It was a very wavering light and at times seemed to disappear altogether. I peered intently into the darkness, trying to discern its source.

'Look away,' Eleanor hissed.

'What?'

'Your eyes are too bright: like socking green fog lamps. He'll fall off his bike if he sees them. Avert them instantly!'

I shut them tightly, too surprised to do otherwise. A few moments later she gave me a prod and said I could open them. When I did so the light had vanished, but instead there was the clear outline of a bicycle propped against the stable wall. Next to it, fumbling with what was evidently the lock on the door stood the familiar figure of a rather short man: Top-Ho.

'Well if that doesn't take the haddock,' I murmured. 'How very purrculiar.'

'I don't know about purrculiar,' Eleanor whispered, 'but it's certainly curious because this is the fourth or fifth time

I have seen him doing that, and it is always at night and long after the birds have stopped their blathering. When I first noticed it going on, there was someone else with him also on a bicycle, but he doesn't seem to have come lately: just this one on his own. And it's always the same: he takes packages out of his saddlebag, disappears inside and then comes out about ten minutes later and rides back up the drive.' She emitted a muted miaow and fluffed out her cheeks, an action that makes her look like the furriest mop I have ever seen.

'Well,' I said, 'let us see if he follows the usual routine.'

We settled ourselves more comfortably in the grass, and I toyed with a dandelion while at the same time keeping a sharp eye on the stable door. This eventually opened and the Top-Ho person re-emerged.

Yes, just as Eleanor had predicted, both hands were now empty; and mounting the bicycle with its dying lamp, he wobbled off into the night whence he had come.

I thanked Eleanor profusely for her vigilance and for showing me yet another case of bizarre human behaviour. And responding to her quizzical gaze I said that it was something I should have to reflect upon more fully before assessing its meaning, but if she would care to partner me at the next rooftop revels I would then doubtless have an answer.

'Right-o,' she mewed, and brandishing that enormous tail, crashed into the undergrowth in pursuit of a passing mouse.

I wandered home in ruminative mood. It was interesting the way that this episode tallied with Bouncer's tale of Top-Ho cycling frantically to the telephone box. The destinations were different, of course, but both journeys had been solitary and both under cover of darkness. My immediate thought was to tell the dog of my adventure. But on second thoughts I think I may bide my time a little – it will only excite him and the barking will be excruciating. I shall wait a while and pick my moment.

CHAPTER EIGHTEEN

The Dog's View

Well, things aren't half hotting up here and no mistake! I mean it's not often you come snout to snout with a cut-off human head – especially when you are in the middle of cocking your leg on a lump of rock. There I was at one end and *it* was at the other. Glaring at me. Cripes, did I yelp! I mean it's not the sort of thing you expect to see at a time like that, is it? Quite put me off my stride it did; made everything go haywire . . . As a matter of fact, once I had got over the shock I went a bit haywire myself. After all, it's pretty exciting to be suddenly faced with a dead head and *then* to see the rest of it floating in the water. I can tell you I didn't know which bit to sniff first! Not that I had much of a chance. P.O. didn't seem at all keen to hang about and kept shoving me towards the car. She was a bit of a spoilsport really. Still it was nice while it lasted.

Mind you after we got home I came over a bit queer. Didn't feel like myself at all. Odd really. Maurice said it was *mislaid sock* or some such. Don't know what he meant by that but he said it enough times so I suppose he knew what he was talking about. Anyhow he was quite matey and stayed the whole night in my basket. Now what do you think of that? I thought it was jolly decent, though there *was* one small problem: he twitches like hell when he sleeps and I kept waking up with his tail rammed in my ear. And you know that white paw of his? Well somehow he had stuck it in my jaw; and I was just dreaming that I was chewing on a nice piece of bacon when there was a god-awful caterwaul and I found my mouth stuffed full of gungy wet fur. Ugh! There was a good deal of pussy-limping around in the morning but he didn't say a word – which I also thought was jolly decent. It just goes to show that cats are not always catty . . . Well not ALWAYS, just mostly.

Anyway, after the Prim had given him his early milk and me my biscuit we had a good bow-wow about it all. Maurice was *very* interested in my adventure and wanted to know every detail about the HEAD. I got a bit muddled – I mean a dog can't be expected to remember everything at that time of day, can it? Still, you know how Maurice is, and he wouldn't let up; kept on firing the questions. When he had finished he shut up for a while and closed his eyes, like he does when he is 'mee-oosing', as he calls it. I quite like it when he *mee-ooses* because everything goes still and I can collect my thoughts, e.g. work out what bones I've got and choose where the next burying hole will be. Then, I had just decided on that patch of ground behind the rabbit hutch when His Nibs opens his eyes, swishes his tail and says, 'In my considered opinion, Bouncer, this whole affair is extremely purr-quewlia.'

PURR-QUEWLIA? Big deal, my arse! What the hell did he

112

think that *I* thought when I found the blooming bonce! I mean I know that Maurice is all very clever and uses long words which I don't understand and can count things without using his paws, but ANYONE could see that a dead-headed stiff in a pond was purr-quewlia! Even P.O. was being as sick as a cat – and it takes a lot to rattle her (unlike F.O. who would collapse at the first cuckoo). If you ask me, Mop Face, the grey Persian, has got something to do with it. Ever since she invited Maurice for a night on the tiles he has been what you might call 'distray'. (I think that's the right word – it's the one he uses anyhow; it probably means mad as a coot.) He keeps poncing about in the tool shed kicking up his heels as if he's practising some daft dance – the Pusstrot or something. He thinks I haven't noticed but I'm a crafty hound and I've spied him through the crack in the broken brick. No fleas on Bouncer!

Yes, that's what I think: he's so taken with trying to make a show for Eleanor that only half his mind is on this head business, the other half being up on the tiles among the chimney pots. Well too bad, I say. Bouncer will go it alone and sniff out EVERYTHING.

And to start with I may chew things over with Duster, that tall man's cairn I was talking about earlier. Maurice heard P.O. on the blower to the tall man saying she would visit him soon and bring the new dog. That's ME, of course. If I like the Duster he could be a useful ally – though it doesn't do to be too sudden. *Always size up the buggers first and don't give an inch without gain.* That's what Bowler, my other old master, used to say about his customers (you know, the bank manager in Molehill who ran off with the cash). But that was a long time ago in my puppyhood and before I met my next master, the vicar, so I don't remember him much. But sometimes in dreams I still hear his voice: 'Bouncer, come here, sir. Come here *at once*, sir!' Of course I never did. Why should I?

Anyway, back to the cairn. I am not quite sure what to expect when I get taken there, because the other day when we met on the pavement on our leads he seemed a bit odd, sort of quiet and queer. Kept staring at the hedge and not looking at me. And do you know? His tail never wagged once; not all the time they were yattering on! I told Maurice about this and he gave me a long lecture about how I had got to be patient and not be neg-a-tive. Huh, he's a one to talk – he's the most neg-a-tive cat I know. If Maurice doesn't like something or somebody then don't we all know it! Still he may be right, I suppose. We'll just have to sniff the bone and see what's what.

CHAPTER NINETEEN

Charles Penlow's Journal

Great drama at the school. One of the masters has been found absent without leave . . . or at least not so much without leave as without his head. Yes, on the downs at the Chalk Hill dew pond. An extraordinary business! The papers are full of it and so are the tea shops. It has set the town ablaze and agog. Apparently he was discovered by some shepherd in the early morning: body in water, head a little distant. The shepherd has been living on medicinal brandy ever since.

Murder not being the mark of a good school, it has made the headmaster acutely embarrassed and at first he tried to suggest that it must have been suicide. 'The deceased was always a little dour,' he had ventured to a reporter. However, a number of people, including the police, pointed out that suicides are not generally adroit enough to hack off their own heads let alone place them at some distance from their torsos. Winchbrooke conceded that they had a point. I also gather that the poor chap was the maths master who had joined the school three years ago and whose *Common Entrance* results were remarkable. Indeed it struck me that perhaps this was the work of some vengeful rival (from St Bede's at Eastbourne?) who, being tired of secondary honours, had decided to nip further triumphs in the bud. I had rung Primrose who I thought might have been amused by the idea; but rather unusually she said nothing, cleared her throat and changed the subject. Probably felt the telephone wasn't the place for such drollery. It's time I invited her here and we can explore the matter more freely.

<u>Later</u>

Primrose came, as did the new dog, Bouncer. At first I was a little concerned in case he and Duster didn't hit it off. But I needn't have worried. They sat quietly just staring at each other for a long time; and then without a word (or a bark) slouched off in tandem to the terrace. I've no idea how things proceeded from there but since no sounds of butchery or mayhem ensued, we assumed they were all right.

Whether Primrose was all right I wasn't entirely sure. She seemed a bit shifty . . . well not shifty so much as distracted. I had the impression she had something on her mind, something which bothered her but which she was hesitant to divulge. Such reticence is a-typical. Normally she is only too ready to give tongue, to seize bulls by horns and give a good toss. But tonight there was a distinct holding back, a restraint which I couldn't quite fathom. We talked of this and that – my tussle with the planners over adjustments to Podmore, the government's blunders, the proposed new housing estate, and inevitably the incompetence of the town

116

clerk *(on which topic she did give tongue)*. But all the while I had the impression that her mind, except when directed to the town clerk, was otherwise engaged; and engaged in a way she was reluctant to share.

I offered a second whisky and by way of broadening our agenda said jovially, 'Well now, Primrose, what do you think of this latest affair, our unfortunate corpse?'

She hesitated and then said, 'Oh I suppose you mean the one in the pond that everyone's talking about. All very sordid I consider.'

'But rather fascinating you have to admit,' I observed encouragingly.

'Not necessarily. It sounds beastly.' She gave a dismissive shrug.

I was slightly surprised at this, not realising Primrose was so squeamish. Indeed it seemed most out of character. I recalled her excitement over the stabbing of the Teddy boy at the rectory fête and her fascination with Beachy Head's latest suicide victim whom she was convinced had been pushed. Both incidents had preoccupied her for days. To be so indifferent towards this current drama was unusual to say the least.

I tried again. 'Of course Winchbrooke is terrified of the publicity; he thinks parents will start withdrawing their children once the facts are fully revealed. On the whole, people object to the idea of their progeny having been taught by one destined for decapitation; unsettles them, the parents I mean. The boys love it, of course. Still it'll give the local police plenty to do: that new man MacManus is itching to get his teeth into something. Eager to win his spurs. You'll see, he'll have drummed up witnesses before you can say knife!'

'Witnesses? Oh I shouldn't think there will be any of those,' she said firmly. 'Not up there at that time of night.'

'Ah, but it's amazing how often people loiter in lonely places. Detective novels are full of them.' I laughed. Primrose did not.

'Well,' she retorted, 'I very much doubt if there are any witnesses in this particular case, and it's hardly a novel after all.' She fixed me with one of those glacial stares which invariably spell immovable dissent.

I took the hint and changed the subject. 'So how's your friend, Topping?' I asked. 'The last time we spoke you told me you felt he was distinctly flaky.' I smiled enticingly.

She brightened. 'Oh he's that all right . . . but you know it's all a bit peculiar. I can't quite make out—' She had lowered her voice and leant forward in the old confiding way, and then stopped abruptly as if having second thoughts. I was about to probe further but was forestalled by a crash from the garden door as the two dogs bounded into the room. Anything that Primrose might or might not have been going to say was instantly swept aside.

'Oh look,' she cried, 'they have been having lovely games!' She threw open her arms in rapturous welcome. Bouncer, always a glutton for attention I have since learnt, relished the role of long lost wanderer and responded with frenzied woofs and head butting. Duster, more circumspect, at first hung back but then submitted manfully to the spate of pats and effusions.

Actually I was slightly puzzled by the display. I knew that Primrose was not averse to animals (why else would she have taken on her brother's orphans?). Nevertheless I was surprised at the force of her reaction; she is not normally so demonstrative . . . And then, of course, I realised: the display had been a feint, a handy means of dismissing Topping and whatever it was she had been about to say. Like dei ex machina, *Bouncer and Duster* had appeared just when needed.

Thus hoping to resurrect the theme I suggested we had a final nightcap, but Primrose declined, explaining she had a heavy morning ahead lecturing to the Women's Institute about the habits of sheep. (Apparently it is assumed that because they feature in her paintings that she must be an expert on ovine psychology. She is not in the least but invents the wildest of anecdotes which entrance her audience and increase her sales.) Anyway, as she and Bouncer were leaving I said brightly, 'Well if you hear anything spicy about the dew pond business do let me know!'

'Oh certainly,' was the vague reply.

CHAPTER TWENTY

The Primrose Version

I don't quite know why I was reluctant to talk freely to
Charles about my experience. Ingaza's fault no doubt for
ruffling me about the police. If, as he says, they really are
intending to grill everyone connected with the school,
then nice as Charles is, I don't think this is quite the
moment to have it bruited abroad that I was there. In fact
it's something to be kept dark at all costs. Of course, I
am sure Charles wouldn't *mean* to say anything; but you
never know, he might just let drop something to Agnes
who is *not* known for her discretion. After all, still being
in Tobago doesn't stop her from writing excited letters
to all and sundry – even telephoning were she sufficiently
intrigued. The mayor's wife is still reeling from Agnes's
gaily started rumour that the lady's long sojourn in
London had been prompted by some facelift blunder.
Actually I think she was merely cat-sitting for her sister,
but the seeds are firmly sown . . . Yes, it has to be said
that Agnes Penlow's undoubted charm is matched only

by the size of her vocal cords. Hence my hesitation to confide in her husband.

Of course when he enquired about Hubert Topping I *very* nearly let slip that I had seen a pink rosebud drifting in 'mysterious circumstances'. Thank goodness I realised in the nick of time that such news would naturally establish my presence there. One can see the headlines only too clearly: 'Respected local artist admits to being at murder spot.' No thank you! Fortunately the dogs' sudden entry made a handy smokescreen and I'm sure Charles didn't notice a thing.

I am *extremely* suspicious about that rose; and the more I think about it the more convinced I am that it had fallen from Topping's smug lapel. Carstairs may have been the corpse, but I wouldn't mind betting that H.T. was the perpetrator, or at least foully involved. It is a shame that I cannot discuss such matters with Charles for he is one of the few people around here who is solid and whose judgements are moderately shrewd. Ingaza's judgements may be shrewd but he is far from solid. However, with no other suitable confidant available (Emily being less than sound) I may have to brave the pain and speak further with him. This will entail the expensive pleasure of inviting him to tea (must remember to replenish the Scotch – grocer's will do). But meanwhile I must get hold of Emily and see what I can prise out of her regarding Carstairs and his background.

Emily has a penchant for cream horns . . . actually not so much a penchant as an indelicate greed. And just as I was passing the newly opened Smugglers' Café I observed her in the window gorging disgracefully. *Two* on her plate if you please: one chocolate and one vanilla. Thus seizing the opportunity, I went in and parked myself at her table. I don't think she was terribly thrilled at that, being too enamoured of the pastry feast to welcome tiresome intrusions even from friends. However, undaunted I stated my business.

'Emily, dear,' I enthused, signalling to the waitress to bring another cup, 'how lovely to see you, and at the very moment when I was wondering how you were coping with that dreadful disturbance at the school. It must be so nerve-racking!'

'Yes,' she replied indistinctly from behind the cream horn, 'it is rather.' And then after a pause she added, 'It does one good to get away for some private peace and quiet occasionally.'

Well, frankly, if Emily Bartlett thought she could give me the brush-off like that I fear she was much mistaken. I flashed a sympathetic smile. 'Oh absolutely,' I agreed earnestly, and pressed on. 'And what about poor Mr Winchbrooke? How is he dealing with the grisly business? Up to his ears with police enquiries no doubt. Must be ghastly for him, especially as good maths teachers are so hard to come by.'

Emily nodded; and embarking on the second cream horn said that things were not helped by the fact that the usual means of advertising, the *Prep School Journal* or whatever it calls itself, was so slow to insert notices. 'It will be weeks before we get a replacement,' she grumbled.

'Well meanwhile you will just have to share someone with St Hilda's,' I said briskly. 'Now tell me about Dr Carstairs. Was he married, for instance?'

'Oh no. He had a mother – or so he said – over at Newhaven I believe. He used to visit her regularly; most weekends and Wednesday evenings too sometimes. He was always scurrying off there – I daresay she did his laundry. Very commendable I am sure.'

I thought I detected an acid note in this last observation, Emily's visits to her own parent at a safer distance on the Isle of Wight being invariably conducted in a mood of Lenten penance. 'Well presumably the police will be interviewing her,' I observed. 'She may well be the key to the whole business.'

Emily scooped up the last bits of the cream horn. 'Really Primrose, you are not suggesting that she *did* it, are you?'

'Of course not but she might know a thing or two . . . about his habits and so forth.'

'What habits? Other than being sarcastic to the boys I don't think he had any – though he did keep a bicycle,' she added.

'Kept a bicycle?' I said in surprise. 'Well, there you are then, *just* like Mr Topping. I expect they were cycling cronies.'

Emily looked bemused. 'I don't think so, or at least not that one was aware. Certainly they both did quite a lot of peddling about, but on the whole in opposite directions.'

'*Very* opposite,' I said darkly. After all, if Topping had had a hand in carving up Carstairs, their interests must have diverged more than somewhat. Needless to say, my point was lost on Emily, who, clearly sated by her gourmandising, seemed ready to depart. But I had one more pressing question: 'Tell me,' I said warmly, 'and how *is* Mr Topping these days? Still sporting that smart pink buttonhole? It has become quite a little trade mark! It's so nice to see a man paying attention to the finer details of his attire. Most seem indifferent to that sort of thing nowadays.'

Emily, in the middle of scrabbling in her handbag for some silver to pay the bill, paused and stared at me. 'That's not what you said the last time you mentioned it. What you said then was that only a neo-nancy or a prissy little fraud would parade a socking great rose in his lapel day after day.'

'Did I say that?' I exclaimed lightly. 'Must have been Maurice's influence; you've no idea how his moods affect one's own.'

Judging from her expression I don't think she was entirely convinced. However, she gave me the answer I had been seeking: 'Since you ask, Mr Topping is most punctilious in his habit. In fact from what I can recall he has broken it only once.' She found a half-crown and was about to call the waitress.

'When?' I asked.

'What?'

'*When* did he not wear the rose?'

She sighed. 'Well really, Primrose, I can't be expected to remember such details, especially when there is this ghastly tragedy looming over us . . . although, as it happens, I rather think it was in early May. Yes, that's right, it must have been the third. I do remember because that was the morning when I was on my way to the dentist and I bumped into Mr Topping coming out of School Hall. At the time I thought he looked a trifle down in the mouth – a bit like me in fact with my bad tooth! We were both in rather a hurry but I did notice that his jacket was without its usual emblem. In fact I made some joking reference to it, but he just shrugged and hurried on, saying something about the bloom having withered in the night . . . Forgot to refill the water, I suppose.' Emily stood up, left the half-crown on the table and with a slightly puzzled smile at me, left the café.

I remained, and lighting a cigarette, hailed the waitress for some fresh tea. There was much to think about. The third of May was, of course, the day that Carstairs and his appendage had been found by the shepherd and when I was barely recovering from my midnight ordeal.

I sipped my tea and brooded. Clearly I should contact Ingaza to fix our rendezvous. Surely with this new revelation he was bound to take things seriously and be of *some* use – if not as an ally then at least as a convenient sounding board. I left the café and started to walk home in a reflective mood.

Absorbed by these thoughts and also wondering whether I should give the dog a treat for its supper, I was suddenly startled by the shrill blast of a bicycle bell and a voice from behind cried, 'Why it's Miss Oughterard, if I'm not mistaken. Walking all the way home? You should get one of these.'

I turned, and smiling politely at the gnome crouched over the bike's handlebars, said, 'Actually, Mr Topping, I have a perfectly good motor car but I often choose to walk – it stimulates thought.'

'How wise,' he exclaimed. 'There's nothing like a good dose of country air to stir the old brain box – although,' and he gave a light chuckle, 'perhaps in your case one should say the paint box. An artist such as yourself must draw great inspiration from the *tangibilities* of nature. All those rambling sheep, rustic churches and enchanted moonlit ponds . . . nature seen in the raw must be vital to the muse!' (Muse? I don't have any muse. Hard graft, that's what.) 'Ah well,' he continued, 'if you will excuse me I must push on. Time and tide and the third-formers wait for no man.' And with a brisk thrust to the peddles he sped off.

I gazed after him. The 'tangibilities of nature' my foot! What extraordinary language these people used . . . And then I froze. What else had he said exactly? 'All those rambling sheep, rustic churches and enchanted moonlit ponds.' What *ponds*? I had never painted a pond in my life, least of all a moonlit one. Not one of my paintings featured such a thing, with or without enchantment! So was this simply part of his vacuous gush, or did the term hold a darker meaning, a sly reference to my presence on that fateful evening? Perhaps, as Nicholas had gaily hinted, I had indeed been observed and this was an oblique way of letting me know. I winced: *not* a happy thought . . . Still, I reasoned, it doesn't do to be overly literal and one should always allow for poetic licence, especially with a smarmy type like Topping. Probably he had included the term randomly to evoke the bucolic style of my pictures. Yes, that was it surely: the term was merely figurative and contained nothing sinister at all. Clearly Emily's revelation about the missing rosebud had made me unduly sensitive and I was seeing connections where none existed.

Thus persuaded, I strode home where I was greeted by

Maurice toting a mangled mouse. He wore that smug, self-satisfied look which invariably hints at further triumphs and whose remains are generally scattered in the kitchen. I entered cautiously. Two more bodies were laid out by the gas stove, their severed heads neatly arranged at their sides. I retreated to the drawing room, and with Carstairs in mind, poured a drink.

CHAPTER TWENTY-ONE

My dear Agnes,
You won't believe this – but since my last letter the
most extraordinary thing has befallen the school:
Mr Carstairs, the maths master, has been found
dead and decapitated at Chalk Hill dew pond.
Yes, can you imagine! No, of course you can't
and neither can anyone else; but it has happened
all right, and to prove it the police are swarming
everywhere like flies or helmeted bluebottles.
Mr Winchbrooke has turned a permanent shade
of gangrenous grey, and Bertha Twigg, the gym
mistress, has taken to her bed declaring that
with this hanging over us she cannot possibly
perform on the parallel bars. In my view no bad
thing . . . the last time she 'performed' was sheer
disaster and there have been complaints ever
since. Anyway, the whole thing is very mysterious
and very grisly.

Now I come to think of it you are probably aware of it all, as I am sure dear Charles will have already informed you of the event. But speaking as one who is willy-nilly in the midst of things – or on the sands at Suez as young Harris and his cohorts keep bleating – I may be able to apprise you of the subtler details.

One such detail is the new chief superintendent for Lewes police force, Alastair MacManus. Actually he is not subtle at all but rather imposing and has taken command in a most assertive manner. Primrose, needless to say, has taken against him, disliking both his manner and the fact that he is (allegedly) teetotal. 'No good can come from such a person,' she informs me periodically. But then, of course, she says the same about Mr Topping – who, as it happens, has turned out to be an absolute gem. Very good with the boys, universally useful and displaying a slightly roguish air which entirely captivates Fräulein Hockheimer. 'He ist zo naice,' she keeps intoning. Mind you, since the dreadful incident the roguish air has been somewhat displaced by a firm sobriety, and on at least two occasions I have overheard him reproving the boys for their ghoulish jokes and lack of respect for the departed. Personally, I feel that Erasmus House can only benefit from one of such sensibility.

Whether Chief Superintendent MacManus has any sensibilities I am not sure but he certainly exudes an air of great competence. I can say this because today he actually took a hand in interviewing the school staff, including Yours truly. I gather from Sergeant Wilding that this is not normal practice, a fact that seems to cause him disquiet . . . well not so much disquiet as mild apoplexy. I think he had been looking forward to doing the job himself and clearly thinks MacManus's intrusion highly irregular. Not being au fait with police protocol, I wouldn't know. However, what I do know is that the chief superintendent is very stern and very searching. Indeed after my session with him I felt not so much 'grilled' as fried to a frazzle! At one point I ventured some light pleasantries but as these were met only with a grunt and a blank stare, I didn't try again.

Afterwards I mentioned this to Mr Topping who said that in his experience the police, particularly the top rankers, were not noted for their frivolity and that I mustn't mind if my little banter had fallen flat. 'Be assured,' he had smiled, 'your piquant wit is not lost on the rest of us.' Evidently Mr Topping has some insight into police psychology and I have to say that I was most reassured, and indeed flattered, by his kind words. When I told Primrose this she laughed like a drain and said that piquant wit was not something she would readily associate with me and it was just conceivable that Topping had been pulling my leg. Really, at times she can be so cynical, not to say rude!

Still, while the chief superintendent may not be blessed with much humour he certainly showed interest when I told him that I knew for a fact that Mr Carstairs had been in the habit of visiting his mother in Newhaven as he had said as much to me on more than one occasion. Yesterday I mentioned this to Primrose who immediately said the mother was bound to be a significant factor in the enquiry – and in this she seems to be right as Mr MacManus lost his grim expression and asked for the address. I explained that not having been on close terms with the deceased it was not, alas, something I could supply. He looked put out by that but wrote a few words in his notebook and said I had been most helpful.

On that cheering note I assumed that was the end of things. Not a bit of it. The next moment he said, 'Now tell me, madam, as school secretary I daresay you have access to quite a lot of correspondence.'

'Oh yes,' I replied, 'you have no idea how much we get: all those edicts from the ministry and the interminable circulars the governors insist on sending out, not to mention shoals of enquiries from the parents. A veritable avalanche! And then, of course, there are all the tradesmen's bills to file, and—'

'Not that sort of correspondence,' he said rather curtly, 'I am referring to letters for the staff. What is the system – are you responsible for their collection and distribution?'

I confirmed that it was indeed my domain and that I was assiduous in personally inserting the letters into the staff pigeon holes. (Being of uncertain eyesight, my assistant Martha is apt to get muddled.)

'In that case,' he said, 'you would doubtless be aware of the volume and provenance of the deceased's post.'

I have to say, Agnes, that I couldn't quite make out whether that was intended as a question or a statement but assumed the former; and nor was I entirely clear on 'volume and provenance' – but took it to mean how much mail did Mr Carstairs get and where did it come from. So I told him that having a demanding administrative schedule it really wasn't something to which I had paid much attention. I don't think he liked that because I noticed one of his fingers beginning to twitch (though, of course, it might just be a congenital tic; Mother has one of those). 'Well perhaps you could pay some attention to the matter now,' he said. 'Naturally my officers searched the deceased's room but rather surprisingly they found no correspondence, either kept or discarded. So it would be helpful if you could recall when he last received a letter – or indeed whether there have been any subsequent to his passing.'

I can't say I was much struck by his tone which held a note of command rather too abrasive for my liking. Still, I suppose that is no bad thing in a policeman – after all they have to deal with some very peculiar types! But, as it happens, I knew I could give him a straight answer: 'Oh yes,' I replied, 'a letter arrived by the late post on the very day that we last saw him. I do remember putting it in his pigeon hole. Indeed who knows, it may still be there.'

This piece of information had a startling effect on my interrogator and he leapt to his feet exclaiming, 'Good God, woman, why on earth didn't you tell me this before? We must get it immediately. Quick: conduct me to the pigeon holes!' As a matter of fact I was feeling a little tired by this time, not to say a mite peckish having missed my usual elevenses; thus I was not especially eager to go traipsing all the way to the staff common room, whoever wished to be 'conducted'. However, he seemed insistent so I did as I was bid.

Was the letter there? No. Only a couple of the headmaster's memos and Harris's hundred lines: something about not catapulting the cat. MacManus asked if I was sure there had ever been such a letter, and rather coldly I told him that I had not been secretary at Erasmus House all this time to make a mistake like that, and that if he wanted my opinion, poor Mr Carstairs had probably retrieved it shortly before his death and dropped it along the way. (I gather his pockets were empty when found.)

At that point, MacManus consulted his watch and said rather abruptly that in view of my heavy schedule he wouldn't detain me any longer. I confess to being very glad about that as I was beginning to find the whole interview somewhat trying. Primrose's remarks about him are unnecessarily scathing; but I would agree that his manner does lack emollience. Still, it is reassuring to know that the case is being handled by somebody of authority and purpose – unlike that idle type from Crawley we had a couple of years ago whose wife was had up for shoplifting and I don't know what else! Yes, Agnes, I am sure that if anyone can get to the root of this disgraceful affair it will be the new broom of Chief Superintendent MacManus.

Your good friend,
Emily

CHAPTER TWENTY-TWO

The Cat's View

Settled in one of my favourite places, the hall window seat facing south, I lay musing upon my experiences of the previous night at Podmore. There was much to consider.

However, I had not got far with my reflections when the dog appeared from the kitchen toting a brand new and assertively orange rabbit with blue waistcoat – clearly yet another toy P.O. had indulged him with. At least it had the merit of being clean. I hastily closed my eyes feigning sleep; not a notably successful tactic but always worth a try.

I could hear him padding around, toenails clicking on the parquet, sniffing this and scratching that. Yet despite these mild irritants there seemed to be something missing which I couldn't quite put my tail on. I opened one eye and shot a discreet look, but he seemed his usual self – tousled and aimless.

I was about to shut the eye but it was too late, he had seen me. 'What are you staring at, Maurice?' he snorted, 'thought you were supposed to be asleep.'

'Just dozing,' I replied casually. 'But since you mention it, do you find that it is unusually quiet in here?'

He frowned and shook himself from side to side, a noisy rat-a-tat action which was only too familiar. But today the racket seemed slightly more muted. 'Where's your collar?' I asked. 'P.O. doesn't generally take it off till after supper.'

'Wearing it,' he said, 'can't you see?'

I peered down trying to discern a glimpse of leather amidst all the fuzz. Yes, he was quite right, it was there. But in that case . . . 'Aha,' I mewed, light dawning, 'Now I know what's wrong. I've been wondering about that for some days: it's your metal name tag, the one that always clinks against the collar studs. It's not there. No wonder things have been a trifle more *piano* recently!' Like my late grandfather's, my ears are acutely sensitive – especially regarding anything connected with Dog. 'P.O. must have taken it off.'

He sat on his haunches and looked thoughtful. 'It's funny you should say that,' he said slowly, 'because now I come to think of it I *have* been feeling a bit odd these last few days . . . it's as if something is missing, like I wasn't quite all there. Do you know what I mean, Maurice?'

'Actually, Bouncer,' I replied, 'I know exactly what you mean; I couldn't have put it better myself.' I raised a paw to my face to veil a smile. I think he was a little surprised at this ready agreement, so I went on quickly: 'I wonder why she has removed it. Perhaps it needs polishing – it is amazing how such trivia will occupy humans.'

'Hmm, don't know about that,' he growled, 'but I want it back. I like the noise it makes, sort of friendly. And besides, it's got my name on; people might not know who I am without it.'

'I shouldn't worry about that,' I assured him, 'they know all right!'

He sighed and looked bleak. 'Even so, I still want it back. Doesn't feel right without it.' Then his ears cocked and he said hopefully, 'Perhaps she is getting me another one, a *bigger* one. That'd be good.'

'Would it,' I remarked dryly. 'And perhaps while she's about it she will also buy you another mammoth rabbit – that one will be eviscerated within a week.' I regarded the orange thing with distaste.

'Huh,' he snorted, 'and bones could fly.' Then he paused and added, 'As a matter of fact, Maurice, I wouldn't mind seeing a flying bone – brighten the day as you might say.'

'Not my day it wouldn't,' I snapped. Really, as if normal ones weren't bad enough, but the idea of an airborne bone was intolerable. Trust the dog to dream that one up!

'Well I think it would be good sport, especially if it had an engine . . . almost as good as a souped-up cat.' He spun round in a circle chasing his tail and then rushed into the garden roaring 'Brroom-brroom! Brroom-brroom!' at the top of his lungs.

I closed my eyes and this time really did try to sleep.

Alas, sleep is becoming almost as elusive here as it had been at the vicar's. No sooner had I begun to nod off than I was disturbed by a loud screeching of tyres and the slamming of a car door. I raised my head, and saw sprawled on the gravel a low-slung black vehicle which I instantly recognised as belonging to the Type from Brighton. I sighed. One had seen quite enough of the Brighton Type when living in that other place and I had always placed him in the category of the Dubious and Dangerous. He had certainly led our master into some very fraught situations. But fortunately P.O. is more resilient than F.O. so I persuaded myself that his arrival here might prove less vexing than in the past.

Vain hope! The moment he set foot in the hall and saw me on the seat he roared with laughter and said to P.O., 'I see you've still got old Scrag-arse keeping sentry. And where's the big fellow, burying bones?'

I am not accustomed to being laughed at and even less to being described as 'scrag-arse'. Thus I leapt to the floor, narrowed my eyes, gave one of the loudest hisses I could muster and stalked off tail at full mast. Disgraceful!

CHAPTER TWENTY-THREE

The Primrose Version

As planned, Ingaza came to tea and was moderately attentive to what I had to say about the Topping matter. Nevertheless his entry was not entirely welcomed by the cat who walked off in obvious ire. I think it was offended by the guest's cavalier manner and to being referred to as 'scrag-arse'; and once we were settled in the drawing room I did murmur a mild reproof: 'It's all very well for you, Nicholas, but you don't have to live with these creatures. I do, and I can tell you they can be very sensitive, especially Maurice.'

'Nonsense,' he replied indifferently, 'that cat has a hide like the proverbial rhinoceros; tough as old boots. And what's more it's not something you'd want to meet on a dark night.'

Actually I was inclined to agree, but said nothing and went instead to fetch the cucumber sandwiches and a bottle of Scotch.

I could see that Ingaza was not enamoured of the

grocer's whisky but I had no intention of raiding Pa's legacy of best malt. He would just have to make do. Besides, after the second glass it is amazing how quickly one becomes attuned.

'So what do you think,' I said eagerly, 'is it really the same Topping that you knew at Oxford?'

He nodded. 'Oh yes, it's him all right. Oddly enough he happened to come into one of the Brighton auction houses last week – only having a general browse, no serious intention. I was there bidding for a pal of mine and saw him at the far end of the room. Older, of course, as we all are, but he hadn't changed really; just as dapper and pleased with himself. Still has those pink cheeks, which was what made me certain.'

'Well, there you are then,' I exclaimed, 'he is obviously up to his fiendish tricks again down here in Sussex. Having been part of Messina's mafia outfit he is bound to be involved in something murky. Leopards do not change their spots,' I said firmly.

Ingaza sipped his whisky, made a sour face and then giggled. 'That's what you said about me once.'

'Doubtless. And I was right too,' I snapped. 'Listen, you may take this more seriously when I tell you what Emily Bartlett has told me about the missing rosebud. I consider the coincidence highly significant.' I gave him a detailed account of what Emily had confirmed about the third of May: the one day when Topping was minus his usual decoration and when only hours previously I had seen a rosebud bobbing about in the water just yards from Carstairs' head.

I also told him about my recent encounter with Topping

astride that ridiculous racing bike. 'He actually referred to a *moonlit pond*,' I cried, 'and I have never painted a pond in my life, moonlit or otherwise. It wouldn't surprise me if it was some kind of covert threat!' My earlier rash dismissal of such fears was by now replaced with nagging doubt.

'Hmm. I suppose you mean a threat to keep your nose out of his affairs and to stop pursuing him like a rabid bloodhound.'

Despite the mocking tone I could see he was intrigued. Indeed long association has taught me that it is in the midst of levity when Ingaza can be at his most lethal – as Francis had so often found. Thus I continued: 'Rabid or not, I intend to get to the bottom of this matter.'

He took another sip of whisky and a large bite of his cucumber sandwich, and rather indistinctly enquired, 'Even if it kills you? Or were you about to add that?'

I said nothing and instead stared at the dog. It saw me looking and gave a friendly belch. 'Bouncer,' I exclaimed, 'you are not to do that! It's disgusting, especially in front of our guest.'

'Oh don't mind me,' said Nicholas graciously, 'you should try living with Eric.'

'Now that *would* kill me,' I said. 'Tell me, how is your lively chum these days – still exercising his elbow with the beer and darts?' Frankly I wasn't in the least interested in Ingaza's loud companion, but thinking of him somehow helped deflect my mind from that last question.

'He sends you his fondest love,' was the solemn reply.

'What?' I cried, 'I barely know the man – I only hear him on the telephone and that's enough.'

Nicholas smiled. 'Yes, that's what your brother used to say . . . But you know, Eric took quite a shine to old

Francis, always referred to him as "that nice vicar geezer".'

'Is that so,' I said dryly, 'and just how does he refer to me?'

He put a finger to the side of his nose and winked. 'Ah well, that would be telling, wouldn't it? But I can assure you he certainly sent his most affectionate felicitations.'

'Affectionate felicitations, my arse!' I snorted.

Nicholas grinned, and then stopped. 'Actually Primrose, since you've introduced the topic yourself, I would suggest you watch your rear. I am being serious. From what I recall of Topping and from what one heard of that particular gang, he is not one to be trifled with. I hate to admit it but you could just be right about his link with Carstairs.'

I watched as he stretched for another sandwich, and felt rather shaken. If Nicholas Ingaza used the expression 'I am being serious', then you knew that this was no light statement and that matters might indeed be dangerous. Thus for a few moments I faltered, tempted to shelve the whole beastly business and instead concentrate my energies on plaguing the town clerk and producing a fresh batch of lucrative sheep pictures – this time possibly featuring a moonlit pond – minus foreign matter, of course.

I had just decided on this when somewhere from the far past I heard Pa's reedy voice recounting yet again his one moment of triumph on the Western Front: *So as Fritz lunged towards me pistol in hand, I shouted: 'Keep back you bastard or I'll have your guts!' And I did too.*

It was a tale that Francis and I had always found faintly curious. That a man as dithering and cack-handed as Pa could have put a spanner quite so firmly in the enemy's works was puzzling. But Mother vouched for its veracity: apparently he had suffered nightmares for years afterwards.

Thus I told myself that if Pa could confront Fritz in his Flanders shell hole, then, with or without bayonet, I could jolly well deal with Hubert Topping here in Sussex.

I leant forward. 'It is precisely because it is serious, Nicholas, that I propose continuing my pursuit. We can't have little toads like Topping behaving unspeakably on the South Downs. *Somebody* has to step in.'

He sighed and took out his cigarette case. 'I was afraid you might say that,' he murmured.

Shortly after he left, I had a phone call. It was from Melinda Balfour. 'I say,' she breathed, 'I suppose you've heard about this dreadful thing on the downs, everyone has. It's too awful for words!'

'Awful,' I agreed tersely.

'Well,' she went on, 'Freddie and I were discussing it earlier, and *he* said, "Sounds to me as if it must have happened when you were just packing up the cards. In fact I imagine Primrose Oughterard would have passed the site on her way home, it's exactly on her route."' Melinda paused and then said, 'My dear, that would be right, wouldn't it?'

'Er, yes,' I replied vaguely, 'I suppose it is.'

'Gosh, just think, you might have *seen* something!'

'Not that I was aware of,' I said hastily, 'it was too dark; and in any case the dog was being difficult – terribly distracting.'

'But don't they say that often witnesses absorb things *subconsciously* and that they just need someone to jog their memory and it all comes flooding back? At least that's what Freddie says. He says it happens all the time.' Oh yes? And how was Freddie to know – Balfour of the Yard?

'Well I hardly think—' I began.

'And MacManus agrees with him, says it's very common,' she added.

I was startled. 'And why was Freddie talking to the chief superintendent? Been nicked on the A27 like poor Mr Winchbrooke?'

Shrieks of laughter from the other end. 'Oh, no, nothing like that. They both attend the same Rotary suppers and Freddie happened to mention the coincidence of you probably passing the pond on your way home from my bridge party. According to Freddie, MacManus seemed quite interested and said something about having to look into it.' There came more loud giggles. 'Just think, you may become one of those people who are said to be "helping the police with their enquiries"!'

I joined in the laughter, while privately planning how to shove Freddie Balfour's stupid pipe down his stupid throat.

CHAPTER TWENTY-FOUR

The Primrose Version

I had spent much of the day in the studio grappling with recalcitrant sheep and ancient hedgerows. My sky was good but the grass poor, and despite the introduction of gambolling lambs and splodges of bluebells, the picture lacked animation. I sighed irritably, unable to settle to the thing. It was not so much that I was bored, but distracted – distracted by thoughts of Freddie Balfour and the likely consequence of his officious comments to the chief superintendent.

I do not like MacManus: his blend of ambition and sanctimony being far from my taste. Doubtless he is more competent than the last man we had here, and his height and jutting jaw seem to impress the more susceptible of our local ladies including, I suspect, Emily. But personally I find his manner wooden and charmless and I certainly did not relish the prospect of being interviewed by him. With luck, I thought, he might send a lackey. But since it was he who had personally appeared at the school, and indeed questioned Emily, it was quite likely that I too might be accorded that dubious honour.

Yet it was not simply the prospect of Alastair MacManus that unsettled me: it was the idea of being interviewed at *all*. As explained, it was clearly in my best interests to steer well clear of any known involvement in so gruesome a matter. Thus to now learn that I was likely to be the object of police probing was distinctly disquieting.

However, as I wielded my brush over sheep and bluebells I told myself that I was becoming absurdly windy. The thing would be perfectly simple: lie like a trooper and tell MacManus or whoever that I had indeed been passing the dew pond in the early hours; and that no, I had not stopped, and that after a merry evening at the bridge table I had been only too glad to get home to my restful bed. Apart from one unsavoury detail this was, of course, entirely true. I could talk rapturously about the silvery moon and luminous sky, the scent of thyme wafting in through the car window and the little lights of Lewes twinkling merrily in the far distance . . . Oh yes, indeed, I would supply lavish descriptions of everything other than that awful balding head, yellowing teeth and staring eyes!

I cogitated and felt slightly better. The point was that other than Freddie Balfour's loose-tongued tattling there was nothing to connect me with the crime scene at all . . . I could await the chief superintendent's approach with relative ease. So with that settled I slung my brush aside and went out to walk the dog.

I say 'walk the dog' – the dog walks me. And I spent the best part of an hour stumbling and bawling in Bouncer's wake as we scoured rutted fields and sodden paths searching for God knows what. Eventually the quest lost its urgency, and with the dog tired and me exhausted we returned to the house to be met by Maurice screeching for his supper. I sometimes wonder how on earth Francis managed. He had never had much stamina (hence the dispatch of Mrs Fotherington), so how he coped with this pair I do not know. Ignored them, I suppose.

As predicted, the following morning I was telephoned by some police cleric asking when it might be convenient for the chief superintendent to call and ask a few routine questions. I was about to reply that if the questions were so routine why didn't he send a minion, but thought better of it. It doesn't do to ruffle their feathers. However, as a matter of principle I did make it clear that being extremely busy, no time was especially convenient, but that naturally I was willing to cooperate as best I could in this dastardly case. Thus an appointment was fixed and I waited.

In due course a black Wolseley rolled up; and leaving the driver in the car MacManus presented himself in my porch. After the usual formal pleasantries (I had no intention of producing coffee), we settled down to brass tacks, or rather he did.

'Miss Oughterard,' he began, 'I gather from Mr Balfour of Hope Vale that you were playing bridge with his wife and a party of friends on the evening of the incident and that you left shortly after midnight. Is that correct?'

'Oh yes,' I enthused, 'we had a splendid session and I actually did rather well. Do you play bridge, Mr MacManus? I should think that with your training and expertise it would be right up your street. It needs a sharp mind.' I beamed encouragingly.

'I dabble,' he replied shortly. Dabble? That probably meant he missed every trick in the book – just like Freddie Balfour.

'So you left after midnight . . . and then what did you do?'

'Do? Well I drove home, naturally. Far too tired to hang about.'

'And you passed the dew pond, of course.'

'Of course, it's the quickest route.'

He nodded, and after a pause said, 'And I take it you didn't stop or see anything out of the ordinary. No cars parked on the verge? There was nothing strange that caught your eye?' Caught my eye? I suppose he meant like a beheaded corpse.

'No, I am afraid I can't help you there. Mind you,' and I gave an embarrassed laugh, 'I have to admit to not having my eye entirely on the road: it was such a glorious night and the stars were utterly magnetic!'

I was about to launch into further poetics, when Bouncer bounded in from the garden. But on seeing the visitor he stopped abruptly, flopped down and instantly fell asleep. It is amazing how discerning animals can be in judging the calibre of visitors.

'And I suppose that's Bouncer,' MacManus said.

I agreed that it was and expressed surprise that he should know his name. He explained that Freddie Balfour had once mentioned the dog, disparagingly no doubt, and then stared thoughtfully at the heaving flanks.

'As a matter of fact,' I said brightly, 'I haven't had him for very long. He belonged to my late brother.'

'Ah yes, of course, that vicar in Surrey – Molehill, wasn't it? The one that flung himself off the church tower.'

148

I was enraged! But biting back caustic fury, I replied evenly that my brother had indeed been the *canon* of Molehill and that his sad death had been occasioned by his gallant rescue of a parishioner dangling from a gargoyle. 'Francis,' I added, 'would never have *flung* himself anywhere, let alone while on church property.' I looked suitably pained; while MacManus looked suitably abashed – as well he might.

'Ah yes, yes, of course,' he muttered; but then added, 'Hadn't he been a friend of that unfortunate woman found dead in the woods? I seem to remember—'

This was becoming irritating. Why on earth was this tedious man raking up things long since buried? It was too bad. Why didn't he just stick to the matter in hand: Carstairs and his beastly cadaver? Thus I said rather curtly that 'friend' wasn't quite the right term but naturally, being Mrs Fotherington's rector, my brother had indeed known her in his professional capacity. I then enquired rather pointedly if he had any further questions.

'Yes, I have actually,' he replied. 'Tell me, do you often go up to the dew pond, Miss Oughterard?'

I was puzzled by this and not a little unnerved. But I told him, truthfully, that I did visit the spot very occasionally, though not nearly as often as Francis and I had when children – and started to give a vivid account of our exploits there.

He cut me short, saying, 'And your dog, does he go up there?'

'My dog? Well, er . . . not without me he doesn't. At least I shouldn't think so, it's rather a long way.' I laughed nervously.

MacManus fished in his pocket and held out his hand.

149

In it there lay a small metal disc, a dog collar tag with the word 'BOUNCER' writ large.

I gazed nonplussed. 'Wherever did you find that?'

'Just by the deceased's head,' MacManus replied.

It was a blow all right. But unlike Francis I have the capacity for fairly quick thinking, and thus despite my shock I heard myself exclaiming: 'Goodness gracious, so that's where it got to. I've been looking for ages!' Then giving a stage gasp, I cried: 'But oh how dreadful – I mean it being found so close to the, er, well to the *remains*.' I shuddered and rushed on before he could say anything. 'You see we *had* gone up there about a fortnight ago and spent such a lively afternoon with all the other dogs. Bouncer enjoyed every minute – splashing about and rabbiting in the gorse; he was having a lovely time. So I suppose with all that rampaging it must have fallen off. Probably been loose for ages and I had never noticed.'

MacManus cleared his throat and placed the disc on the table. 'So you think it dropped off the dog's collar a fortnight ago and has been lying on that same spot ever since?'

'Well yes, evidently; unless, of course, some sheep picked it up from under a gorse bush, and then wandered about and spat it out.' There was I fear just a hint of ice in my tone. Whether MacManus had noticed I am not sure. But to compensate I said forlornly, 'You know, Chief Superintendent, I really don't think I want it back now. After all, it would always be such a ghastly reminder of that poor man's fate!' I endeavoured to look stricken.

'Hmm,' he grunted, and slipped the disc back into his pocket.

Little else was said, and after thanking me politely for my time he returned to the waiting Wolseley and was driven away.

The moment he had gone the dog woke up and shook itself. 'Short commons for you this evening,' I said, 'how could you have been so crass!' He looked blank and mooched off into the kitchen.

CHAPTER TWENTY-FIVE

The Primrose Version

The morning after MacManus's visit I had an unexpected encounter; not especially congenial but interesting all the same. I was in the queue at the baker's, rather keen to get my hands on some of that new loaf he has just produced – the Lewes Lozenge or some such esoteric name – when I realised I was standing behind Bertha Twigg, the gym mistress at Erasmus. I had only spoken to her twice, neither time enlivening, but since I was eager to learn more of what was afoot with the Carstairs case, I made my presence known.

'Why it is Miss Twigg, isn't it? How nice to see you,' I gushed. 'I wonder if we are after the same thing, Mr Dexter's exciting new recipe. Emily Bartlett tells me it is the best thing since Chelsea buns.'

'I wouldn't know about that,' Bertha replied, 'I only buy the rye wafers; bread of any kind is bad for the thighs.' She wore the look of the stoutly righteous, and stealing a glance at her lower limbs I felt like murmuring something about things past redress; but intent on my agenda instead asked if she would care to join me for a coffee at the adjacent bookshop.

This she did and I began to pump her about the situation at Erasmus House.

'It must be dreadful for you all,' I said, 'especially for Mr Winchbrooke. I gather that two pupils have been withdrawn already. I hope there won't be many more.'

'Shouldn't think so,' she replied. 'Half-term has just finished and the parents will be gagging for a rest. Besides, those two were in line for expulsion anyway, so it saves a lot of messing about. As I always say, even the worst things can produce good results.' She stretched for a chocolate biscuit, while I visualised Carstairs' conveniently propped-up head.

'Well, there is that, I suppose,' I agreed doubtfully. 'But then, of course, there is also the mother. Poor woman, she must be desperate – her only child I believe.' I had a vision of the lonely widow in Newhaven bereft both of her son and the ritual of his weekly laundry, and did indeed feel sorry.

'Oh there's no mother,' Bertha said briskly. 'That was all my eye.'

'But whatever do you mean? Emily Bartlett told me that—'

'Yes, that's what he told us all but when the police checked, there was apparently no trace; not a single trace. Mr Winchbrooke is very annoyed. If you ask me it was simply a ruse to get more time off than the rest of us.' She eyed the biscuits indignantly and took another. It struck me that for one so solicitous about the condition of her thighs, Bertha Twigg was pretty sharp in the chocolate stakes.

'But presumably Dr Carstairs must have had some sort of family or relatives. I mean, where did he come from?'

She shrugged. 'Apart from the mythical mother he never spoke about anything like that; though now that you ask, I do remember he mentioned Australia a couple of times. Something about an ex-wife being there – but frankly I wasn't very interested. As a matter of fact, I found him rather rude and stand-offish.'

'Oh really? Why was that?'

Bertha Twigg's face darkened. 'Well,' she said, planting her elbows firmly on the table, 'he very rarely joined in with anything – you know like nature rambles and healthy hikes; and he certainly lacked what you might call *zeal*. For example, there was one time when the whole school was getting ready for Founder's Day. It's a most important occasion with prize-giving, tugs-of-war and all that sort of thing, including the ten-minute rugger scrum that young Mr Fairley organises. But the best part is the grand finale in the evening –the seniors' gymnastic display for which, naturally, I am responsible. This is a very popular event and *much* appreciated by the parents.' She paused, presumably allowing me time to absorb the fact.

'I am sure it is,' I murmured sceptically, wishing she would get to the point.

'And, of course, as a prologue to the boys' performance I always do a little display myself – it reassures the parents that their offspring are being instructed by a true professional.' I wasn't entirely convinced of that but said nothing.

'Anyway,' she continued, 'to this end I was in the gym one afternoon practising a backward flip on the horse – jolly difficult things to get right you know – when I realised

154

that one of its legs was a bit wonky and that if I wasn't careful the whole thing might keel over. As it happens, Dr Carstairs was in the corridor, and since he didn't seem to be doing anything useful I asked him if he wouldn't mind kneeling on the floor and gripping the leg to anchor it while I did one or two quick vaults . . . And do you know what he said?' I shook my head, a number of possibilities coming to mind.

'He *claimed* that he had weak wrists and couldn't possibly risk such a manoeuvre. I told him that holding the horse steady was hardly a manoeuvre; to which he replied that it all depended on the context – and walked off!'

'Oh dear,' I said vaguely, 'that wasn't very cooperative of him.'

'Not cooperative? I should think not!' Bertha snorted. 'If you ask me it was downright ungallant, not to say disloyal.'

I was puzzled by the disloyalty bit and asked her what she meant. She explained that as someone doing her physical best for the honour of the school she should surely have been able to rely on support from a fellow member of staff, and that clearly Dr Carstairs had been indifferent to the athletic prowess of Erasmus House.

It crossed my mind that it was possibly less the honour of Erasmus House that Carstairs had been reluctant to support than the weight of those pounding and formidable flanks. However, such an observation might have been injudicious and I hastily changed tack: 'But I think you mentioned he rarely joined in with things. Does that mean he didn't have any cronies among the rest of the staff?'

She sniffed. 'Well not until Mr Topping arrived he didn't. They played chess and cleaned their bicycles together.'

'Cleaned their bicycles?'

'Oh yes. You know how men are about that sort of thing – they get obsessed. It was a sort of ritual: every Wednesday evening after Evensong. As a matter of fact, I found it rather tiresome.'

I asked her why and she explained that the 'ritual' often took place under her bedroom window just when she was engaged in her deep-breathing exercises, and that the sound of the men's voices and the relentless scraping of mudguards had been most distracting. 'In fact I looked out once to ask them to go elsewhere but there was rather a wind blowing and I don't think they heard. But Mr Topping saw me and gave a charming wave; he is really most mannerly, *unlike* Dr Carstairs.'

'So no wave from Dr Carstairs?' I asked lightly.

'Oh he just kept his head down. Typical!'

It was increasingly evident that Bertha Twigg harboured a simmering antipathy to the deceased. Had such dislike occasioned his unfortunate fate? An excessive reaction perhaps, but these days one does hear of people doing the most extraordinary things. It flashed through my mind that perhaps Hubert Topping was blameless after all . . . But surveying the figure opposite, I thought this unlikely. There was something wholesomely bovine about the gym mistress which would seem to preclude such an enterprise. Yes, Topping was definitely the surer bet.

I stood up, and murmuring blatant lies about pressing engagements, left her toying with the remains of the chocolate biscuits.

Out in the High Street I considered the news: admittedly not much but intriguing nevertheless. Why had Carstairs fabricated the mother in Newhaven? Was it really just a means of ducking his professional duties as Bertha had insisted? If so, it did indeed put him in a rather feeble light. After all, why continue at an institution like Erasmus if he found its routine so distasteful? But if it wasn't that then why the pretext for goodness' sake?

A secret mistress? Doubtful; he had sounded too dull for that sort of caper. So what had he been doing in those absences, or whom had he been seeing? And then what about that curious liaison with Topping? What on earth had they had in common? Surely more than the compulsive cleaning of mudguards. Something else must have drawn them together. I thought of Topping's smarmy bonhomie and very much doubted if it could have been a mutual chemistry. And according to Mr Winchbrooke several of the masters are keen on chess, so why should Topping have singled out Carstairs as his partner? It was obvious, I told myself, there was some *other* matter which had linked them: a matter which conceivably had led to Carstairs' death . . . I walked down the hill feeling rather pleased with my deductions.

However, the pleasure was eclipsed by the sight of the chief superintendent emerging from the fishing tackle shop. He was in mufti and accompanied by a wan little woman whom I presumed was his wife. He strode ahead while she padded behind carrying a weighty shopping bag. Seeing him I was reminded that it was, of course, through police enquiries in the Newhaven area that the fiction of Carstairs' mother had been exposed. I felt a prick of annoyance to think that MacManus had been in possession of such information well before I had it myself.

I wondered what he was making of it and what else he might have unearthed relevant to the case – other than

Bouncer's wretched name tag, of course. Did he, for example, know of Carstairs' friendship with Topping? Presumably only if the latter had volunteered such information, unless Bertha had told him. But I rather suspected that the gym mistress had not been among those interviewed. Had she been so, she would surely have told me during our recent conversation.

CHAPTER TWENTY-SIX

The Dog's View

I visited that pair of droop-eared wonders yesterday, Boris and Karloff. Hadn't seen them for a bit and thought it was time to remind them who's boss. So I was just sneaking up to their cage to give 'em a fright, when from inside I heard the most awful racket: Boris on the rampage – and he hadn't even seen me! When I got to the wire there was Karloff's fat face pressed up against it. He looked a bit put out.

'What's up,' I asked, 'P.O. poisoned your mangy carrots?'

'No,' he snarled, 'but I wish she would poison those poxy foxes. They were here again this morning *and* with their screaming cubs; dancing and barking and making a hell of a shindig. We couldn't sleep a wink.'

'Tough,' I said, and wagged my tail.

He narrowed those pink eyes and had the cheek to say, 'If you were a proper dog you would see them off. But not being a proper one I suppose you're not able to.'

Me not a proper dog? What did the bastard mean! I

stood on my hind legs and rattled his cage. 'Don't you come that with me,' I roared, 'Bouncer can fix any poxy fox!'

'Do it then,' the rabbit said all hoity-toity, and lolloped into the rear to shut up its mate.

At that moment I saw Maurice skulking in the long grass so I told him what had happened. He seemed to find it very funny. 'Well, Bouncer, there's a challenge for you: a chance for Bouncer the Bold to show his mettle.' I didn't know what he meant by mettle – one of his foreign words, I suppose. But he had given a sarky miaow so I knew he was being RUDE. I had had enough of rude for one day, so I was just about to bite his tail when he snatched it away and said, 'As a matter of fact, dear friend, there is a rather bigger challenge to deal with and one much more satisfying than poxy foxes.'

'Oh yes?' I said. 'You mean like beating up snooty cats?'

He pretended not to hear and stared at a butterfly. And then he said, 'What I mean is getting to the bottom of this Top-Ho mystery. Our mistress is getting increasingly *agitato* and—'

'*Agi*-what?' I said.

He sighed and batted the butterfly. And then I twigged it: the *agi* thing is cat-speak for buggered up.

'Oh yes,' I agreed, 'she's that all right. Do you know, she left some extra Dog Chocs in my bowl last night – masses; couldn't believe my luck. Generally she's pretty stingy with 'em. Just goes to show her mind's not on the job; probably keeps thinking of that grinning bonce I found.' I barked, thinking of the Dog Chocs . . .

'Control your lungs!' the cat hissed. 'Do you want those two loons in the hutch to hear us? This is not for everyone's ears, least of all theirs.'

Personally, I couldn't see why it should matter a hoot what the idiots heard, but the cat is a secretive sod and likes to keep things to himself. In fact I'll give you a jolly good example of how cagey he is. You see it was only yesterday that he was *good* enough to tell me about his evening visit to the tall man's house, the place where Duster lives. Yes, he had sneaked off without a miaow to anyone and met Mop Face. And do you know, they had an ADVENTURE without ME! I can tell you I was a bit fed up about that and nearly cut up rough, but he said that it was quite by chance that the adventure had happened and that in any case he had been going to tell me but he had needed to get his mind straight first. Huh! That'll be the day. If you ask me, Maurice's mind is about as straight as a knot of barbed wire.

Anyway, I lowered my voice to a nice growl and said that I had a jolly good idea – JOLLY good.

'Oh yes,' the cat said, 'and what might that be?'

I told him that we should enlist Duster; that since the cairn lived at the place which seemed to interest Top-Ho, he could do some useful spying for us. He could be 'Our Dog in Podkennel' or whatever it's called, and report back whenever he saw the weedy one come snooping towards the stable. 'You see,' I went on, 'because Duster is titchy and twitchy, like you, his master has made him a special cairn-flap so he can go out and about any time he wants. That could be pretty handy for spying.'

At first I thought I had made a gaffe by calling Maurice titchy, because he flattened his ears and narrowed his eyes. But then he suddenly beamed and said, 'Well done, Bouncer. That is a most useful suggestion. Kindly alert Duster immediately.'

Well, howzat! You don't often get a pat on the head from Maurice. If he had been normal I would have offered him a bit of my bone to gnaw; but not being normal, I just tweaked his tail which he secretly quite enjoys.

So that's what I am going to do: talk to the cairn and tell him that he's got to make himself useful. I'll put on my Great Dane voice; that should do the trick.

CHAPTER TWENTY-SEVEN

The Cat's View

'Phew,' the dog panted, 'it's getting a bit hot these days; time I had my coat clipped. I wonder if she'll remember.' He shook himself and blew out his jowls.

'It would be more to the point,' I said, 'if she gave you a bath. You have not had one since we arrived.'

He wagged his tail. 'You're right; I could do with one of those.'

Unusually Bouncer is partial to being bathed and invariably converts what for most is a prosaic ritual into a theatrical performance of epic scale. At the vicarage such events were fairly rare as I do not think F.O. had the necessary stamina, but when they did occur the dog would be in his element. Thus for his delectation and my relief I hoped that our new owner would soon put her mind to the canine ablution.

But what if she didn't? Obvious: sad for Bouncer and smelly for me. Perhaps I could devise some subtle hints. The matter required careful thought and to this end I

163

retreated to my usual place under the dining-room table, being mindful to tuck my white paw well into my chest out of sight of intrusive eyes.

An hour later I emerged, pleased with my plan and ready to activate proceedings at the earliest convenience – that is to say *my* convenience. In the meantime I thought I would take a stroll up to the school to see what further intelligence might be gleaned regarding the Top-Ho specimen: a reconnaissance of the kind my grandfather would have termed 'a pry and a prowl'. The route to the school is not short, but having no immediate engagements and the weather being fair I looked forward to the walk. The scent of cow parsley and the tantalising hint of butterfly wings would lend pleasant distraction, and there was, of course, always the chance of a brisk skirmish with a passing field mouse . . . Thus filled with such prospects I set off on my mission with sprightly step.

On arrival, I picked my way carefully and kept my head well down – not so much out of fear of being seen than of being hit. These human kittens are not noted for the accuracy of their aim whether with ball or conker, and when in their midst it is wise to move with caution. Luckily, it being early in the day there did not seem much midst about and I was able to proceed on my prowl unmolested.

With Top-Ho's recent bicycling escapade in mind I thought that my first port of call should be the bike shed. I do not mean the general one for the boys but the small one assigned to the pedagogues. As mentioned, I am not keen on bicycles – dangerous contraptions – but I felt that by inspecting the vehicle I might learn a little more of its rider.

My grandfather always taught me that if you wanted to make an assessment of human beings you had to examine their kit – 'helps you get the feel of the buggers' he had said. Over the years this has proved sound advice; and thus suppressing instinctive distaste I slipped in through the open window.

There were several of the machines slung about and at first I was a little confused. But not for long. Slightly apart from the others and distinguished by its lowered handlebars and smart appearance – the others were dull and battered – stood the one that surely belonged to Top-Ho. I noted too the large saddlebag attached to its rear: exactly the same as the one observed on my stroll with Eleanor. Yes, this was undoubtedly his, and I commenced my inspection.

I circled the wheels, sniffed the tyres, flicked the spokes with my claw and pawed the pump. Then with an agile leap I landed upon the saddle. This exuded a smell of polished leather and old trouser. Shifting my paws carefully I was able to get at the saddlebag. This was open and apparently empty. Nevertheless I am nothing if not thorough, and thus with a little craning was able to stretch down and thrust my head inside. My nostrils were met by an unfamiliar smell. But I had no time to give thought to this, or indeed to indulge the sneeze which had just assailed me, as the next moment there was a crash as the shed door was flung open, and hastily withdrawing my head I was confronted by the figure of Top-Ho.

In a trice I had leapt to the floor only to be met with a hail of abuse: 'Get away from that frigging bike you effing little toad!' he snarled, and lunged towards me.

Well really! For one who made a fetish of flaunting a rosebud on his lapel and wearing obsessively polished shoes, I considered his outburst disgraceful. I mean even Bouncer doesn't use language like that. I slunk into a corner and emitted one of my more poisonous hisses; and then with nice judgement shot between his feet and out through the door.

Gaining the sanctuary of a large holly bush, I crouched quietly and brooded. Either the specimen was morbidly fond of his bicycle or he had an aversion to my own species; and if the latter then it was certainly reciprocal. Admittedly s*ome* of their kind are tolerable. But the majority – such as my erstwhile mistress of whom the vicar so clumsily disposed – are crass or obnoxious. Quite clearly Top-Ho was of the larger category. I studied a rummaging beetle and considered my next move. The simplest would be to turn tail and return home. But I was so incensed by the man's behaviour that I was determined to stay and see what else might be unearthed. Thus I bided my time until he re-emerged from the shed, and then with utmost stealth and keeping a good distance, followed him back to the school building.

At the door I slipped in behind him, and was just slinking along the corridor keeping his heels well in sight, when there was a sudden splutter of noise and the overpowering waft of sausage and lavender; and the next moment I had been swept up into the arms of some human female. She gabbled excitedly in a tongue utterly foreign to me. But as I struggled to get free she screeched something that I did comprehend: 'Oh Herr Topping, do stop. Look what I have found – ein sweet little katze. Do come and stroke him. He ist zo naice!'

Top-Ho turned and walked back towards us. 'You are mistaken *Fräulein* Hockheimer,' he said smoothly, 'I suspect the creature is far from agreeable and I advise that you keep your distance from it. After all, you wouldn't want a flea in your ear, would you?' He smirked, while I glared.

A flea indeed! I wondered whether I should pee on his rose. When a kitten I could have done it with ease, but age restricts both range and impact; so instead I gave a couple of sharp scratches to the arm of my captor, and as she shrieked, jumped down and sped to the open door.

This time I decided that I had endured enough. Such treatment is anathema to one of my breeding. Besides, I was beginning to be aware of an odd sensation in my nostrils and to feel just a trifle light-headed. Perhaps I was sickening for a dose of cat flu, and thus all the more reason to return home where I could be suitably nurtured by our mistress. With luck she would have replenished the store of my special pilchards and ordered fresh cream from the milkman. Thus pausing only to give a skittish kick to a lolling snail, I set off on my journey home.

I have to say that the inward journey was even more congenial than the outward. The country scents seemed stronger and the spring colours brighter. And despite the tingling in my nose, by the time I had squeezed through the hedge bordering our domain I was in quite a merry mood. Bouncer was mooching in the garden and raising my paw I gave a cheerful wave.

His mouth fell open slightly and he fixed me with a puzzled stare. As he approached, I beamed benignly.

He looked a bit shifty and then said, 'I say, Maurice, what's that white stuff all over your nose and whiskers?'

I replied that I had no idea what he was talking about but that doubtless it was the pollen from the cow parsley.

'Doesn't look like pollen to me,' he grunted, 'more like that powder the Prim puffs on the ants or on her face.'

'Oh fiddley-dee,' I mewed gaily, 'I daresay it will come out in the wash.'

The dog looked blanker than usual, and cocking his head on one side, said 'Wot wash?'

'Don't be so pedantic; there's bound to be some wash or other, there always is,' I yawned.

The dog moved closer and shoved his snout in my face. 'Have you seen your eyes?' he said, 'because if you ask me they look a bit skew-whiff.'

I smiled and riposted that unlike some of our human friends I was not in the habit of carrying a face-mirror around with me. I thought the observation quite witty but the dog's mouth fell open again, this time even wider. Then with a long yawn I stretched my length on the grass and with paws in the air contemplated the sky.

Bouncer swivelled his head to worry his rump, and then said solemnly: '*I* think you're up the spout, Maurice. You should go inside. It's probably the sun; too much isn't good for cats . . .'

Those were the last words I heard that day.

CHAPTER TWENTY-EIGHT

The Dog's View

You know that cairn is sharper than you might think and I am beginning to get the gist of his funny way of talking – not that he does talk much, which is just as well as sometimes I really have to cock my ears to make out what he's saying. It's all growly and gurgly and full of words that sound like 'sporran' and 'och aye' and 'something-ken'. I mean it's almost as bad as talking to that big French dog the time when we were AB-RORD. I liked him, he was a good sport; though I'm not sure if Duster is – a bit of a dark horse if you ask me. But I expect I'll get his measure, especially once I grasp what he's actually saying. Maurice says he speaks Garlic, and I suppose the cat knows – or thinks he does. Anyway, garlic or not, I've got to persuade him to be our lookout at Podkennel and to report if Top-Ho comes peddling down the drive again like he did the night Maurice and the Persian were there. You see because Duster is small, grey and mainly silent he can melt into the shadows and spy with uhm . . . with . . . IMPOONITI. That's one of Maurice's words and I was a bit puzzled when he first used it so I asked him what it meant. The cat must have been in a good mood because he kindly explained, so now I know . . . Im-poon-i-ti means you can do something without being caught and getting a kick up the backside. I'll tell Duster that: it might make him more ready to play the game.

And going back to the cairn's lingo, when you *can* understand him he's quite interesting. For instance, he says that he has seen Top-Ho wobbling down that drive a number of times. In fact he saw him on the same night that the two cats were there. While *they* were watching Top-Ho, the cairn was watching *them* and the mogs never knew! I think that's very funny and I would like to tell old Maurice but he would only get shirty and go into a sulk so I'd better not.

Anyway, Duster seemed to like my suggestion that he should do a bit of spying for us; said he had always thought he was meant for higher things. I told him I didn't know about *higher things*, especially with his legs being so short, but that the great thing was to keep his snout and ears well primed . . . Oopsie! I think I put my paw in it there because he suddenly looked very fierce and asked who did I think I was talking to, some bloody dachshund?

I don't have the cat's tact (or so he keeps telling me) but there are times when Bouncer can be JOLLY canny. So I told Duster that it was a well-known fact that all the best spies have short legs as it means they can keep their noses close to the ground, and that, *of course*, his legs were far taller than any short-arsed dachshund's.

He gave a sort of grunt and I could see he was thinking

170

that over. And then he said, 'So if dachshunds are so short-arsed does that mean they make better spies than cairns?'

I tell you, old Bouncer had to think pretty quickly! 'Not at all,' I growled, 'they can't hear a thing with those flapping ears; deaf as posts. But a cairn's ears being so pricked can hear *everything*. I mean to say, short legs and sharp ears – what could be better for DI6?'

Well that did the trick because he wagged his tail and nosed his rubber ball towards me. 'Hmm, so you think I would suit Dog Intelligence, do you?' he asked.

'You bet,' I said.

'And who should I report to?'

'ME,' I barked.

He wanted to know where the cat fitted in and I said that in my experience he didn't fit anywhere very much except by a lily pond netting goldfish; but since he had asked, I could tell him that Maurice was a sort of behind-the-scenes chap issuing orders which *I* saw were properly carried out.

'Och aye,' the cairn said, 'so you're the gofer, are you?'

'No,' I roared, 'I am not the gofer! I am NUMBER ONE DOG, the lynch-bone of the whole outfit!'

He didn't say anything for a few seconds but just twitched his ears and stared bleakly, and then trotted off and cocked his leg against a lavender bush. This took quite a long time so he must have been thinking because when he came back he said, 'When do I start?'

'That's the biscuit!' I barked; and told him that there was no time like the present. (That's what the cat is always saying, so I expect I had got it right.)

Mission completed I went home over the fields. It's slower than on the road because there are lots of different trails and funny smells and a chap can get sidetracked. But though it's slow it's also safer because that way you don't meet humans banging on about the 'poor little lost dog' and then trying to catch your scruff to read your collar disc. (Well that's one thing they won't be able to get hold of – P.O. still hasn't got me a new one.)

Anyway, when I got back I found Maurice snoring on the terrace so I gave his tail a jolly good pull.

'Good Fish,' he screamed, 'what the hell's that!'

'Only me,' I said.

'*Only* you,' he hissed, 'that's enough, isn't it?'

I pretended I hadn't heard that and did what Duster does and just stared into the distance. And then I said, all sniffy, 'You might like to hear that I have nobbled the cairn. He has agreed to be Our Man in Podkennel.'

I could see that Maurice was impressed. 'Well done, Bouncer,' he mewed. 'Now be a good dog and go and fetch me that carton of cream the Prim has left in the larder. This calls for a celebration . . . Oh and by the way, I note that there is some treacle cake on the sideboard; you like that, don't you?'

So we had a really good nosh and then made ourselves scarce in the garden for a LONG time!

CHAPTER TWENTY-NINE

The Primrose Version ·

There was an agitated telephone call from Erasmus House, from Emily. 'Oh Primrose,' she breathed, 'you couldn't possibly do the headmaster a favour, could you? It's all rather tricky.'

'Rather depends,' I replied guardedly. 'What is it? *Fräulein* Hockheimer struck with German measles and someone is needed to take her art classes?'

'Not so simple,' she said. 'You see it is poor little Dickie Ickington, he's been left in the lurch and he was *so* looking forward to everything.'

'Looking forward to what?' I enquired.

'Being taken out by his grandfather Mr Justice Ickington. They have a rendezvous every half-term. But this time the judge is caught up in some complex fraud trial and simply can't get here and the parents are away on the Riviera so there is no one to give the little chap a treat. He is being awfully brave about it, which somehow makes it worse. I don't suppose you could take him off our hands for the afternoon, could you? I mean now that you have Bouncer and Maurice I expect you are quite good at that sort of thing . . .' Her voice trailed off hopefully.

What on earth did she expect? For me to throw the child a bone and a piece of haddock? Kind though Emily is, she sometimes has the strangest notions. 'Er, possibly,' I replied, 'if you are sure it's only for the afternoon. I've got rather a lot on at the moment and can't spend too much—'

In a trice the plaintive note had vanished to be replaced by brisk assertion. 'Excellent,' she cried. 'Meet him at the school gates at two o'clock and take him to Drusilla's the children's zoo at Alfriston. Bring him back at five.' The line went dead.

So that was my brief: to entertain Sickie-Dickie for three scintillating hours feeding the llamas and chimpanzees, taking multiple rides on the model railway and staring endlessly at the repellent denizens of the reptile house . . . *And you can damn well put a brave face on it too*, I heard Pa's voice say sternly.

In fact my charge turned out to be quite companionable: polite and enthusiastic, and chattered authoritatively on a whole range of topics from Hornby rolling stock and the mating habits of moths to Bertha Twigg's serge gym knickers. 'They're awfully big,' he confided. And then after demonstrating his skill at plunging head first down all three slides while I dutifully clapped, he suddenly remarked breathlessly: 'I say Miss Oughterard, do you know anything about hacked-off heads – you know like what happened to Dr Carstairs at the dew pond? I bet he got a shock! I wonder what size axe they used, a pretty big one I should think.' He gazed at me, seeking enlightenment.

I told him that I had no idea and it really wasn't something one talked about in polite company. He protested that we weren't in polite company as it was just him and me (!)

'Yes, Dickie,' I said, 'but it's still not a very nice subject and it was obviously done by someone very wicked involved in something very wrong.' I glanced at the sky, hoping to point out an odd shaped cloud. There weren't any.

The little boy nodded solemnly: 'Oh yes, bound to be dope I expect. Grandpa says there's a lot of it about these days.'

'Really?' I said mildly. 'Well I suppose he would know. He probably has to deal with quite a number of those nasty drug smuggling people.'

The child nodded again. 'Grandpa says he hates the bally buggers and he'd string 'em up given half a chance and it wouldn't be by the neck either.' He frowned. 'How else would he string them up, Miss Oughterard?'

'I have no idea,' I said hastily. 'Now Si – er, Dicky, why don't we go and have some nice ice creams? They do some very tasty vanilla cones at that little tea shop.' I smiled indulgently.

The smile faded somewhat when he explained that on the whole he would prefer a Knickerbocker Glory – a whopping big one with chocolate fudge, cream, cherries and a long spoon, as that was the kind that he and his grandfather always ate when they visited Drusilla's. I felt like telling him that he would do no such thing and that he could eat a fourpenny cone like any other child. However, not wishing to fall out with the judiciary I bought him a small sundae – with a short spoon.

As it happens, it was quite a useful move since it entailed our sitting at a table and ordering lemon squash and tea.

Not only did this take the weight off my feet and delay gazing at yet another baboon's bottom, but more to the point it allowed me to ply Sickie with some subtle questions, such as what was his opinion of poor Dr Carstairs and nice Mr Topping?

This produced the answer that he had thought Dr Carstairs pretty stupid because he hadn't liked baked beans and that Mr Topping wasn't nice anyway.

'Really?' I asked eagerly. 'And why is that I wonder?' I splashed more squash into his mug and considered whether I should order him another sundae, but stayed my hand. Bribery can be overdone – as I am sure Mr Justice Ickington would have agreed.

'Well,' he began, licking his spoon, 'for a start he doesn't laugh at my jokes, says they're silly. I think that stinks because I tell jolly good jokes. They are some of Grandpa's, and *everyone* laughs in court when he cracks one, even the fellow in the dock. Shall I tell you a few, Miss Oughterard?'

'Not just now,' I said hastily. 'Er, but you were saying about Mr Topping and his lack of humour . . . Is that the only thing he lacks?'

The boy looked thoughtful. 'Reverence,' he announced earnestly.

'*What?*'

'Reverence – you know, it's how you've got to behave in church.'

I was intrigued. What on earth was the child talking about? And how had Topping flouted the laws of churchly convention – orgies in the vestry? Card-sharping in the organ loft? My mind whirled with curiosity.

'Oh I cannot imagine Mr Topping not showing respect in church. Perhaps you've made a mistake.'

'No, I haven't,' he said stoutly, 'I saw them at it.'

I cleared my throat, and then rather cautiously asked at what exactly.

'Passing notes; him and Dr Carstairs when we were singing "All Things Bright and Beautiful". They weren't joining in at all, just scribbling away and shoving these bits of paper at each other.' Sickie-Dickie looked indignant. 'I mean if *we* pass notes in class we get lines and a cuffed ear. It's not fair, is it? And after all, this was in the middle of *chapel*! I think that's a bit sneaky, don't you, Miss Oughterard? I mean telling us off and then doing the same thing yourself – it's what Grandpa would call hyp, hypo something or other.'

'I am sure your grandfather is right. But it may have been something rather urgent or conversely rather trivial, or perhaps simply comments on the excellence of the choir's singing.'

He shrugged. 'Shouldn't think so, not with old Travers conducting. The writing was all in Latin anyhow.' He glanced around, eyeing the cake counter. 'They look pretty good,' he said pointedly.

'In Latin?' I exclaimed, ignoring the cakes. 'How do you know that?'

'What? Oh Dr Carstairs dropped one when we were marching out, so I picked it up. I was going to give it to him and say, "Oh, sir, I think you've just dropped this piece of paper that Mr Topping passed to you when we were saying our prayers after that nice hymn." But he was moving too fast and I missed him . . . Anyway, like I said, it was only a bit of old Latin.'

'So what did you do with it?' I enquired softly.

He screwed up his face in an effort to remember.

Chucked it away I feared. 'Oh,' he said vaguely, 'it could be in my hymn book or p'raps my blazer pocket.'

There was a long pause as I surveyed the child opposite me. 'Do you mean,' I said casually, 'the blazer you are wearing now, the one with those smart stripes?'

He gave a surprised toothy grin. 'Oh *yes*, that's it, I'd forgotten all about it! It was ages ago.' He dug his fingers into the top pocket and drew out a screwed-up piece of paper. 'Yes, this is it, it's still here. Do you want it?' He pushed the paper across the table while again casting a speculative eye towards the cake counter.

This time I summoned the waitress. 'Two cream buns for the young man,' I said. My request was no bribe, merely a token of gratitude . . .

Back at home and the child safely returned to the school, I unfolded the crumpled note. It was indeed in Latin and its hasty scrawl did little to aid translation. In any case my own memory of the language was sparse to say the least. How maddening – and how typical of Topping to communicate in this way. Smug little showman! I stared irritably at the pencilled words, one or two striking distant chords – *navalia*, *ad tempus*, *onus* – and then to my surprise I discerned the name *Caesar*. What on earth had he to do with anything! I studied the other three terms: something to do with a dock and a punctual burden? Unlikely, as the only other word I recognised was *mater*: mother. Perhaps the wretched man had coded it as well. There was only one thing for it: the dubious help of Nicholas Ingaza. With a first in Classics (*and*, as Charles had let drop, at Bletchley during the war) he would surely crack the thing in an instant.

178

I dialled straightaway and was answered by Eric. Ingaza's telephone voice is silkily wary; Eric's has the subtle lilt of a costermonger.

'Wotcha!' he roared.

'Good evening,' I began, 'this is Primrose Oughterard. I wonder whether—'

'Well stone the crows,' he exclaimed, 'if I haven't just put money on you!'

'I *beg* your pardon?'

'Yes, five good smackers at Kempton Park. Miss Primrose, fifty to one. A blooming outsider, of course, but with a name like that you never knows your luck, do yer?' He gave a dark chuckle. 'Yes, the moment I saw that one among the runners I said to His Nibs, "That's my girl. I'll back her any day!"'

'Oh really?' I said, feeling faintly flattered. 'And what did His Nibs say?'

'Ow he didn't say nuffin', just gave one of those looks. Know what I mean?'

'I do indeed,' I replied dryly. 'And where is Nicholas? I need to speak to him rather urgently.'

Eric explained that his friend was out closing a deal, after which he was due for a tango lesson. 'Been shortlisted for the South Coast Latino Cup,' he said with pride, 'so he don't want to miss a trick.'

'I am sure he rarely does,' I murmured.

'You can say that again!' was the bellowed response.

Thus it was eventually agreed that unless I heard to the contrary, Nicholas would meet me in the lounge of Brighton's Old Schooner at eleven o'clock the following day. And with that settled and feeling a trifle fatigued after parleying with

Eric, I sat down and toyed with a gin. Haunted by the insistent rhythms of 'Hernando's Hideaway', I mused upon Ingaza's passion for fancy footwork and glanced again at Topping's note. Really, was there to be no end to this Latin nonsense!

As arranged, and not having heard otherwise, the next morning I drove over to Brighton, managed to park the Morris on the seafront and strolled along to the Old Schooner. My companion was already there, lounging in an armchair and looking rather smug. At my approach he stood up and executed an extravagant bow.

'Getting in the mood for the Latino Cup, are we?' I asked.

'But of course. Just wait, by the end of next week the title will be seen everywhere. "Ingaza of the Plaza", that'll be me!' He smirked.

'How nice. And what about your partner, Mona – what will she be?'

'Much the same I imagine: Mona the Moaner.'

I sighed. 'I don't think you are nice to know, Nicholas. Now hurry up and get me a drink, I have an important matter to discuss and I need your wits if you can spare them.'

When he returned I told him about my session with Sickie-Dickie and produced the note. He scanned it quickly, and then said, 'Yes, the Latin's easy enough, but as to what it actually *means* is anyone's guess. Presumably it would have been perfectly clear to Carstairs.'

'He is not in a position to be asked,' I said. 'So what does it say?'

'It says: "Caesar arrives with the stuff on Wednesday night at nine. I can't be there as have to see the others in the usual place, so it is up to you. Be at the dock promptly. If necessary tell them your mother is ill again."'

I frowned. 'What do you mean "stuff" – where do you get that from?' He explained that it was his version of *onus*. 'There's a whole gamut of meanings – load, burden, tax, freight, cargo. Indeed even—'

'Yes, yes,' I said impatiently, 'I don't need a Latin lesson, "cargo" will do. So this Caesar person was going to arrive laden with a load of stuff and expecting to be met on some quayside by Carstairs . . .' I paused, and then yelped in triumph, 'who was spinning a line that his *mother* was ill. It's obvious . . . *Newhaven* – that's where he had to be, somewhere down on the port!'

Ingaza raised a quizzical eyebrow. 'If you say so.'

'I do say so,' I cried. 'Carstairs had a mythical mother in Newhaven!'

He looked puzzled. And I explained what Bertha Twigg had told me about the police having pursued that line of enquiry and drawn a blank. 'So there was no mother and thus the redoubtable MacManus will have to think again,' I said this with a tinge of satisfaction. 'In my view he doesn't have the liveliest brain. In fact, frankly, if ever I do get proof of Topping's villainy I shall think twice before laying it on *his* desk.'

Nicholas gave a faint smile. 'Actually, Primrose, he is brighter than you think – and possibly a little more flexible too.'

'Huh, he hasn't struck me as flexible – wooden features, wooden mind.'

'I don't mean mentally flexible, I mean morally.'

'Oh really? Like you?' I asked.

'Or Francis,' was the quick retort.

I nearly upset my drink. 'Francis was *not* like you. He was under considerable strain as well you know, and was simply not up to coping with taxing situations – some of which were your devising!'

'Perhaps,' he admitted smoothly, 'but not, you must agree, the first one.'

'*Force majeure*,' I said stiffly; and quickly moving away from the subject asked him what he meant by suggesting MacManus was morally flexible.

'Ever heard of the Bognor Bordello?' he asked.

'I don't move in those circles. What is it – a superior knocking shop?'

'Superior is not a word that comes readily to mind, discreet might be more accurate . . . But yes, that's it: half a mile back from the seafront. MacManus has been known to go there, used to at any rate; and not conducting a raid.'

'Do you mean as a punter? Goodness, no wonder the wife looks so sour. I take it he doesn't don his uniform for such occasions?'

'Apparently not. Merely the proverbial raincoat plus moustache, though whether either is removed when occupied I wouldn't know.'

I asked him how he had acquired such intriguing intelligence. He tapped the side of his nose and said it was from all the little birds that fluttered around his shoulders.

'And what else do your feathered friends tell you?'

'Nothing much except that not only is he moderately bright but also ambitious, ruthlessly so. He did the dirty on some poor little snout a couple of years ago: had promised him immunity and then fitted him up and got the chap sent down before you could say knife. Won his promotion on that.'

'In that case, I am surprised he is so free with his favours in Bognor. Bit of a risk I should have thought, given his position.'

'Ah well,' Nicholas observed magnanimously, 'we all have our little weaknesses and vanities. Besides, it's probably part of the challenge: skating across frozen ponds, testing the ice, it probably gives him a kick.'

'Like it did you in the Turkish bath?'

The lazy lids came down and he gave a slow leer. 'My dear girl, nothing frozen there: that was *steamy*!'

CHAPTER THIRTY

The Primrose Version

You know I am beginning to wonder about those two animals, or at least about my own sanity. I used to think that Francis was exaggerating when he complained of their mysterious antics. But now I am not so sure. For example, when I arrived home this evening after asking *searching* questions at the town council meeting concerning their absurd attachment to personal parking spaces, I found the kitchen in the most extraordinary state. I do not mean untidy exactly but things most peculiarly arranged.

Smack in the middle of the floor, between the oven and the larder door, lay a neatly assembled collection of articles: scrubbing brush, a packet of soap flakes, a dog collar and an apron . . . Well, as you may imagine *I* had certainly not left them there like that, and for a few seconds it occurred to me that Mrs Maggs, the treasured char, had had another of her turns – or worse still it was some coded message indicating she was about to give notice. However, relief and wonder mingled as I recalled she was currently savouring the delights of Skegness in a charabanc. Clearly some other agency was responsible. Nervously I checked the windows and back door, fearing the house might be harbouring an escaped lunatic with a cleaning fetish, or at best some small prankster from the school. But all seemed normal. I continued to stare, fascinated by the 'crop circle' on the floor; and then doubting my own sanity retreated to the sitting room for a restorative brandy.

After a couple of these and thus comparatively sobered, I brooded upon the scene in the kitchen. There could be only one answer: the source was indigenous; *they* had done it! Clearly something was being signified – or did the dog and cat regularly engage in such random high jinks? Had they perhaps been playing some arcane version of mah-jong or Cluedo – versions known only to the animal world? I pondered the possibility and then decided to take another look. With luck the vision would have disappeared.

Luck was out. And as I stared a pattern emerged. Yes, how obvious; not only were the items linked but they added up to one thing: a *laundering*. Of the dog's bedding? Possibly – but far more likely of the dog itself!

As I tried to digest this uncanny hint, Bouncer pottered in. I shot him a covert look but he caught my glance and responded with a sheepish grunt, and then proceeded to sniff at each object in turn. The cat appeared, surveyed the scene and with a brisk hiss pounced on the collar and began to play with it, pawing and prodding as if it were some hapless mouse. I watched the performance, impressed by the creature's dexterity; but then with an excited swirl of the tail he sent the soap packet flying, its contents spilling everywhere.

This was too much. 'Oh really,' I cried, 'for goodness' sake get out of the way the pair of you!' I was about to clear up the mess but was anticipated by Bouncer who rushed forward, started to lap up the flakes and then with spume drizzling down his chops began to gag in the most disgusting way. That galvanised me: 'If that's what you want, you shall have it,' I said grimly. I stooped down, hauled him up, and staggering to the sink, shoved him in it and turned on the taps.

I won't go into the details of the ensuing ten minutes. Suffice it to say that the dog clearly enjoyed itself while I did not. Then with ordeal over I raked him with my electric hair dryer, a process which elicited further yelps of prancing joy. The resultant sight was of a bear whose front and rear were indistinguishable. Maurice, I noted, had scarpered.

And talking of Maurice, he too has caused me some concern. Indeed for at least a day I was convinced he was ill and had it not been the weekend I would have taken him to the vet. Fortunately this no longer seems necessary as he has become his normal self, aloof and difficult. However, while it lasted the phase was really most peculiar.

He had disappeared on the Saturday morning – one of his not infrequent absences; and then just before lunch as I was scanning the *Telegraph* on the terrace, I saw him slip through the hedge and start talking to the dog. I say 'talk' but you know what I mean: circling, sniffing and twitching – the usual ritual. Bouncer's ears, normally drooping, had sprung bolt upright and he seemed to be staring intently at the other.

Anyway, I resumed my reading. But all of a sudden there was a piercing screech, and the next instant the cat had landed on my lap like a bolt from the blue – literally, the sky being a June azure and the air blissfully still. The screech was followed by a manic purring as Maurice tried to drape himself around my neck while at the same time rasping my cheek with his scouring-cloth tongue. I *think* it was a sign of affection but can't be sure as it has never happened before. I was startled to say the least, and in the general confusion sent my coffee cup flying. This clearly distracted the cat who ceasing its endearments – if such they were – leapt off my lap and attacked the cup, rolling it obsessively on the crazy paving (porcelain chips everywhere, of course). I was about to hurl the newspaper, when just as suddenly the creature stopped; curled up and fell fast asleep . . . for the *rest of the day*. Yes, didn't even surface for its pilchards. I ask you!

Later, when recounting this to Charles Penlow, I remarked jokingly that from my experience the display bore all the signs of the cat being as tight as a tick, i.e. crazed and maudlin antics followed by stupefied slumber. Charles laughed and asked if I had ever considered that Maurice might be an undercover dope fiend. I told him that fiendish and undercover though Maurice was, I had never pictured him as a junkie – a term recently encountered in a Chandler yarn and of which I was rather proud. For a while we discussed the curious habits of domestic pets and I enquired whether Duster ever went similarly berserk.

'Oh no,' said Charles, 'the blighter is as sober as a judge. Pompous little basket – it's high time he was mated.'

Putting aside Duster's amatory needs and changing the subject, I said, 'Talking of pompous little baskets, I don't suppose you've seen any more of Hubert Topping, have you?'

'Funny you should ask that,' Charles replied. 'No, I've not seen him but I have heard him – this morning on the telephone. He said he was fascinated by my restoration project and wondered whether we might meet for a drink tonight and talk about it. Apparently he had once had an uncle who was an architect and thus he has always been interested in such matters. Someone had told him I was hoping to site an orangery in the grounds and he said that if I was interested he might have one or two suggestions.'

I sniffed. 'Oh doubtless he will be brimming with suggestions. Where does he propose having this drink – in that dreary cottage he rents from Miss Dunhill?'

Charles laughed. 'No, he suggested the White Hart. But since it is my building plans we are going to discuss it seemed the obvious thing to invite him to Podmore and then I can give him a conducted tour.' He paused and added, 'As a matter of fact Primrose, I was wondering whether you might care to join us, it would give you a chance to get to know him better.' He gave a sly grin.

'Hmm,' I replied, 'nice though it always is to share a drink with you, Charles, I very much doubt whether Mr Topping improves on further acquaintance. Thanks for the offer but I think I'll give it a miss if you don't mind . . . besides I am rather tied up this evening,' I added vaguely. 'I think Emily might be coming.' She wasn't. But still rattled by my recent encounter with Topping and his peculiar allusion to midnight ponds I was in no hurry to engage in more small talk of that ilk!

But by the time I got home I was having second thoughts. 'Know the enemy,' Pa had always counselled. Indeed it had been one of his favourite dicta – although who the enemy was had never been entirely clear. I cannot recall his having had any notable opponents, and rather suspect that apart from the shell hole incident most hostilities were enjoyable figments. Nevertheless it was sound advice and which, given the present situation, it would be foolish to dismiss. Obviously if I wanted to verify my suspicions about Topping, let alone protect myself, the more I had the chance to scrutinise the man, the better. So supressing instinctive reluctance I telephoned Charles to say that Emily's visit had been most unfortunately cancelled and that I should be delighted to join him and his guest if the offer were still open.

He said that it was, adding gnomically that he had rather thought I might come round in the end. What that was supposed to mean I really have no idea.

Thus shortly after six o'clock I drove up Podmore's potholed back drive and parked outside the east wing (the only habitable part). As I approached the side door, I noticed a bicycle propped against the wall, and judging from the drop handlebars and spruce condition assumed it to be Topping's. I thought grimly that it was typical of the man to have arrived bang on the hour . . . doubtless eager to make the most of his host's whisky and to give him the full benefit of his architectural expertise.

I smoothed my hair, straightened my seams and gave a smart blast on the bell . . . well it would have been a blast had the thing been working properly. As it was, there was a sort of death-throe whimper and then silence.

Fortunately from the other side of the door I could hear a canine scrabbling and whining; and as I waited I couldn't help comparing Duster's muted response with Bouncer's. In similar circumstances the latter's bark would by now have reached full throttle.

'Your doorbell's buggered,' I announced when Charles finally greeted me.

'It's not the only thing,' he said ruefully; 'the whole place is in rack and ruin.'

'Obviously. But I thought that was supposed to be all part of the great challenge,' I replied briskly.

'In principle, yes; but I've been stuck all afternoon with the county planners. It dampens the ardour.'

'Well I am sure Mr Topping must have some bright ideas,' I whispered. 'Where have you put him?'

'We are in the library for this evening – or what will be one day. The sitting room is getting too cluttered: Agnes has shipped some more stuff from Tobago. Just where I am expected to store it all I have no idea. Anyway, come on in.' He took my coat and I followed him across the hall to an open door.

It was a large room and doubtless one day will be lovely. But currently, apart from a large pouffe, small console table and a couple of leather armchairs, its space was magnified by scant furniture and empty bookshelves. However, I was cheered to see the console sporting an array of decanters and glasses – one of which Topping was grasping. At my entry he rose, smiled unctuously and – rather commonly, I thought – clicked his heels. But at least this time one was spared the Peter Lorre white tuxedo, although the usual pink embellishment was on full display. Ridiculous.

Cigarettes were exchanged and small talk commenced: the weather and its forecast, the latest test score, the vicar's petulant paddy during Communion, the Anderson girl's unfortunate condition, Macmillan's latest witticism and Rod Laver's prospects for Wimbledon.

By now we had reached our second round; at least *I* had – the punctual Topping being naturally well advanced. Thus I was just wondering whether I could subtly introduce the topic of Carstairs' cranium when I was anticipated by Charles. 'I say,' he said, turning to the guest, 'I daresay poor Winchbrooke wishes he were somewhere else, a ghastly business to deal with. His nerves were never good. How is he coping?'

'Given the pressures, remarkably well,' Topping replied. 'But then, of course, he does have the help of the estimable Mrs Bartlett, *so* adroit!'

I was startled. An image of Emily being adroit was not within my mental scope. 'In what way adroit?' I enquired curiously.

'With the parents. She parries their questions, talks volubly and wears them down. They go away dazed and silent and none the wiser. Invaluable really.' He smiled.

Yes, it made sense. I had often been in that condition myself after talking with Emily. Nice to know the effect could be so useful . . . I was about to give a merry laugh and say I knew just what he meant, when at the next moment his smile transmuted into a knowing leer and he said, 'And I gather *you*, Miss Oughterard, are very adroit at cards – quite formidable in fact. A lady after my own heart!' And before I had a chance to make modest denial, he went on, 'A little bird tells me that you virtually swept the board at Mrs Balfour's not so long ago – a veritable slaying apparently!'

'Well I—'

Charles gave a bark of caustic mirth. 'Not the only slaying, I fear. It was the night of poor Carstairs' demise.'

'Ah yes, yes, of course,' Topping purred. 'It must have been sickening for you, Miss Oughterard, sickening. A ghastly shock.'

I was about to say, 'You bet!' but stopped abruptly. What was the little creep getting at? Why should I have been so sickened unless I had been present at the scene – and why should he suggest that unless he himself had been there also and seen me?

Playing for time I took a sip of my martini, trying to decide whether to look utterly blank or make some light agreement. But before I had decided, he added, 'Mrs Balfour mentioned that you and the redoubtable Bouncer had left at midnight. Rather unnerving to think that you drove past the very spot where it had been – or indeed *was* being – enacted. A bit gruesome I should think.' He regarded me quizzically.

I shrugged and said coolly, 'Who knows? Had I stopped, it might have been. As it was, I was eager to get home and had no plans to loiter on the downs at that time of night, far too tired!' I gave a polite smile.

This was not returned. Indeed the ingratiating expression had entirely vanished and was replaced by a hard, impassive stare. 'How wise,' he remarked. 'It doesn't do to jeopardise one's safety, however long the odds. But as a bridge player you would know that, of course.' The stare hardened. And perhaps it was my imagination but I couldn't help feeling that the smoke ring which he had just so neatly expelled had been deliberately cast in my direction. I averted my eyes to the vase of azaleas on the mantelpiece. I don't think Charles had heard our exchange, being too busy hoisting Duster out of the window to sprinkle the plants; and as he regained his chair Topping had swiftly turned the conversation towards his host's building plans and the projected orangery.

Clearly eager to discuss the proposals, Charles suggested a brief tour of the grounds and led us out into the rear courtyard which housed the dilapidated stable block. He gestured towards it and said, 'Originally I thought I might convert this into a set of garages; that way our pernickety house guests couldn't complain that there was no shelter for their precious motors. It's the Bentley owners, they're so damned fussy. Well they'll just have to take their chance with the rest of us because I've decided to raze the whole lot. Unless they decide to go on strike, the bulldozers will appear in a fortnight's time. Once it is all cleared away the view will be superb.'

'Oh what a good idea,' I agreed, 'and then you will catch the evening sun over the downs. As you say, blow the Bentleys!' We laughed gaily but I couldn't help noticing that Topping did not join in. In fact he looked decidedly grim, sullen really.

And then once our mirth had subsided and Charles had started to walk on, he suddenly said, 'If you don't mind my saying, I think that would be a bit of a blunder – considerable in fact. Personally, I would delay the bulldozers.'

'Oh really,' Charles asked, 'and why is that?'

'Well I know you said you wanted to tag it on to the west wing, but the position of that stable is ideal for an orangery. It will not only catch the westering sun but get the full benefit from the south as well. Besides, don't you see that the aesthetics would be so much better? Far more harmonious, and then you wouldn't need to dismantle the whole thing but use some of the original materials for flooring and a nursery section. Yes, I would certainly shelve demolition for a while and meanwhile concentrate on putting the west wing to rights before those planners change their minds. You know how mercurial they can be – and that's putting it politely!' This time the laughter was threefold.

'You could be right,' mused Charles, 'I won a major tussle this afternoon; perhaps better exploit it while the iron still glows . . . Yes, I suppose that might be best: deal with essentials first and leave the stable question till later.' He grinned and added, 'And then I can decide whether I want a perfect view or perfect oranges.'

'*Exactly*,' chimed Topping, 'a tantalising choice and thus not one to be hurried. Bide your time. Besides, as said, one mustn't give those planners a chance to renege. Forge ahead on the west wing while the going's good, that's what I say!' He chuckled and turned to me: 'Wouldn't you agree, Miss Oughterard?' As one who has experienced a number of run-ins with pettifogging officialdom, I certainly did. However, I was loath to give Hubert Topping the satisfaction of my support.

'Well,' I said, 'I am sure Charles will do whatever he thinks fit but it is always useful to hear others' opinions.' I flashed him a dazzling smile – of the sort that our school matron would give whenever she was feeling particularly vicious – which was often.

We sauntered on, Charles expatiating on the niceties of building materials and treating us to what he termed 'Podmore's potted history' . . . Very potted actually, as apart from some tale of an ancestral crank given to taking covert rifle shots at his guests, it consisted largely of a tirade against the listed building people for their cavalier refusal to allow modern pots for the refurbished chimney stacks. 'The cost for originals will be extortionate,' Charles fumed. It was clearly an issue of some moment and on which he waxed not so much lyrical as incandescent. Fortunately the tirade was curtailed by Duster loping from the bushes, his head covered in some sort of briar.

'Poor little man,' I cried, 'if he's not careful it'll get into his eyes!' I rushed forward and did the necessary. 'Good boy,' I crooned gratefully, by now bored with brickwork and the finer details of dry rot. From the distance came the faint chimes of the church clock.

'Ah,' Topping exclaimed, 'alas, it tolleth the hour and duty calls. I must be off to supervise prep; a tiresome but necessary task. No rest for the wicked I fear!'

I was about to express pointed agreement but he was already babbling his thanks to his host and making tracks for the bicycle. Mounting this, he gave a gay wave, and shouting something like 'Remember, *festina lente*,' to his host, peddled rapidly out of sight.

'Funny little chap,' remarked Charles as we returned to the house, 'clued up on architecture all right and he's probably quite right about the west wing and delaying the stable business, but he did seem to rush off rather abruptly. I was going to suggest a digestif.'

'It's Winchbrooke,' I explained, 'he has an obsession about the masters starting prep punctually. He is invariably late himself but is a stickler for others.'

'Ah yes, that follows. Poor old Wichbrooke – a pity about Carstairs and his head. Can't be easy for him . . .'

'Don't suppose it was for Carstairs,' I replied. 'I say, did you mention a digestif?'

Driving home in the gathering dusk and musing on what had surely been Topping's veiled malice, I saw a small figure marching along the side of the lane: Emily. I drew up sharply, and winding down my window offered her a lift.

Detaching herself from the hedge, she exclaimed, 'Really Primrose, you shouldn't creep up on people like that, it's highly dangerous.'

'I wasn't creeping up,' I protested, 'surely you heard the car's engine.'

'Yes, but I hadn't expected it to stop, least of all with such loud brakes!'

'Oh well,' I countered, 'beggars can't be choosers. Here, hop in and I'll drive you to the very gates of Erasmus, or Elysium if you prefer.' She tossed her head and eased herself into the front seat.

'So what have you been doing?' I asked. 'It's not bell-ringing night, is it?'

'As it happens, I have been attending one of Dr Bracegirdle's lectures on the mechanics of the mind.'

'Was it enlightening?'

'Not really.' Having long been sceptical of Bracegirdle's mental balance this did not surprise me. 'And what about you?' she asked.

I told her that I had been at Podmore being taught the mechanics of renovation and enjoying the dubious company of Hubert Topping.

'Oh funny you should say that: he passed me in a Humber a couple of minutes ago. In fact I waved but he was with somebody and didn't see me.'

'You were mistaken,' I laughed, 'it couldn't have been Topping; he's doing prep duty. No wonder the occupant didn't return your wave – doubtless thought you were flagging him down for a little nocturnal dalliance.'

'Really, Primrose, you can be so vulgar,' she expostulated. 'I assure you it was no mistake; and anyway I know for a fact that he is not on prep duty.'

'How?'

'How? Because there is never prep at Erasmus on Wednesday evenings. It is the boys' night off when they are permitted to play with their Dinky cars and Meccano sets. The noise is appalling.'

'But he *told* us that he was—'

'Then in that case you must have misheard . . . mistakes are so easily made,' she added smugly. I said nothing, thought the more and squeezed the throttle. Soon we had reached the school gates where Emily got out, thanked me for the lift and bade a rather cool goodnight.

As she turned to go I put my head out of the window and said casually, 'By the way which direction was it going in?'

'What?'

'The *car*, where was it going?'

There was an impatient sigh. 'Well really how should I know? You do ask the most absurd questions, Primrose!'

'Just *think*,' I directed her.

There was another sigh followed by a pause; and then she said, 'It turned off on to the Newhaven road, that's all I can tell you . . . Now if you don't mind I propose having an early night. Dr Bracegirdle's lectures can be rather wearying; they probably need a certain calibre of brain to be fully grasped.' Yes, I thought, unhinged most likely.

CHAPTER THIRTY-ONE

The Primrose Version

When I arrived home my mind was in what you might term as quiet turmoil. 'A tiresome but necessary task', was it? What a downright lie – and delivered with such casual ease! Oily little charlatan! Anyone else would have just mumbled something about having to feed the proverbial cat or some such; but not Hubert Topping. Oh no, he had to gild the lily by inventing specious detail. Well, he hadn't reckoned on the *adroit* Emily Bartlett blowing the gaff.

I gave a rueful smile: yes, dear Emily did have her uses. She would certainly have known about the school prep schedule. But, I reflected, had she been right about the car? You would need to be pretty sharp-eyed to see the occupants as it sped past. But then, of course, Emily *is* sharp-eyed, as the Erasmus boys have frequently found to their cost. She may be gullible but she does take note of things . . . and remembers – a trait which renders her so indispensable to Mr Winchbrooke.

I looked down at the distinctly *un*proverbial Maurice

lazily toying with his woollen mouse. He must have sensed my gaze for his ears twitched, and lifting his head he gazed back in that truculent fashion which used to so unsettle Francis. 'Well, Maurice,' I murmured, 'what do you think of this then?' He continued to stare defiantly, and then with a flick of his tail returned to the mouse. And I returned to Topping.

Clearly the man had peddled swiftly home, jettisoned the bike and met his companion. Probably there had been an arrangement for the car to pick him up. I pictured Topping poised in readiness at his front gate all ready to jump in . . . to be transported where? To the cinema in Newhaven? Like hell. To the port, of course, to take delivery of the *onus* or to do whatever else Carstairs' regular missions to his 'mother' had entailed. I delved into my handbag and drew out the scribbled note purloined by Sickie-Dickie. My Latin had not improved since last time's scrutiny, but with Ingaza's translation in mind I was able to check its gist and confirm that the previous assignation had been set for a Wednesday evening at nine o'clock. Today was also a Wednesday, and glancing at my watch I saw that it was now nine-forty. If Topping and his accomplice had calculated correctly and their vehicle hadn't blown a tyre, then they would have arrived at the Newhaven quay at approximately nine o'clock. So quite possibly this little trip was part of a regular event, an event in which the hapless Carstairs could no longer feature. Ingaza had earlier suggested he may have blotted his copybook and thus grown surplus to requirements. I wondered if Topping's driver was his replacement. If so, he would have to watch his step – and neck!

There was a sudden movement from the hearthrug.

Tired of the mouse Maurice had cast it aside and was regarding me with what I can only describe as a look of quizzical scorn. He gave one of those strangulated miaows as if to say 'Surmise! Surmise!' and strolled from the room. The languid progress was abruptly checked by an explosive snarl followed by a howl of fury: Bouncer was evidently in one of his playful moods and had been patiently lying in wait for his friend. 'Shut up,' I shouted, 'I'm thinking.'

Growling and spitting they retreated to the kitchen and peace reigned once more. Well silence at any rate, for I was far from peaceful – too busy trying to decide on my next move: whether to enjoy an early night with the crossword or to race to the Newhaven docks on the off-chance of spying Topping and pal . . . No, far too long a shot; and besides it was now nearing ten o'clock. Whatever they were doing on the quayside – *assuming* that that had been their destination– by the time I arrived it would doubtless be finished and the birds flown. Yes, I argued, no point in embarking on a fool's errand. Clearly an early night was indicated.

I looked at the newspaper but was unenticed by the crossword. Monday's puzzles are manageable and can be completed with smug satisfaction, others are more difficult but intriguing; while occasionally there is one where the clues are not only abstruse but simply fail to engage, and thus even the frisson of challenge is forfeited. Tonight's was such a one; and my mind returned to a more tantalising conundrum: Carstairs' head. (That copybook must have been more than blotted – total saturation I'd say!)

The clues here were few but specific: the floating rosebud, and, according to Emily, Topping's naked lapel on the morning after the event; his close liaison with the victim (for as the passed note had made clear it was more than chess and the cleaning of bicycles that the pair had in common); and then there had been that private telephone conversation during his drinks party: *But I checked it myself, there was at least fifty grand's worth . . . Are you sure of that? Because if so I think a little action is required, don't you? We can't allow that, there's far too much at stake. Listen carefully. What I suggest is . . .* What was it that had been worth fifty grand? Part of the '*onus*'? Had Carstairs done the dirty and helped himself to some of it? And indeed what exactly had Topping suggested – to pre-empt further theft by killing Carstairs and cutting off his head? It seemed a bit extreme . . . but then what vital thing was 'at stake'? Hardly a coveted prize for Latin prosody! It was just typical of Emily to have appeared at the crucial moment – a few minutes longer and I might have heard the whole thing. She really can be so annoying.

With these fragments whirling in my mind, earlier thoughts of bed had completely vanished and I found myself increasingly restless and eager to learn more of Topping's current activity. As decided, it was pointless to drive the five miles to Newhaven; *but* perfectly reasonable to drive the mile or so to Miss Dunhill's cottage and check if her tenant had by chance returned from his evening's venture. It was shortly after ten, and if he was at home the lights were bound to be still on. And if not? Well one could simply park the car round the corner and wait upon events. Who knew what clues might be gleaned! I could hear my brother's voice of protest: *Oh really Prim, must you be so nosy? It will be frightfully embarrassing if you are seen, he'll think you are snooping. Don't interfere so!*

'I shan't be seen,' I inwardly retorted. 'And I am not interfering, merely gathering information. Besides, why shouldn't I take the dog for its late night walk? He doesn't know that part of the locality yet and it'll do him good to get a fresh perspective.' Yes, that was it: Bouncer would be my pretext, my cover. I went to fetch him from the kitchen and discovered that unlike me he had retired for the night and was snoring heavily in his basket.

'Time for walkies,' I announced briskly, rattling his lead and nudging the basket with my foot. He leapt up with an indignant roar and despite the sight of the dangling lead seemed reluctant to cooperate.

'Be like that,' I said indifferently, picking up my handbag but still trailing the lead. 'I'm off for a nice car ride.' I turned to the door, and seconds later heard the thudding of paws and a sort of grumbling yelp.

As we neared Miss Dunhill's cottage, I doused the headlights, slowed to a dignified pace and cruised past. The little house was swathed in darkness with not a glimmer to be seen. At the crossroads I turned the car and slowly glided back again. Absolutely nothing; not a movement or light.

I rounded the corner and drew up at the kerbside. From here I could just see over the low hedge into the garden and despite an overhanging apple tree had a partial view of the front gate. It was a good vantage point – although whether likely to provide an *ad*vantage one couldn't be sure. After all, he (or they) might not return for hours. Bouncer evidently felt the same, for having first shown interest by shoving his face against the side window he then gave a weary grunt and settled down to sleep.

I lit a cigarette and prepared for boredom. It came. And I lit another cigarette while the dog slept on. I started to fidget: retrieved a squashed toffee from the floor, dusted the dashboard, and then winding down the window a couple of inches, listened to an owl hooting. From the nearby wood came the eerie wail of a vixen. The dog slept on.

And then it stopped sleeping and suddenly raising its head, emitted a low growl. I was startled and quickly wound up the window and stubbed out my cigarette. For a moment there was nothing; but then I could just discern the low hum of an engine in the distance and seconds later caught the pallid shaft of an approaching headlamp. As I watched in the mirror, the beam broadened and then round the bend came the car. It slowed and drew up smoothly a few yards from Topping's gate. I tensed, as did the dog.

I gripped his collar, sensing a bark welling up. 'It's all right, Bouncer,' I whispered, 'we must just be very quiet.' Rather to my surprise I felt his flanks relax and he stayed silent.

The car lights were extinguished and I listened for the opening and shutting of doors, perhaps the murmur of voices. But there was nothing. Presumably the occupants were still engrossed in conversation. I swivelled round in my seat trying to see if the vehicle was a Humber mentioned by Emily but it was too dark to tell. A couple of minutes went by and still no movement from the car. I began to feel not just impatient but uneasy: its silent anonymous presence only yards from my own was vaguely unnerving. Why didn't someone get out or why didn't it move off?

And then a disagreeable thought struck me. Suppose my car was as visible to them as theirs was to me? The angle at which I was parked made this unlikely but I couldn't be sure. Perhaps the top of its roof could be glimpsed and they too were watching and waiting, biding their time, trying to assess if it was occupied or not . . . But that's absurd, I thought, what if it *can* be seen? A parked car is hardly suspicious! No, not in a well-lit street in early evening it isn't . . . but late at night in a dark country lane it might be considered so, especially in a place with no houses around only a solitary cottage. Maddening!

I could do one of two things: give up and drive off discreetly having learnt nothing, or take the bull by the horns, or rather Bouncer by the collar, and do the dog-walking charade. After all, just to depart empty-handed, as it were, seemed rather feeble; as pointless an exercise as driving to Newhaven. Yet the dog excuse now seemed a bit clumsy. Would I really be dragging the hound out of the car at eleven o'clock to give it a run just by Topping's cottage – particularly as, I suddenly recalled, the road led to a dead end? One could hardly be 'just passing'. However, it also dawned on me that a quiet retreat too was debarred. The dead end would necessitate turning the car, re-tracing my way and thus driving past the other. So much for discretion.

Debating the quandary I must have missed the footsteps, but I did hear Bouncer's sudden, throaty growl . . . and the subsequent thump of fist on window.

CHAPTER THIRTY-TWO

The Cat's Views

I am glad to say that after my strange little incident I am feeling perfectly all right – quite my old, alert self in fact. I don't really know what came upon me but it was all very strange, albeit not *un*pleasant. I recall vividly my visit to the school and the encounter with that odious pedagogue Top-Ho – and indeed with the smothering foreign female – but after that things begin to blur, although I do vaguely recall coming home and chasing a saucer across the terrace. Can't think why it was there – presumably dropped by P.O. It is amazing how careless she can be; although mercifully not as bad as the brother.

Bouncer seems to have found my *petit mal* highly risible, and when I finally awoke after apparently long hours of slumber, he bellowed: 'Out for the count and no mistake, Maurice! Thought you had nearly kicked your ninth bucket!'

'I have no intention of kicking any bucket yet,' I told him irritably, 'ninth or otherwise. Now kindly fetch me a sardine.'

Rather to my surprise, he trotted off dutifully to the larder and returned moments later toting a slither of silver in his jaws. He dropped it in front of me and made the most distasteful gagging noise. Absurdly the dog has an aversion to fish, thus in its way it was a noble gesture and one I must recall when next he vexes – as vex he surely will. Currently, however, he is being quite useful. For example, he fully cooperated in my masterly tactic to alert our mistress to the bathing ritual (a great success – he has become almost fragrant!) and arranged the various items exactly as instructed. And I have to admit that his suggestion of our appointing Duster to report any curious comings and goings at the tall man's place was really most thoughtful.

Meanwhile, it rather looks as if I might enjoy the luxury of another quiet evening. Having gone out earlier, our mistress returned not long ago in high dudgeon. It was obvious that something had occurred to annoy her as there was much irritable sighing and drumming of fingers on the card table. And the occasional imprecation directed at 'bloody Topping' and 'idiot Emily' more than hinted at the cause of her mood. It was all very *well*, but I had my woollen mouse to consider. I mean how could one concentrate on garrotting its neck on the hearthrug with that din raging above? I shot her a few stern looks but these had little effect and the fuming continued. There was nothing for it but to leave the room.

Thus teeth clamped firmly to the woollen infidel, I started to make my exit, only to be ambushed by the dog who wanted to play Murder in the Dark. Really! Did I say he was being useful? A rash statement I fear. However, he calmed down, retreated to his basket and dropped off to sleep.

And then to my surprise P.O. suddenly appeared at the kitchen door demanding that he wake up and go with her for a ride in the car. This struck me as a trifle odd, it being a late hour for humans to start gallivanting. But then as I have often remarked, their psyche is not noted for its logic. However, given the earlier agitation I assume her motive was somehow connected with the Top-Ho business. Still, intriguing though this may be, the point *is* that with the two of them out of the way for a while I am now left to my own devices and can do exactly as I please without being frustrated by P.O.'s whims or raucous horseplay from the dog . . . Ah, the bliss of an empty house, a warm fire and unimpeded access to the pantry!

Of course, now I come to think of it, the last time I was in such a happy position was the night they returned from that little contretemps at the dew pond. It would be unfortunate were they to encounter a second head, though I imagine the likelihood is remote. But then one can be certain of nothing in this life – least of all if living with one of the Oughterards. Now, what shall I do first – revisit the mouse or liberate the haddock? Fish first, I fancy, and then a light grapple with the grey one . . .

CHAPTER THIRTY-THREE

The Primrose Version

The fist on glass? The Long Arm of the Law, to wit Chief Superintendent Alastair MacManus, and in full uniform, if you please, intrusive oaf! My initial terror melted to indignant fury. What was he up to, lurking around innocent cars and affrighting their respectable occupants?

I wound down the window and said frostily, 'What *are* you doing, Superintendent?' I had no intention of dignifying him with the addition of Chief. 'You have just upset my poor dog. He has been in rather a fragile state and you have now made him much worse.' I turned to Bouncer and gave him an uncharacteristic hug. 'Poor little boy,' I crooned, 'you are quite safe with Mummy!' I think Bouncer was rather surprised but he gave a most plausible whimper.

I turned back to the shape at the window. 'Is there something bothering you, Mr MacManus?' I enquired dryly, 'or is this tapping a random procedure?'

There followed a gravelly clearing of throat. 'My

apologies, Miss Oughterard, I thought you might be somebody else, a case of mistaken identity, if you see what I mean.'

I certainly did not see what he meant, and with the merest note of sarcasm said, 'Ah, someone else you know who drives a two-toned Morris Oxford in Lewes with a Rutland number plate? I daresay there are quite a few of us about.'

'Yes, there are,' he replied woodenly.

There was no answer to that. So patting the dog I said quickly, 'Well we must be getting home, Bouncer's had his little run,' and reached for the starter.

But before I had time to press it he said, 'If you don't mind my saying, isn't it a little late for you to be out at this time of night? I mean an unaccompanied female parking in a lonely lane does make herself rather vulnerable. After all—'

'Oh you mean vulnerable to being frightened by sudden knocks on her car window? Yes, I so agree; it doesn't do to loiter, does it!' I gave a merry laugh.

'No it doesn't, Miss Oughterard,' he murmured, his fingers gripping the sill, 'especially after that incident on the downs. I should have thought you would be a bit anxious. I know my wife would.' Yes, having seen that mouse of a woman I could well imagine. He paused and then added, 'In future it might be wise to exercise Bouncer in a less secluded place, the lane outside your own house, for example.'

The cheek of it – instructing me where to take the dog, if you please! But I could see his point: why drive to this particular spot late at night to let the dog out? There were indeed more convenient places.

'You obviously don't know our canine friends, Superintendent,' I replied. 'Just like us they have their whims and preferences. Bouncer adores this field and the wood above it too. It must be something to do with its brand of rabbit,' I added jocularly. 'I bring him here on special occasions when he has been very good or when he is under the weather, as he is just now. A little jaunt in fresh pastures perks him up no end. Now if you don't mind, we really must be off.' I pressed the starter, and not caring if I trapped his fingers, wound up the window. The car shot forward rather more suddenly than intended but I managed a brisk three-point turn and away we zoomed.

Ruffled by the encounter but also pleased by my handling of it, it was only when I got home that I began to wonder what exactly he had been doing there . . . I mean it was all very well his enquiring why I was parked in a lonely lane, but what about him? Presumably it had been he and not Topping sitting in that car; he was unlikely to have wandered there on foot, especially wearing formal uniform.

He had *said* I had been a case of mistaken identity. Whose identity? Some known local felon? Or perhaps another police officer in an unmarked vehicle if you can describe my battered Morris as such. Maybe they were engaged in a sort of dragnet operation connected with the Carstairs case, and my sally about random window tapping was closer to the mark than I thought. Was it perhaps part of a surveillance job entailing spot checks on motor cars thought to be harbouring would-be executioners? But if so, did such manoeuvres merit the presence of the senior man, and in full dress uniform to boot? It seemed a mite excessive. But then what did I know of police practice and convention? That is, other than the little gleaned from my late brother's experience?

CHAPTER THIRTY-FOUR

The Dog's Views

Well, I don't know, it's all getting a bit dodgy. What with Maurice coming home from that school place wearing face powder and then going berserk on the terrace, and the Prim waking me up and forcing me to go walkies at God knows what hour, it's a wonder that a decent dog like me doesn't go under. It's just as well that I'm tough (which is why I was such a good ally of F.O.) because living here is not what you would call the smoothest of picnics. But then if it was, would I like it? Nah, not on your best bone I wouldn't! BORING.

Still it's quite a strain on the old brain box trying to puzzle things out. And living here I don't have that nice hidey-hole under F.O.'s church to go into, the crip or whatever they called it – that place with all those old tombs and burbling ghosts. I liked it down there because it was quiet and away from Maurice and I could THINK . . . I wonder if those ghosts are still nattering on. Probably. I expect they are saying: 'Whatever happened to that nice

Bouncer fellow? He was a really smart dog and no mistake. Ah well, *canis fugit*!' (You *see* I can even remember a bit of their weird patter – no fleas on me!)

And talking of weird, I don't know what game P.O. is playing but my part in it the other night was JOLLY IMPORTANT and she called me a clever boy. I was a bit fed up at first when she hauled me out of my warm basket and into the cold car. But I decided to behave as it doesn't hurt to keep the old snout in good nick.

The Prim drove like a cat out of hell to some dark place and stopped near a house. She didn't get out or do anything interesting (except dust the steering wheel) but just sat and sat until I got bored and went to sleep. I had a dream that the car was full of bones and bunnies and that we were sitting close to Top-Ho. When I woke up nothing had changed, of course: no bones or bunnies and there was no sign of Top-Ho either. BUT do you know, I had this really sure feeling that we were by his house – I could sniff him in the air. I get these feelings sometimes, it's all part of a dog's sixth sense (which Maurice is so sniffy about), and I just *knew* that that's where we were. And then when I was in the middle of working things out and deciding that the Prim was doing a spot of SPYING (like what Duster is doing for us), there was a noise and this big car comes and parks round the corner. 'Ho, Ho,' I said to myself, 'what's up?' And I was about to signal my DISKWART, as the cat says, when P.O. told me not to make a sound. So I closed my jaw and shut my eyes tight.

We stayed like that for some time with not a move from anywhere and I very nearly dropped off again. But then I heard these heavy feet coming nearer and nearer and my hackles didn't half shoot up! The next moment there was this cat-awful crash on the window. Cor, I nearly jumped out of my skin! A whopping great shadow was looming outside and I could see that the Prim was shaken. But I tell you what – she wound down the window and gave this shadow a right old ear-bashing, and then all of a sudden clutched me round the scruff and cried 'My poor little man, look what you've done to him!' or some such.

At first I was a bit flummoxed by this but then I got the message. So I flattened my ears and let out a really good whimper and started to quiver all over. That did the trick because the shape at the window began to cough and mumble. And that's when I remembered where I'd seen him before: it was that big police type who had come to talk to her about our adventure at the dew pond. I thought he was daft then and still thought so . . . But he's not as daft as *all that*. Maurice tells me there are degrees of human daftness (made a study of it he says), and I think that this man is only half daft. Anyway, I don't like him. He's the sort that would grab your bone as soon as look at it. So I went on playing my part and pretending to be two crumbs short of a biscuit (I'm good at that), until P.O. shoved the window up to shut him out and we buzzed off.

When we got home she gave me lots of pats and some special chews, so I knew I'd done well. Of course the cat wanted to hear all about it straightaway. But it doesn't do to please him too often so I said he would just have to wait till the morning, and curled up in my basket and kept my TRAP SHUT!

CHAPTER THIRTY-FIVE

The Primrose Version

I had just emerged from the grocer's when I saw Melinda Balfour flapping towards me. She had news to impart for her face wore an expression of suppressed excitement. It frequently does and thus it's as well not to be too intrigued for fear of disappointment. I mean does one really want to hear about Freddie's increased golfing handicap or her sister-in-law's laryngitis?

The words came tumbling out. 'My dear, it's so funny! Polly Fox-Findley is on the prowl again. Lance is away for weeks on some business trip and she's at a loose end. And you know what that means!'

'Looser than usual?' I enquired.

'A whole Victor Stiebel cocktail dress looser,' she giggled. 'Looks good in it too, she gave me a fashion show. The waist is stunning.'

'That must have set Lance back a bit,' I laughed. 'So who's the target this time? Someone in London presumably.'

'*Well,*' Melinda said with relish, 'principally no doubt. But *I* think there's a second-ranker in the offing – rather more local, you might say.' She gave a broad wink and stood back, waiting for my reaction.

'You mean like Mr Winchbrooke of Erasmus House?'

This was met with peals of laughter. 'Don't be silly, Primrose! Have another go.'

'I really have no idea. Besides, this is sheer speculation and I must get back to feed the creatures. If I leave it any longer they'll have destroyed the house.' I was about to move off.

'MacManus,' she said.

I stopped instantly. 'Surely you don't mean the police person?'

'Ah,' she crowed, 'I thought that might amuse.'

I replied that I was less amused than surprised. 'I mean he's so dull, bleak really.'

'Yes, but you must admit he is rather handsome. Tall and broad-shouldered and—'

I sniffed. 'Well if one likes the lantern-jawed variety; he's certainly not my style.'

'I am not sure that style is part of Polly's criteria, and generally any variety tends to do. I mean, consider Lance . . .' We considered Lance but did not linger.

'But what on earth gives you this idea?' I asked.

She explained that she and Freddie had been at a recent Rotary Club dinner (Ladies' Night or some such thing), and Lance being on his business trip they had invited Polly to go with them. 'I can't say that it was the most enlivening evening and in fact the only bright spot was MacManus cutting quite a dash in full rig and—'

I frowned. 'Full rig? I thought they only wore that for

217

Church parades and on Armistice Day etc., surely not for minor local bean feasts.'

'Ah, but you see he was the guest of honour and giving a talk on police procedures. I suppose the organisers thought people would pay more attention if he looked the part. Anyway, Primrose, the point *is* that he was placed next to Polly at dinner with Mrs Mac opposite. Polly was vamping him like crazy and poor little Mrs M. was casting the most poisonous looks. I shouldn't be surprised if there weren't another decapitation soon, though I rather doubt if she could lift the axe.' Melinda emitted a bellow of mirth which sent a loitering dachshund scuttling for cover.

'But Polly vamps anything in uniform; and besides I doubt if she would get far with MacManus, he's far too stolid.'

'Ah, but I think she has!' Melinda cried with glee.

I asked her what she meant and she explained that at the end of the dinner MacManus had sent his wife home in a taxi saying that he had urgent reports to attend to at the station which couldn't wait till morning; and that the moment she was safely installed in the taxi he had turned to Polly and suggested he give her a lift home as it was on his way – an offer which was readily accepted.

'But I thought Polly was with you,' I said. 'Weren't you and Freddie going to drop her off?'

'Oh that was the *plan* all right, but she babbled something about it taking us well out of our way and it being much quicker with MacManus. The next moment she had gone racing across the car park, skirts up to her knees and making a beeline for his car. I ask you! But the silly girl had to hang about on the tarmac looking an idiot, because at that moment one of the hotel staff appeared and said that MacManus was wanted on the telephone. Rather embarrassing I should think. Just shows, more haste, less speed.'

'So what did Freddie say?' I asked with interest.

'"Thank God for that. Now we can get home pronto and have a nightcap."'

'But wasn't he puzzled by the sudden flight?'

'Freddie? No. Fortunately few things puzzle him . . . unlike yours truly.' She gave a dark chortle. 'Anyway, my dear, I must fly. But *do* come over for some more bridge – though I think this time you ought to stay the night: after all one never knows *what* might be encountered on the downs these days!'

I returned to my car in a state of some amusement. Admittedly Melinda was the most inveterate of gossips but in this case she might just be on to something for once. When Polly Fox-Findley had the bit between her teeth few things were known to stop her, let alone the complaisant Lance. Perhaps she viewed MacManus as a sort of challenge, though frankly I shouldn't have thought it worth the effort. Still, I mused, no accounting for tastes, especially those of the Fox-Findley kind.

And then I stopped short, staring at the clouds above the church spire. Oh my giddy aunt . . . in his dress uniform and a couple of nights ago? That would surely have been the night when he had accosted me near Topping's house. Had he been alone in that car or had there been some covert lover there – Mrs F.-F. shrouded under a rug in the back seat, resplendent in her Stiebel dress? Would that account for his skulking movements? Checking if the coast was clear before . . . well anything you care to mention, I suppose. Disgraceful!

* * *

I have to admit that I found Melinda's speculations so engrossing that the issue of Hubert Topping rather slipped from my mind. However, after lunch I collected my thoughts, and forgoing the crossword turned back to the crucial question: what had he been doing and with whom on that Wednesday night travelling the Newhaven road? Had they collected the *onus*, the 'stuff' as Ingaza had termed it – and if so, what had they done with it? Was it taken back to Topping's place much later that night or stowed somewhere else? It irked me to think that had it not been for the intrusive MacManus and his amatory nonsense I might have been able to wait long enough to see Topping return to the cottage and thus get some inkling of his activity. As it was, I remained clueless. Hell!

A genuine ally would have been handy, a confidant with whom I could chew things over. Alas, Francis was no more (though I am not entirely sure his views would have been helpful; always a ditherer). Charles, of course, is *sound* but seemed to be unduly indulgent of Topping. I mean to say, did he really need to be quite so amenable to his cocksure advice the previous night? 'Mark my words,' T. had insisted, 'leave the stable renovation and get on with the west wing; it's the obvious route.' Huh! Obvious to Topping maybe but not necessarily to anyone else. But Charles had seemed quite impressed and besides which there was the liability of Agnes. Much as I like her, discretion is not her strong suit. Emily? Well, not the brightest spark in the box except where timetables and wayward parents are concerned. Melinda, of course, is a good egg but as mad as a coot – and there is always the Freddie problem . . . which left only one possibility. Nicholas Ingaza.

Certainly Nicholas has the brains, and, unlike Charles, nobody could accuse him of being even-handed, but did I really need to involve him more than necessary? After all, despite the tears at the funeral he didn't exactly ease Francis's plight! . . . I lit a cigarette and brooded. A risk? Quite possibly. But better the devil you knew (more or less) than the devil of that unctuous little Latin-spouting toad. I was determined to expose him; and if that meant further engagement with Ingaza then so be it.

Thus decided, I marched to the telephone and dialled the Brighton number, keeping fingers crossed that it wasn't Eric who answered; I was in no mood for thunderous jollity.

'Hello,' the nasal voice said cautiously, 'I thought you weren't going to phone until Ted had wrapped up the deal. I take it there's no hitch because if so—'

'No, Nicholas,' I said, 'there is no hitch and neither am I Ted nor any other of your dubious contacts. This is Primrose Oughterard speaking.'

'Well what do you know,' he replied silkily, 'found another head, have we?'

'Don't be absurd. But, as it happens, I would appreciate your views on one or two small matters – *not* unconnected if you see what I mean. Should an empty slot appear in your busy schedule I would be most obliged.'

'Always time for you, dear girl,' was the smooth response. 'Six-thirty tomorrow at the Masons' Arms? I have to be over in your neck of the woods later in the evening so that would be fine.' He paused and then added, 'Do I take it we shall have the pleasure of Bouncer's company? Because if so I must come suitably clad. The last time we met he thoughtfully smeared my jacket with some bone residue. Rather difficult to remove I recall.'

'In that case, you'd better be a wise boy scout and come prepared. Bring a mackintosh.'

I was about to ring off when he said, 'Oh by the way, I saw your little friend the other day.'

'Do you mean Topping? Where? Footling around on his bicycle, I suppose.'

'I didn't see any bicycle. He was with another chap, footling about on the Newhaven quay. I couldn't quite make out—'

'On the quay!' I exploded.

'Good lord, Primrose, you'll bust the line or my eardrums! Now if you don't mind I've got some urgent business to attend to. Toodle-oo.' The line went dead, leaving me in a state of suspended triumph.

CHAPTER THIRTY-SIX

The Primrose Version

So I was right. He *had* been at Newhaven and down by the docks. Vindicated! I couldn't wait to meet Ingaza the following day and press him to be more precise about their movements. He must surely have noticed something more revealing than the mere absence of a bicycle. Typical of Nicholas to be so cryptic and to clam up just when one wanted to learn more. Yes, just as I had surmised, they must have been hanging about waiting to receive the mysterious cargo, the consignment of stuff, whatever it was. Obviously it was something illicit otherwise why all the subterfuge, such as that ridiculous lie about taking prep? What was it that was being collected on those Wednesday evenings? Hardly 'brandy for the parson' – these days cognac is plentiful enough, and in any case, judging from the suspicious quantities of orange squash the Reverend Hollis consumes I rather imagine that gin is the preferred tipple, a commodity obtained at any off-licence. 'Baccy for the clerk' also seemed unlikely, our own municipal jobsworth being obsessed with the obnoxious sucking of pear drops.

I wondered who Topping's accomplice had been. Emily hadn't specified the gender of the driver but I think if it had been a woman she would doubtless have remarked. Yes, the other man was surely the same figure Ingaza had seen with him on the quay.

Despite my buzzing thoughts that night, I slept remarkably well and the following day I felt so full of energy that I completed my current canvas and started a fresh one – its foreground taken up by a shimmering but placid dew pond. Perhaps Winchbrooke would like it for his study. Other than a break to exercise the dog and feed the chinchillas I continued in my studio all day. And thus come five o'clock it was quite a relief to put down my brush and get ready for our rendezvous.

I looked at Bouncer mooching about on the terrace and wondered if I should take him but decided against it. It would be gracious to spare Ingaza's jacket. And in any case the hound had had quite enough drama the other night with that absurd MacManus creeping all over the place. I made a mental note to direct a sly innuendo at Polly Fox-Findley the next time I faced her across the bridge table. With luck it might put her off her stride and win me a trick; one should never pass up an opportunity as Pa had constantly reminded us. The context of the opportunity was rarely defined but I think it generally had something to do with confounding the enemy – whether at a game of cards or in the game of life, a piece of advice which Nicholas would surely endorse. I hurried to the car not wanting to keep His Nibs waiting: there were important matters to discuss and I certainly didn't want him slipping away before they were fully aired.

In my haste I reached the pub well before the allotted time. It had only just opened its doors and was in that semi-somnolent state that prevails just before the onset of homing farm workers and businessmen. This meant I could secure a cosy corner in what was ambitiously called the lounge bar – distinguished only from the public one by its hideous carpet and plastic flowers. Both rooms are dingy but the beer is good and the publican pleasant.

'Good evening, Albert,' I said (he won't answer to Bert), 'I'll have half of Harveys' best please, and I don't suppose you could rustle up some cheese and pickles, could you? I have been painting all day and if I don't have sustenance I shall faint immediately.'

He grinned and nodded. 'Can't have that, Miss Oughterard, bad for trade. And speaking of which, how's yours these days – still raking it in with the old sheep and churches?'

'Oh one hobbles along,' I replied genially, 'but actually I've just introduced something new: a water feature. It doesn't do to get stuck in the same mould, however popular.' My eyes swept the smoke-encrusted bar with its fake horseshoes gathering dust.

'Ah, you mean a river? Which is it – the Ouse or the Cuckmere? I bet it's the Cuckmere: artists like all those meanders. Or do I mean ox-bows?'

'It is not a river, it's a pond. A downland pond.'

Albert gave a low whistle. 'Well, now that is inspired! I suppose it includes the headless stiff; that's bound to pull

225

in the punters.' He gave a sepulchral chuckle and lumbered off to fetch the cheese and pickles.

I took my beer to the table and picked up the evening paper. No news of the murder except a couple of lines to say the police had matters in hand and that the chief superintendent was expecting a speedy resolution . . . Huh, I thought, most likely the only thing that MacManus has in hand is Polly Fox-Findley. As to the speedy resolution, it would rather depend on how soon her husband returned from his business trip.

So absorbed was I by the image of weedy Lance squaring up to his strapping rival that I did not at first see Ingaza. He had slipped through the door unnoticed and like a thin shadow had settled himself opposite. He flashed a brilliantined smile. 'My drink on order, is it?'

'Not really,' I replied, 'didn't know what you wanted.'

He sighed theatrically. 'Just like your brother, ever tight-fisted.'

'I am *not* tight-fisted,' I retorted, 'merely thrifty. Why should I waste money on something you might not appreciate? And besides, Francis wasn't tight-fisted, it was simply that his mind was frequently preoccupied.'

'You bet it was. Trying to work out how to elude Mr Pierrepoint.'

'Really, Nicholas, I consider that remark most uncalled for. Utterly tasteless.'

He had the grace to look contrite. 'Yes,' he murmured, 'you're right. It was rather.' He got up abruptly and went to the bar to order a Scotch. When he returned my bread and cheese had arrived.

I pointed to the plate. 'You may have a pickled onion,' I said graciously.

'How kind . . . Now, dear girl, tell me: what's in the wind?'

And so I told him my suspicions, starting with my evening at Podmore and the Latin master's sinister flash of hostility. 'It was quite obvious, Nicholas, he was distinctly menacing. Only a few seconds admittedly, but it was the look as much as the words. It was most unpleasant! It was if he knew I had been at the dew pond and was deliberately taunting me.'

'That's a bit subjective, isn't it?'

'Things often are but that doesn't invalidate them.'

He nodded.

I then told him about Topping inventing the tale of having to get back to the school and then shortly afterwards being seen by Emily sitting in a large car apparently en route for Newhaven. 'And *that* isn't subjective. In fact in view of what you said last night about seeing him down at the docks with another man it is the plain objective truth. Not even circumstantial. And by the way, what were you doing there – and more to the point what were *they* doing?'

He explained that he had been on his way to a nearby public house to support Eric in one of his darts matches, a regular contest between the Brighton Warriors and the Newhaven Newts. However, other than noticing the pair talking on the quay amid the boats and oil tankers he had seen nothing. 'The weather was filthy and I wasn't going to hang about; but it was him all right – a bit like a sodden weasel.'

'There you are then,' I said eagerly, 'it all fits with that note you translated. He's obviously in some racket to do with smuggled goods and using the school as his cover. And Carstairs' death is all part of it!'

I suppose excitement made me speak louder than I meant for I saw Ingaza wince and he muttered, 'For God's sake, Primrose, keep your voice down, you're not calling the odds at Epsom.'

'But what do you think it is,' I asked in a suitably hushed tone, 'gun-running? Although there don't seem to be any wars at present – unless the Irish are restive again. The venerable de Valera is still in the cock-pit you know . . .'

He laughed. 'No, I think those times are over; he's a pussy cat now. If Topping is in the receiving game it will be something simpler and smaller – drugs I shouldn't wonder. London has become full of the stuff these days. It's a very lucrative business . . . In *fact*, dear girl, it might be right up your street: I am told that hollow picture frames make excellent carriers.'

'Oh very funny,' I said. 'Now kindly apply your mind and suggest something useful. What's our next move?'

He looked startled. '*Our* next move? Look, I don't wish to be a skeleton at the feast but I have no intention of getting embroiled in this unsavoury affair, and if you take my advice neither should you. I've told you before, little Topping can turn nasty. He wasn't with the Messina brothers for his charm, you know.'

'And that is precisely why I propose spiking his beastly gun,' I retorted tartly. 'Now, I am sure there is one thing you could do for me: check the shipping timetables and find out what boats come into harbour on Wednesday nights. At least that would be helpful.'

He took a sip of his Scotch and flicked a length of ash into the tray. 'Actually Primrose, I am rather busy at the moment. The Sussex Art Dealers' Convention is looming and I have a couple of rather special clients to accommodate.

Things are a trifle delicate and need my fullest attention. So if you don't mind—'

'So I suppose you won't,' I said impatiently.

He sighed. 'Just like Francis, always jumping to conclusions. What I was *going* to say was that I can't but Eric can. It's the sort of thing he likes doing: nosing around and imagining he is being crafty. He'll be only too pleased especially when I tell him it's for you. Probably make his day. Now, one for the road and then I must be off. Got to see a man about a dog.' He winked.

I was pleased with this concession and when he returned to the table started to tell him about my vigil outside Topping's cottage and MacManus's tiresome intrusion. 'And do you know what? I've just learnt via the grapevine that he was more than likely romancing Polly Fox-Findley on that night. She is one of our local ladies who he had given a lift to after the Rotary dinner. I suppose he chose that area because it's secluded. Stupid idiot.' I started to laugh.

'I doubt it. She was at home by then.'

I stopped laughing and stared at him. 'What do you mean? And how on earth would you know?'

'Because I know the Fox-Findleys, professionally at any rate. They come into the gallery and Lance puts an occasional bit of business my way. She's a fool but I don't dislike her. Anyway, she appeared the other day effing and blinding about your new police chief. Said he had the manners of an oaf and she never wanted to see him again. Apparently she had accepted that lift, hoping they might stop for a drink en route, or something equally jolly, and instead of which he drove like the clappers, reached her house in record time and didn't even get out to open the car door. According to her she tripped on the running board, snagged her dress, and by the time she had scrabbled for the latchkey her gallant escort had zoomed off into the night leaving her in the middle of the drive. She was none too pleased I can tell you!' Nicholas tittered and added, 'Just goes to show, a gal can't always trust a uniform.'

Well, I thought as I drove back from the pub, that's scotched that piece of gossip. How disappointed Melinda will be. Indeed I was mildly disappointed myself. It had been satisfying, risible really, to think of the starchy MacManus falling prey to Polly's predatory glad eye. And I wondered vaguely how much it would cost to repair the stitching on the Victor Stiebel cocktail dress . . .

Once home and unsated by the pub's cold collation I stirred the stew and pondered Ingaza's tale of Polly's speedy delivery to her house. Clearly, if anyone had been hidden in that silent vehicle outside Topping's cottage it had not been her. Had the superintendent been alone there after all and, as I had originally surmised, intent on some perfectly legitimate police business – business which necessitated prowling around and peering into innocently parked cars? Presumably. Yet according to Melinda he had sent his wife home after the dinner saying there were mountains of urgent paperwork awaiting him at the station. But if that were so, and not, as assumed, a pretext to dally with Polly, why had he been knocking on my car window at midnight and not sitting at his desk toiling over reports?

I took a ruminative sip of wine and addressed the dog: 'You know what, Bouncer? *I* think he was on the Topping trail, and just like us was there to spy out the land. Perhaps he had received a sudden tip-off. What about that phone call to the hotel, for instance?' The dog gave a gormless stare and then promptly went to sleep. So much for animal empathy.

I have to admit to being annoyed at the thought of MacManus conducting the same speculative vigil as myself, and wondered irritably whether he had learnt anything. What had happened, for instance, after my hurried departure? Had Topping and accomplice turned up staggering under the weight of drug-laden cargo conveniently shouting out words of triumph? Or had the prey returned empty-handed and alone, slipped quietly through his front door and retired meekly for the night? Or had he not appeared at all? Or had the waiting MacManus grown impatient and driven off to the comfort of his bed, and like me none the wiser? I sighed. It was all very frustrating.

CHAPTER THIRTY-SEVEN

The Primrose Version

Thursday brought the Erasmus House Founder's Day dinner, an event from which Winchbrooke excluded all staff but assiduously invited the patrons and local notables – presumably in the hope that their presence might bring fiscal benefit. Since I had donated a couple of my paintings to the school – and I suspect was marked down for more – my own name featured on the guest list; as did that of Chief Superintendent MacManus. I rather doubted whether the latter's presence would be of pecuniary value but assumed he had been invited to confer a whiff of legal probity should the Inland Revenue turn wayward.

Being taken up with an expectant daughter in London, Mrs Winchbrooke was unable to play hostess, and thus Melinda Balfour, escorted by ubiquitous Freddie, had been asked to deputise. To my distaste – and given our last encounter some slight unease – I found myself seated next to MacManus. Why Melinda had decided to place me so I cannot imagine; she knew very well my lack of sympathy for the man. Doubtless revenge for my having trounced her at the last bridge supper. Anyway, whatever the reason, there I was being charming in the teeth of a bleak challenge.

'Tell me, Chief Superintendent,' I began earnestly, 'now that you are well established in our neighbourhood, how are you finding things? It is a lovely part of Sussex but new places always take some getting used to, however attractive. Wouldn't you agree? . . . Or perhaps you miss the bright lights of London,' I added vacuously. 'I fear we are a little dull down here.'

There was a pause while he seemed to consider. And then after an unduly protracted sip of his soup, he replied, 'I wouldn't go so far as that, Miss Oughterard, not with this current tragedy still looming over us. From my observations, it is not something that the majority of Lewes's residents would term "dull". But, of course, you being an artist might think it small beer in comparison with some of the bohemian excesses one hears of these days.' He gave a wintry smile and I felt justifiably rebuked.

'Oh no,' I gasped in horror, 'of course I didn't mean *that*, far from it! Naturally, we are all appalled by this dreadful business and are only too anxious for the villains to be found. I suppose I really meant *generally* speaking, that is to say, in your recreational time.'

He observed soberly that as a senior police officer he had little time for recreation and that the current case in particular was absorbing most of his energies. 'But it will be resolved I assure you, Miss Oughterard, have no doubt of that. These things just require tenacity and patience – *and*, of course, the cooperation of the public.' He gave me a hard look. 'Some people take their civic duties rather lightly.'

'Oh I am sure they do,' I agreed quickly, 'so thoughtless!'

(Oh God, was he still brooding on Bouncer's wretched name tag? Did he really suspect that I had witnessed something?) I turned smartly to my neighbour; but before I had managed to catch the attention of the colonel's deaf ear, MacManus said abruptly, 'And how is Bouncer?'

'Bouncer? Oh *he's* always all right.'

'That's not what you said the other night. I gather he had been poorly which is why you had taken him to that field below Barking Wood. One of his favourite haunts you said.'

I gave a smile of lying agreement, wondering nervously what this was leading up to. Was he suspicious of the excuse I had given (true, exercising the dog did seem pretty limp) and suspected some other motive for my being there? Quite possibly. But then I still couldn't make out what *he* had been doing since amatory dalliance was evidently not the reason. Perhaps my earlier notion was correct and he really had been staking out Topping's cottage, lurking around in the hope of surprising his quarry. If so then he was sharper than I had given him credit for. It was, I supposed, just conceivable that this stiff-necked man was streets ahead of me in the affair, had everything sewn up and was on the brink of busting Topping. Was he perhaps already anticipating his triumph and the prospect of another rung up the chief constable ladder? Well, I thought sourly, if he was so damn clever then he didn't need the help of Primrose Oughterard. I turned again to my other neighbour and this time did manage to get his attention. 'How's tricks, Colonel?' I asked gaily.

'Damned godawful,' was the growling reply, 'and so is this claret. Can't think where they get the stuff!'

We spent an amiable ten minutes disparaging the claret,

the price of coal and most other things. But such pleasantry could not be sustained, for when the colonel stooped to retrieve his fallen napkin I received a light tap on the elbow from MacManus, who with no preliminaries said: 'By the way, Miss Oughterard, how often do you and your dog go wandering in Barking Wood?'

'We do not wander, we march,' I replied curtly, puzzled by his interest. 'And as to how often, I really couldn't say.' I fixed him with a cool stare, stung both by the question and its bald delivery. Really, anyone would think we were down at the police station rather than in the headmaster's dining room.

He must have sensed my annoyance for he said quickly, 'One doesn't like to talk shop on such occasions, but you see with your local knowledge there's something you might be able to help me with.' He lowered his voice: 'Something in the wood.'

'In the wood? Whatever do you mean?' I exclaimed.

He cleared his throat and dropped his voice further. 'Yes. You see there is an old shed there, a disused charcoal burners' hut which according to local legend was used by smugglers to store their contraband. Of course that's all history now but we have reason to believe that recently it has been used for storing something else equally illicit.'

'Absinthe, not brandy?' I quipped.

'Of a similar potency,' he said solemnly, 'cocaine.'

I was startled. Ingaza in talking of Topping's *onus* had certainly surmised the existence of a drug dealing ring in the area, but it had been mere speculation. Yet here was the chief superintendent voicing the same theory – although coming from such a source it was less likely to be theory than fact.

'How extraordinary,' I replied, 'but I really cannot see what that this has to do with Bouncer and me; we are not familiar with drugs.'

'Possibly not,' he replied, 'but you might be able to supply information all the same.' (*Possibly* not? The cheek of the man!) 'You see as you and Bouncer frequent that area I thought you may have seen something untoward, persons hanging around the shed, for instance.'

Since I had never taken Bouncer anywhere near the wood before that evening, the question was irrelevant. However, having fabricated the lie I was bound to stick with it. Thus I frowned, trying to give the impression of deep thought. 'No,' I said slowly, 'I am afraid I can't help you there. I don't recall seeing anybody on our little walks, not a soul.' I endeavoured to sound regretful. And then a thought struck me: 'But have you asked Mr Topping, that nice Latin master from the boys' school? Living so close he may well have seen something.' I beamed helpfully.

MacManus gave a non-committal nod and after a pause said, 'I expect you were wondering what I was doing there on that Wednesday night. Sorry if I startled you.'

I shrugged. 'Not really. Presumably some police matter . . .'

'Exactly. We had had a tip-off that there might be activities at the hut that evening; but other than seeing you in your car, there was nothing.'

'Oh dear,' I murmured, 'a false trail.'

'Hmm. You could say that I suppose.'

He didn't sound especially convinced and seemed to be regarding me with an unnecessarily fixed gaze – at least so it seemed; but perhaps that was simply the effect of the heavy eyebrows which rather got in the way of things. It occurred to me afterwards that perhaps he suspected I was one of those 'persons hanging around'.

Anyway, at that moment I was dug in the ribs by the colonel, who in a rasping stage whisper said, 'I say, my dear, if you are not going to eat any more of that trifle you can pass it to me. Our host's puddings are considerably better than his wines.' Thankfully, I turned away from MacManus and gave the colonel my plate.

After the cheese we broke for the port – the men for the port, we women to gossip in Mrs Winchbrooke's bedroom followed by coffee in the drawing room. I always feel glad of such interludes. I mean if one has been grappling with some ponderous type like MacManus it is very refreshing to be amidst the scent and idle chatter of one's girlfriends.

However, nothing lasts and once we were all reassembled sipping liqueurs, to my annoyance I again found myself sitting next to MacManus. (I really must have a word with Melinda regarding the logistics of such matters.)

I didn't think the port had done him any good. He looked flushed and his voice had taken on a distinctly conspiratorial tone.

'I expect you are wondering where my wife is,' he said.

'Er, not really,' I replied indifferently.

'You see,' he continued, 'she has gone to stay with her mother.'

'How nice,' I said vaguely.

'Yes, in Norfolk.'

I was about to quip 'very flat, Norfolk' but thought better of it. I mean what on earth was the point?

And just as I was thinking that I was sitting next to the

biggest bore in Christendom he suddenly said, 'I met a friend of yours recently.'

'How nice,' I said again. 'And who would that be?'

At first the name Sidney Samson meant absolutely nothing to me. And it was only when MacManus cleared his throat and added, 'Chief inspector as he now is,' that it suddenly struck a chord. That was the name of the beastly little detective sergeant who had been so irksome to Francis during the Fotherington débâcle. He and his superior, March, had been most persistent, and while the latter was civil enough his ferrety sidekick, Samson, had been obnoxiously tiresome – and dangerous. After the shelving of the case and Francis's death, I heard he had gone to Scotland Yard – destined for higher things apparently. Judging from this new title he was progressing briskly.

As these memories stirred, I sensed that MacManus was regarding me intently. I smiled vaguely and took a bolstering sip of Benedictine. 'I do remember but I don't think "friend" is quite the right term, we met once, that's all.'

He shrugged. 'Oh just a *façon de parler* you might say.' (No actually, I wouldn't bloody say I thought savagely.) 'Anyway,' he continued, 'I was up at the Yard recently and we happened to bump into each other and had a chinwag about old times. He remembers you from that unsolved case in your brother's parish. Says you were very sharp – says you were both very sharp in fact. Uncommonly so.' Frankly I don't think that I had ever heard Francis described as 'sharp' – although since he had succeeded in foiling Detective Sergeant Samson at a crucial stage of the investigation some might regard him as such.

'I am flattered,' I replied. 'But I'm even more surprised that the chief inspector should remember me.'

'Oh our Sidney remembers everything, particularly people. That's useful really, very useful – especially in our line of work.' He gave a flaccid smile and a puff at the cigar someone had been fool enough to offer him. 'Yes,' he mused, 'it's amazing the role memory plays in unravelling forgotten cases.'

If he was trying to unsettle me he had certainly succeeded. What the hell was the wretch getting at?

'*Now*,' Freddie Balfour suddenly bellowed from across the room and clapping his hands, 'we are all going to play Murder in the Dark. Chop, chop, everybody! No excuses!' I don't think the headmaster had been expecting that and I saw him crumple as if hit by a cricket ball.

'Just up your street, Chief Superintendent,' I said winsomely, and promptly volunteered to play the victim.

Later in bed that night and worn out with being the corpse, I reflected on my conversation with MacManus. Normally this might have sent me off to sleep pretty quickly. As it was, it kept me staring at the ceiling, irritable and worried. The allusion to Samson was a shock. It would suggest that the two had been discussing the details of the Molehill murder. Hearing of the Sussex killing and perhaps recalling that Lewes was where the Revd Oughterard's sister lived, Samson may have been moved to speculate about all manner of things with MacManus. I could picture the pair of them hunched over a table in some drab office: the Whippet, as Francis had always called Samson, still sallow and scrawny and his nicotined fingers rolling the inevitable fag, while our 'handsome' Sussex gauleiter grimly lapped up his every hint and suspicion.

I sighed and switched off the light. The things one has to put up with! I mean, not to put too fine a point on it, having a murderer in the family is not something one is especially anxious to shout from the rooftops. And the fact that Francis escaped detection, and indeed died a hero's death, makes it no less tricky: one is so vulnerable to officious enquiry. Naturally, *I* know that the foolish boy simply lost his head and blundered, but others might not see it in that light, least of all Alastair MacManus. Thus it was with considerable disquiet that I eventually slipped into a fitful sleep.

CHAPTER THIRTY-EIGHT

The Cat's Views

Bouncer continues to be useful(!) and I like to think that he is at last benefitting from my example. His approach to the cairn at Podkennel has been productive and Duster has presented his first report. This was brought by Eleanor, Duster being entrapped by his master who had insisted he accompany him to the dentist. Apparently the tall man has a pathological fear of dentists and always takes the dog as a kind of moral support; says he likes to see a familiar face when he is pinioned in the chair. The cairn is scathing of this and complains that anyone would think he was a frigging teddy bear . . . a view with which, despite the language, I have some sympathy.

Anyway, as said, Duster's observations were relayed to us by the Persian. Lavish of face, Eleanor is also lavish of word and gesture. Thus we were treated to an operatic version of Top-Ho's movements. This required close attention as it was not easy to discern hard content amidst the florid delivery. However, after a careful sifting of ornament from fact it transpired that the man's midnight visits to Podkennel were becoming more frequent and that on the last occasion he had been accompanied by another person, long and lanky and on foot. This person had arrived before Top-Ho and skulked about filing his nails until the other turned up on his bicycle. The latter removed several bulky packets from his cycle bag, and carrying these they entered the building and shut the door.

Naturally, I enquired if the cairn had followed them into the stable. Eleanor said she had asked the same question but that Duster had looked shirty and answered that since he was neither a beetle nor a ghost the task would have been difficult. The Persian seemed to find that very funny, so for five minutes we were treated to a hail of spit and spluttering merriment. I think even Bouncer found that a trifle prolonged as in the middle of it he nipped off for a quick pee.

Once Eleanor was recovered and Bouncer returned, she told us there was something else in Duster's report. We cocked our ears expectantly but being theatrically disposed the Persian kept us waiting while she twirled around and played with her tail, what I believe is known as a dramatic pause. Performance over, she announced that there had also 'been words'.

'"Words"? What do you mean,' I asked, 'a quarrel?'

She said that was what the cairn had inferred because Top-Ho had looked very angry and said something that sounded like 'you are becoming a liar bubble and I'm not having it and neither will headquarters. They don't like your brand of humour; this isn't a pantomime you know, so just watch it!'

'*Liar bubble?*' I expostulated. 'What on earth is that

supposed to mean? The cairn must be mad or deaf.' Eleanor shrugged and replied that she wouldn't know about that but it was what he had definitely said.

I began to ponder but was interrupted by Bouncer who suddenly barked: 'LIABILITY, that's what.'

I gazed in astonishment. 'You don't know a word like that!'

'Oh yes, I do,' he growled, 'it's what F.O. used to say about me – "A blooming liability, that's what you are, Bouncer." He was always saying it, especially when I had chewed his cigarettes.'

One is tempted to agree with the vicar's assessment – but there is more to Bouncer than meets the eye and just now and again he is uncannily sharp. This was one of those rare moments. I beamed at him – such flashes of perspicacity merit reward – and said: 'That is a most helpful observation, Bouncer, and one that in the fullness of time will doubtless assist our enquiry.' His response was to wag his tail so vigorously that I felt quite dizzy.

I wanted to reflect on the cairn's report but was too diverted by Bouncer's incessant tail and Eleanor's incessant giggling. 'Let's play a game,' the latter suggested. 'We'll have a quiz.' She turned to Bouncer and demanded to know how many bones make five.

'Don't care,' he growled, 'but five bones make a very happy Bouncer!'

She sighed and turned to me. 'I bet you don't know how many studs are on Bouncer's collar.'

'Of course I do,' I replied wearily, 'there are seven.'

'How do you know that?' the dog asked.

I shrugged and murmured that I knew quite a lot of

things. 'It's all to do with cat curiosity,' I explained. 'As a species we are as some human once put it, "snappers up of unconsidered trifles".'

'I like trifles,' Eleanor mewed. 'I ate a whole one once, straight off the dining-room table. *They* didn't like it, of course, but I did!' She made rather distasteful slurping noises as if to emphasise the point.

I was about to explain that it wasn't exactly the kind of trifle I had in mind, when I was rudely interrupted by Bouncer. 'Ho, ho,' he chortled, 'if you ask me it wouldn't be trifles you snap up, Maurice, but unconsidered *chickens*.'

He emitted a howl of mirth and fell on the path waving his paws in the air. To my irritation Eleanor joined in . . . I think I may have to revise my opinion of the Persian, she may not be as bright or refined as I had first thought. I withdrew with dignity to sulk amidst the catmint – and also to muse in peace on Duster's report.

CHAPTER THIRTY-NINE

The Primrose Version

I had been looking forward to spending a quietly diligent day in my studio, so was not particularly pleased to be disturbed by the telephone. I cursed and hoped it wasn't Emily trying to wheedle me into accompanying her to another of Dr Bracegirdle's mind-numbing Mental Mechanics. Wiping my hands on my smock I traipsed down to the hall and picked up the receiver. I was met with a gust of heavy breathing followed by a series of squeaks.

'Is that Miss Oughterard?' a tiny voice asked.

'Yes,' I replied guardedly, 'who is that?'

'It's me, Dickie Ickington. You took me to Drusilla's.'

I told him that I remembered it well. (Surely the child didn't want to go again!)

'You see,' he continued, 'Matron says that I've got to telephone you to ask if I can have my cap back. She says I must have left it with you and it would be good practice for me to ask politely on the telephone like grown-ups do.'

Now that he mentioned it I did recall a cap – or at least something striped – in Bouncer's basket. So assuming that was it I asked when he wanted to fetch it.

'Today if you please because that's when we have to go to Mr Topping's house to see his slides on the Roman forum. Matron said I should pick it up on my way back.' I sighed. How thoughtful of Matron.

I told him that would be all right, and was about to put the phone down when he cleared his throat and piped, 'That is most exceedingly kind of you, Miss Oughterard. I am only too grateful – uhm, uhm, *toodle-ooey*!'

'Toodle-ooey,' I said, and went off to retrieve the trophy from Bouncer's basket.

The boy arrived fresh from the Roman forum and clearly hoping for some more cream buns. There weren't any and he had to make do with crisps and Tizer. He took the deprivation in good part and launched into a long description of Topping's slides of the ancient ruins. At the conclusion he observed, 'I don't think I really like all those old stones and things; I like *landscapes* and dogs and pretty ladies in crinolines.'

'How right you are,' I agreed, 'but it was very good of you to sit still through the whole of Mr Topping's little exhibition.'

'Well I did *nearly*,' he said, 'but I was itching to spend a penny, so when Mr Topping had his head down by the lantern slide I slipped into the passage to look for the lavatory. And then on my way back I sort of went into his study where the door was open. You see it was a bit boring looking at all those grey columns and crumbling water spouts.'

'One can imagine,' I said, 'but I don't suppose you stayed long in the study, did you?'

He hesitated and looked shifty. 'Well,' he said slowly, 'I did just stay for a *little*. You see there were these funny pictures, three photos on his blotting pad; so I did sort of have a squint at them . . . but not for long,' he added quickly, 'and then I went straight back into the sitting room.'

'What do you mean "funny pictures"?' I asked.

'Pictures of a man in a bear suit – one with the head on and two with it off. Actually it wasn't a very good bear suit, a bit tatty – sort of mangy round the edges.' He giggled. 'I say, I sound just like Grandpa! That's what he says about most of the people who come up before him in the dock.'

Ignoring Judge Icktington's personal views of his clients, I asked Dickie if bears were the only things the photos featured, and was slightly taken aback when he said that from what he could make out there was also a blonde lady dressed up as an ostrich – with very thin legs and carrying a whip.

'Ostriches don't carry whips,' I said sternly.

'She did, she did!' he cried. 'I don't tell porkies any longer – Grandpa said if I told any more he would send me down for a hundred years! . . . I say Miss Oughterard, why do you think they were dressed up like that?'

'Rehearsing for a pantomime,' I replied. '"Goldilocks and the Three Bears", I daresay.'

He nodded sagely; but then looked puzzled and said he hadn't realised that 'Goldilocks and the Three Bears' contained any ostriches. I assured him that there were various versions and that this was clearly one of the rarer ones.

However, prurient curiosity got the better of me and I

enquired casually whether by any chance he had recognised the bear suit's incumbent.

'Oh yes,' he replied simply, 'it was that policeman: Mr MacManus.'

To say I was shocked is to put it mildly. However, despite my astonishment I was able to say laughingly that I was sure he was mistaken and that the chief superintendent had far more pressing things to attend to than pantomime rehearsals.

The child stood its ground, explaining that the bear was very tall and broad-shouldered like the policeman; and besides, he had recognised the heavy eyebrows and the dark wart on the left side of his nose – 'You know, the one that bleeds sometimes.' I did not know but did recall the wart. He then asked a question which had been in my own mind: 'I wonder why Mr Topping had the pictures on his desk.'

'Probably keen on amateur theatricals,' I said quickly. 'Now, Dickie, what about some nice éclairs? I've just remembered that I have a tin in the pantry; we'll have a feast.'

His eyes lit up. 'And have they got jam as well as cream?'

'Not yet, but you can help me put some in – lots.'

'Oh *yes*, Miss Oughterard. Whizzo!'

An animated but sickly half hour was spent filling and devouring the éclairs, during which the conversation ranged widely across newts and frogspawn, his new Winsor & Newton paint box, his grandfather's latest pronouncement on the dope-dealing fraternity ('sodding buggers'), his chances of being picked for the second eleven and the weediness of Mr Hutchins.

Just before bundling him into the car to return to the school I said earnestly, 'You know Dickie, I think it would be best if you didn't mention seeing those photographs in Mr Topping's study – either to him or anybody else. After all, you wouldn't like him to think you had been snooping, would you?'

There was a shrill protest to the effect that he hadn't been snooping and that it was pure chance etc. etc.

'Oh yes, you and *I* know that Dickie – but schoolmasters can be a bit odd sometimes. They get touchy and tend to exaggerate.' There were vigorous nods. 'So I think it's best if we keep this very firmly under our hats. Don't you?' More nods. 'It will be just our little secret.'

He grinned. 'That's what Grandpa says when he slips me a ten bob note. And I don't breathe a word!'

Well, I thought cynically, if that child imagines he is going to get a ten shilling back-hander from me he is out of luck. He had done quite well enough on the éclairs. But judging from the ingenuous expression I suspected such cynicism was misplaced; and besides, now being privy to his illicit raid on Topping's study did rather put me at an advantage. Thus exchanging conspiratorial smiles we speeded off back to Erasmus House.

As I drove home I had only one thing in my mind: the ridiculous image of MacManus in the mangy bear suit, cavorting with the whip-brandishing ostrich woman. Thank goodness Sickie-Dickie was only ten and not sixteen and still wore the bloom of innocence. But distasteful though the image was, it certainly had its funny side . . . though really it comes to something when a senior officer of Her Majesty's law enforcers stoops to such shenanigans, especially one so starchy. What had he said at dinner the other night? That he had no time for recreation? Like hell he didn't. What a humbug!

But then I thought of the other humbug, the glib-tongued Topping. That particular aspect of the child's tale was what really intrigued me. How extraordinary that the Latin master should be in possession of such incriminating photos. Where had they come from and why on earth should he want them? Were the two men participants in some circle of unsavoury charades? And if so, what costume did Topping favour: an elf's garb, a cap and bells, leotards of spangled rosebuds? Or perhaps simply sock suspenders and a cream tuxedo . . . For a few seconds I allowed my mind to spin all manner of sartorial possibilities – and indeed in my mirth nearly spun myself off the road.

However, luckily I sobered as the answer suddenly danced before me. It couldn't be a case of blackmail, could it? Or perhaps something similar. Maybe Topping was weaving some insidious web of control, a means of deterring the chief superintendent should his investigations of the Carstairs case grow too close for comfort. Were the photographs a sort of indemnity, a handy brolly for a rainy day?

I stopped the car, got out and lit a cigarette. Leaning my elbows on a five-barred gate I gazed out over the placid fields towards the jutting profile of Firle Beacon and cogitated. From what Nicholas had hinted of Topping both at Oxford and in his tutelage under the Messinas, such self-defensive strategy would be typical. And indeed from my own observations he was not someone to leave things to chance; a cool customer was Hubert Topping and, I rather suspected, one who would derive sly amusement from ruffling the dour MacManus. Yes, that must be it.

The photos were his hold over the man should the latter get too nosy: aces at the ready to be flourished as and when required.

I lit another cigarette and listened to a blackbird whistling its evening solo. *Surmise! Surmise!* the notes fluted.

Yes, I mentally answered, but the photos were tangible enough. They had been there on Topping's desk; ludicrous and compromising. The boy had been adamant about the man's identity and there was no reason to doubt his sincerity – especially with his grandfather's hundred-year sentence hanging over him! Yes, Topping must surely have had them for some calculated purpose, i.e. to safeguard his own guilt in the murder of Carstairs!

Evidence? Evidence? the insistent bird continued.

'Oh do shut up,' I muttered. Admittedly, hard evidence for his guilt was scant but there were definitely bits and they were mounting. Besides, the very fact that Topping had the photos at all looked shady. Why have them unless for something dubious? Clearly the police chief posed a threat of some kind inimical to the Latin master's interests. I felt a stab of satisfaction: it had been Topping's bad luck (not to mention MacManus's) that Sickie's intrusion should have coincided with the photos being spread out on his desk . . . just as it had been my *good* luck to overhear that curious telephone conversation at his dreary drinks party. Well whatever it was I would trump him all right! But *how*, that was the question.

As I turned to go, a car pulled up behind mine and honked: Charles Penlow. He got out, and hauling the sober-faced Duster from the back seat came to join me at the gate. 'Ah, well met!' he cried. 'I was going to phone you this evening but now I can plead in person.'

'I can't imagine you pleading, Charles. It must be very important.'

'Hmm, well it is really. You see I was just wondering whether you might be prepared to take charge of this little tyke for a couple of days or so. I have to go to London to see the solicitors and one or two other chores and it wouldn't be the best thing to drag Duster up there. I had hoped Agnes would be back by now but she's been delayed and isn't due for another fortnight. I don't want to leave the little fellow at the kennels as he is a bit picky about that sort of thing.'

'So you don't think he would be picky about me?'

'Probably. But with luck Bouncer might distract him; they seem to be getting on all right now.'

I regarded the cairn. It was standing four-square, staring intently at a cow pat in the centre of a group of thistles. Did it have artistic leanings? Such close absorption in still-life might suggest so.

'Of course I'll take him,' I smiled, 'but I can't vouch for Maurice's language, he can get peevish with strangers.'

'Oh that won't worry Duster,' Charles replied cheerfully, 'he ignores cats just as he ignores most things. Lives in a world of his own.' He turned to the dog. 'Don't you, Duster old boy?' The dog looked up briefly, gave a perfunctory snort and resumed its study.

'Well, if he is as silent as that I am sure we shall get on famously,' I said. 'When can I expect him?'

Charles said he would drop him round the following afternoon along with his bowl and special biscuits. He also said he would bring a spare key to Podmore.

'What, in case Duster cuts up rough and insists on going home?'

Charles laughed. 'Oh don't worry, he can be quite obliging when he wants.' Well that was a relief.

CHAPTER FORTY

The Primrose Version

So that was the arrangement: Charles would deliver the cairn in the afternoon of the following day and then take off for London. 'Goodness,' I said brightly to my fellow residents, 'aren't you the lucky ones! We're going to have a little visitor for a few days. Won't that be fun? Now just make sure you treat him nicely.' The news was greeted with blank indifference and they swiftly went to sleep.

The visitor's arrival was prompt and decorous. That is to say, no offence was given and none apparently taken. The cairn slipped quietly into the house, sniffed the rugs in the hall and was greeted with uncommon grace by Bouncer and in silence by Maurice. Having expected noisy hub-bub I was much relieved, and leaving them to their own devices retired upstairs to the studio.

When I came down the cat had disappeared but I saw the two dogs in the garden trotting out of the shrubbery, muzzles smeared in earth. Presumably Bouncer had been showing off his bone collection.

I started to prepare supper but was interrupted by the telephone. 'I say,' said Charles's voice, 'I am most fearfully sorry, Primrose, but would you mind awfully going over to Podmore to fetch Duster's harness. I quite forgot to bring it with me. I know it's a bore but if you wouldn't mind—'

'Why ever does he need a harness?' I asked in surprise. 'I mean he's not exactly a leaping greyhound; seems pretty docile to me. Does he often wear one?'

Charles laughed. 'Oh no, he doesn't *wear* it, just sleeps with it. And the point is, if he doesn't have it by him he won't settle and makes a shindig all night.'

The prospect of the cairn making a shindig all night was not enticing. And thus amid further rueful apologies from Charles I assured him all would be well and that I would go over after supper and collect it from the downstairs cloakroom. I stared at the dog. 'No one told me you were a blithering neurotic,' I said irritably. Duster gave a sombre wag of his tail.

Supper over and after completing a corner of the crossword, I reluctantly rallied myself to fetch the wretched harness. Podmore being barely a mile away and the night clear and dry, I decided to walk. Stuck in the studio most of the day made me ready for exercise. Thus, taking a torch but eschewing the company of the two dogs I set out on my mission. Anything to keep the cairn quiescent!

In fact it was quite a pleasant stroll and there was enough moonlight not to need the torch. Podmore's main gates were locked but Charles had directed me to the back entrance which would take me down the old east drive to the side door. Here I did need the torch as the path was rutted and overhung with trees. Driving along it in daylight the previous week had been easy enough, but on foot and at night it was a different matter and once or twice I nearly caught my ankle in a pothole. However, I reached the entrance all right, and using the key let myself in. Pitch dark, of course, and I groped vainly for a light switch. I shone the torch and saw a door which I vaguely remembered as being either to the cloakroom or the kitchen . . . Yes, the cloakroom-cum-lavatory. Here I did find a switch and after peering about under the forty-watt bulb saw the dog's harness hanging on a peg. I shoved it into my bag, switched off the light and prepared to leave.

But at that moment the silence was cut by a noise – the low purr of an approaching car, and through the high, narrow window I caught the glow of a headlamp. How strange. Who was calling on Charles at this time of evening? It was well past the supper hour, almost midnight. And anyway didn't they know he was away? Would they ring the bell and if so should I answer it? My own presence though perfectly legitimate might seem odd – especially if I couldn't find the light switches to welcome them in. I had an absurd vision of myself on the darkened threshold trying to explain who I was and what I was doing. But then what were *they* doing? Or could it possibly be Charles himself returned from London with a change of plan, or to collect some vital item he had left behind such as his cheque book or a file for one of his meetings?

I hovered uncertainly, standing on tiptoe to peek through the rather grimy pane. The car had stopped, its headlamps doused but sidelights still on. To get a better view I clambered onto the lid of the loo and cautiously opened the window a few inches. A door slammed, followed by the sound of footsteps on the gravel; but rather to my surprise these did not seem to be coming towards the house but stayed crunching about where the car was parked in front of the old stable. I could just detect the murmur of voices and saw the sudden gleam of a cigarette.

I continued to squint through the window and then heard what sounded like a bolt being drawn back or the clank of a padlock. I screwed up my eyes and saw that the stable door had swung open and the car boot was gaping wide. Then in the next moment two vague shapes disappeared into the stable. I let out my breath which I realised I had been holding for a good two minutes . . . What on earth was going on? It hardly seemed that Charles had returned, and besides the car certainly wasn't his (a low-slung Alvis which Agnes regularly cursed). This was much bigger, though from my vantage point it was impossible to discern the make.

As at other moments of tension I suddenly seemed to hear my brother's voice. *Oh really Prim, nosy as always. I suppose the next minute you'll want to go and take a closer look. Typical!* 'Actually,' I mentally riposted, 'that is exactly what I propose doing. I consider there is something deeply suspicious about all this, and as Charles's friend it is my duty to investigate.' Thus resolved, I found my way to the side door and slipped outside, quietly locking it behind me. For a moment I loitered in the shadows, assessing how best to approach in safety.

The corner of the stable was only a matter of yards: if I could get there I would have a clearer view while at the same time using it as cover. I started to move stealthily but stopped abruptly – the gravel seemed horribly loud! But there was a patch of thick grass to my left stretching as far as the corner. I tiptoed on to this and stumbled my way to the lee of the wall.

Being now that much closer I had a clear view of the waiting car: very classy – a Humber Hawk. For a couple of seconds nothing impinged except the car itself, and then with a jolt I thought of Emily and her swearing blind that it had been a Humber she had seen bearing Topping towards Newhaven. Surely this couldn't be the same, could it? I nearly let out a yell of triumph but curbed it just in time, for out of the stable came the tall figure of a man carrying what looked like a large box or case. He tottered towards the open boot, heaved the thing over the sill and then went back inside. Two minutes later he was out again with another load.

Fascinated, I gingerly inched my way along the wall to the shelter of a climbing magnolia from whose foliage I could peer out like the legendary Green Man. *Oh lor' Primrose*, came Francis's voice again, *do leave off. You are bound to be seen and then we shall all be in the cart!* Again I ignored his words and doggedly stood my ground, determined to get to the bottom of it.

Squeezed thus between the rough wall and the shrub's branches I recalled a similar situation an age away, when as children we had spied on the neighbours, casting them as enemy agents UP TO NO GOOD. I smiled into the darkness; but the next instant froze, hearing voices again and then footsteps as this time both men re-emerged from the stable each now burdened by boxes. I strained eyes and ears trying to make out if the shorter was Topping but really couldn't be sure. Certainly the height was the same but other features were shrouded by a mac and slouch hat. One of them spoke. 'That's it then. Let's get the hell out of here. It's cold. Hurry up, I need a drink.' (Hear! Hear!) There was a murmured response and I saw the lid of the boot being pushed down. The next moment they were in the car, and with headlights reignited the Humber trundled back up the drive; the sound of its engine gently fading into the night.

For some seconds I remained stock-still – like some playgoer surprised by the fall of the curtain and numbed by the sudden black silence. But I knew that this scene had been no make-believe. It had been real all right and I was jolly well going to find out more. Something very peculiar was afoot and I had a good idea of what it was. Thus disentangling myself from the magnolia's branches I walked briskly towards the stable entrance.

The door was shut and, needless to say, had been re-padlocked. Curse! I wondered if there was a side entrance or even a window I might squeeze through, and was just about to make a reconnaissance when my foot clinked against something on the ground. Yes, miraculously it was the key . . . Hah, not so clever are we, I thought: fancy racing off and dropping that! Presumably it had been haste for the drink that had prompted such carelessness.

Shining the torch I saw that the ancient stable was just as one might expect – a filthy uneven floor, desolate loose boxes, broken hay byres, and here and there even bits of abandoned tack slung forlornly on rusting hooks. I looked up at the cobwebbed rafters and imagined bats; and then flashing the torch into grimy corners thought of rats. I flinched. There were bound to be some. But curiosity stifled distaste and I began to hunt around for some sign of the intruders' purpose. If the shorter of the two men

259

had indeed been Topping then the reason for his being here humping boxes about could mean only one thing: the place was being used as a storage depot. And if Ingaza and MacManus were right then in all probability the goods were drugs – consignments of which were being regularly collected from the Newhaven docks.

I mooched about feeling increasingly cold and seeing nothing to suggest recent activity. The stable had that eerie static quality hinting of death and the decaying past. But then as I gave a final glance round I noticed a half-opened door in a far corner at the end of the row of stalls. Gingerly I pushed it wider and went in. The torch displayed a dingy narrow room, perhaps a place for forgotten grooms to sling their gear or clean their boots. There was a small table and a ramshackle set of shelves. Other than these the place was bare except for several cardboard cartons, a few on the shelves and others strewed haphazardly on the floor. In the pallid light I inspected these but all appeared empty and apparently hastily discarded. Some bore what looked like stamped numbers but otherwise there was nothing to indicate either contents or address.

Whatever had been stored here was obviously all gone; and judging from the earlier comings and goings it looked as if the place had been deliberately cleaned out – made redundant through change of requirement or plan. I stood there cold and dispirited. Sneaking about watching those two had been a strain, and yet despite my vigilance I had nothing to show for it. No proof had emerged either of the goods themselves or indeed the identity of their handlers. The Humber *might* have been the same one that had transported Topping the other evening, and the short man in the raincoat *might* have been him. And yes, the contents of the cartons may well have been drugs – but then again for all I knew it could equally have been pots of jam. In Wilkie Collins' parlance there was a distinct dearth of tangible evidence. Gloomily I started to make my way back to the main door, caught my foot in the sluicing gulley and fell flat on my face.

Amazingly, other than being badly shaken and with tingling knees I was moderately all right. However, to regain both breath and equilibrium I elected to stay temporarily on all fours staring furiously at the hard brick floor. And it was from this ungainly pose that I saw the packet. It lay by the stable door, a few yards from my nose and spotlit by the ray from the fallen torch.

Still on bruised knees, I gazed at it curiously, puzzled by the shiny whiteness of the wrapping. It had the neat, clinical look of something prescribed from a doctor's surgery. I crawled forward and reached for both it and the torch; and on closer inspection saw that its cover wasn't paper at all but cellophane, cellophane sealed tightly around what looked like white powder or castor sugar.

Starting to ache from top to toe and having had enough excitement for one night I was eager to leave and get home as quickly as possible. Thus I levered myself up from the floor, thrust the packet into my handbag, padlocked the door and – unlike the other visitors – slipped the key into my pocket.

The return journey seemed far longer than when coming, fatigue and painful knees taking their toll. But it gave me time to think and review matters.

The first thing I thought about was the packet at the bottom of my bag. Other than vital aspirin I knew nothing about drugs but vaguely recalled Nicholas referring to cocaine as being 'white goods in handy packs'. Was this the sort of thing he had meant? To me the description suggested self-raising flour, but not being abreast of the underworld and its terminology, who was I to cavil? The likelihood of some solitary addict wandering into the stable and negligently losing his supply seemed remote, and in any case it was far too clean to have been lying there long . . . It must surely therefore have slipped from one of the boxes the men had been carrying to the car.

The more I thought, the more certain I was of what had been going on. Unbeknown to Charles his disused stable had been commandeered as a drugs cache; and now for some reason it had grown surplus to requirements and what I had witnessed were the dealers making the final clearance. For a while I felt highly delighted. At least now there was a piece of tangible evidence. What luck!

But then an awful thought struck me . . . supposing Charles himself had known about it all the time, had perhaps sanctioned the whole thing! Or maybe he had hired out the stable for a business he had chosen not to confront; had taken the rent and conveniently turned a blind eye to its usage. And as to why the 'clients' should now decide to end the arrangement – well conceivably it was do with the projected orangery and his conversion plans. Had he given them notice on the grounds that nurture of oranges took precedence over storage of dope?

I trudged along more than a little dismayed by such reflections. And then I suddenly stopped, transfixed by an even greater fear . . . Oh my God, if Charles were somehow involved in, or aware of, the drugs operation, could he also have been party to the fate of Carstairs? My heart pounded at the thought of such an appalling possibility.

And was Agnes in it too, raking in ill-gotten gains to fund her sojourn in Tobago? After all, she had been there long enough, swanning about in all that Caribbean sun. Supposing I had been wrong all along and that it had been *she* and not Topping who had been the engineer of Carstairs' misfortune . . .

Ablaze with such visions and now indifferent to my bruises I thrust forward grimly. If my conjectures were correct it was utterly scandalous. And how on earth should I treat Charles when we next met – with a casual nonchalance or steely disdain? A problem indeed!

Fortunately it was Maurice who brought me down to earth. Seeing the cat's disapproving face peering out from the bars of my garden gate had the effect of a douse of iced water, and I felt suitably ashamed and sobered. How ignoble to be maligning poor Charles and Agnes, a more decent and upright pair it would be hard to imagine. A wave of guilt flooded over me. How could I possibly have entertained such thoughts? Doubtless a nervous reaction after the night's alarming events. Of *course* it was none of their doing . . . a certainty which took me back to my odious quarry. If Hubert Topping could make a daily fetish of wearing a pink rosebud then he could also sport a slouch hat gone out of fashion at least a decade ago. Oh yes, the smaller man had been him all right!

That settled and firmly clutching my handbag with its vital contents, I rounded up Maurice and – as far as knees would allow – marched to the house and the sanctuary of bed.

CHAPTER FORTY-ONE

The Dog's View

'Do you think she is round the bend?' I asked Maurice.

'Who?'

'The mistress, of course.'

'They are all like that,' the cat replied, licking his foot, 'take F.O., for example.'

'Ah, but he wasn't right round, only half.'

'As good as.'

'But Maurice,' I told him, 'you have always said that there are degrees of human bonkers and that we shouldn't confuse one degree of bonkers with another.'

'Hmm,' he agreed sleepily, 'I daresay I did. But frankly, after tonight's charade I may have to revise my view somewhat. There may be fewer gradations than I had imagined.'

I frowned, trying to work that out. Then I gave a puzzled snort. 'Isn't that just what I said? THE PRIM IS BARKING!'

'In-dub-i-tab-ly,' the cat murmured and closed his eyes.

* * *

I stared at the shape under the table – Duster who was snoring his head off with some stupid harness clamped in his paws. I wondered if all cairns were like that, secretly off their chumps like humans. I mean why did he want to have that? Any normal dog would have settled for a ball or a toy rabbit or some old sock. But oh no, the cairn has to have its harness. And what's more the Prim had gone to fetch it for him . . . all the way to Podkennel she went. Can't see her doing that for me! Mind you, it's just as well she did, because as we started to think about bedtime and closing the hatches for the night the ruddy cairn didn't half set up a rumpus – chasing his tail, growling at shadows, tossing the cushions about. It was driving Maurice berserk. In fact he went outside and started yowling at the moon, and I could see him through a chink in the curtains stalking round and round and swishing his tail fit to bust (always a bad sign), which is probably why he is still sleepy today – worn out with wailing!

Still, the point is that at last the Prim came back and things calmed down a bit, or at least *we* did; but she seemed in a right old lather – effing and blinding about her knees (don't know what she'd done to them but they looked sort of blue and murky) and at the same time grinning like a daft Cheshire cat. Her hair was a bit odd too – all fuzzy with a couple of leaves stuck in it. Perhaps she had gone through one of those hedges Duster seems so keen on.

As a matter of fact, I am getting to quite like that fellow, though as said he can't half be a funny beggar. Take last night. You see the first thing P.O. did when she came in was to put her bag down and fish out that harness. That did it! He let out a godawful yelp, leapt up and nearly snatched it out of her hands. 'WAIT!' she roared. Well, of course, he didn't wait and kept snapping the air and dancing round her feet like Maurice when he's practising his cat-tango. So she slung the thing under the table and said 'Fetch.' He shot after it, grabbed it, and after a quick scrabble flopped down like a stone – for the rest of the night. (In fact he is still out for the count now – and it's morning with the sun shining through the window!)

Anyway, after the palaver with the cairn the mistress took something else out of her bag and put it under the cushion on the kitchen chair. I was a bit puzzled by that, because if I've got a bone that I want to keep hidden I wouldn't put it there . . . I mean there's bound to be some great arse who would come along and sit on it. Still, like the cat says, humans are not known for their brightness. And talking of Maurice, I could see him watching her like a lynx. So when she had gone up to bed I said to him, 'What's that about, then?'

'I don't know, Bouncer,' he purred, 'but we shall have to find out, won't we?' And in a tick he had darted to the chair, lifted up his left paw – the strongest and the one with the white patch – and tipped the cushion onto the floor.

Underneath was something white in slippery paper. I stood on my hind legs and was about to clamp it in my teeth, when the cat cried, '*Desist!*'

Now you might think I don't know the meaning of 'dee-sist', but I jolly well do. You don't live with Maurice without learning a word or two. And I know that 'dee-sist' is cat-speak for 'Stop it, you bad boy' or 'Don't do that, you little bugger.'

'Keep your fur on,' I said, 'just testing.'

He ignored that and started to prod it with his paw and gave a couple of licks.

'Well?' I said eagerly, 'what is it?'

'Hard to say,' he replied, 'there is no taste and no smell.'

This time I pushed him out of the way and put my own muzzle on to it. 'Huh!' I said, 'you bet there's a smell, anyone can smell it!'

The cat didn't like that, because he said all hoity-toity: 'Fortunately not all of us have bloodhound in our genes.' (Of course what he really meant was that I am the best sniffer in the business.) And then after a bit he added, 'So if you don't mind my asking, what does it smell like?'

'It smells,' I said, 'like the white stuff you had all over your whiskers that time you went doolally in the garden.'

There was a hiss and his ears flattened. 'I did *not* go doolally! I merely had a mild turn – doubtless brought on by the challenge of living with you.'

I grinned and wagged my tail. 'But you like it really, don't you, Maurice? Helps to exercise that old steely brainbox; keeps it sharp and top-notch.'

That did the trick. He smirked and examined his claws, something he does when he is pleased – which isn't often – and even gave a sort of purr.

'Well now, Bouncer,' he said, all matey, 'we must put our heads together and pursue this further, but meanwhile I propose to retire. What with the cairn's antics and P.O.'s nonsense I am really quite shattered.'

'Right-o,' I said, and jumped into my basket.

CHAPTER FORTY-TWO

My dear Agnes,
Doubtless Charles has apprised you of the current
situation here – his ongoing fight with the town
planners and the Podmore proposals – all rather
technical and not entirely understood by yours truly
(though I am sure <u>you</u> will have grasped it quickly
enough). However, what you may not have grasped
is Primrose's insatiable fascination with dear Mr
Topping which seems to be growing more intense day
by day. She and Charles had a little drinkie the other
night with Hubert Topping, and all I can say is that
she has been most peculiar ever since. For example,
on that same evening I happened to be wending my
way home having been attending a lecture by Claude
Bracegirdle (couldn't understand a word, of course
– but you know what he's like) when a large car
passed me carrying Hubert T. with someone else at
the wheel and going in the direction of Newhaven.

When I mentioned this to Primrose she went very quiet and then accused me of having been mistaken. Naturally, I told her that this was certainly not the case, whereupon she became not so much peculiar as positively apoplectic. She seemed to think that something deeply sinister was going on and kept muttering, 'I knew it! I knew it!'

Frankly I rather suspect that this ghastly business of the maths master's decapitation has gone to her head (if you will excuse the pun!) and that she is seeing skulduggery wherever she looks. Actually, I have to admit that while this is tiresome I cannot entirely blame her. I mean to say, the whole affair is extremely grisly and not at all what one expects in Lewes or indeed the vicinity. Fortunately, as mentioned in my last letter, we have a good man here now in the form of Chief Superintendent MacManus who has everything under control – something which, needless to say, Primrose will not admit – and thus one likes to think that peace and justice will be restored . . . But alas NOT JUST YET. You blink? I am not surprised, and so do I!

You see there has been <u>another</u> body found – at the foot of Mount Caburn, if you please. One can only be grateful that this time the head is firmly in place, but it is very nasty all the same. Stabbed through the heart from behind, or at least that is what the national news says. It was on one of those police messages that they tag on after the nine o'clock news. From what I could gather the man's name is Respighi and he is foreign (well, dear, with a name like that he's bound to be, isn't he?) but is generally unknown.

I don't quite know what they mean by 'generally' – I mean either he is known or he isn't, but you know what these press people are like. They say anything to disturb or intrigue.

Anyway, known or not, his discovery has quite unsettled poor Mr Winchbrooke who does nothing but wring his hands and cry, 'We are ruined, ruined!' I have told him most firmly that this second fatality has nothing whatever to do with the school and that if anything is to ruin Erasmus House it will not be a dead body but the obstruction of the auditors. I think that sobered him somewhat but he is clearly very worried, being convinced there will be a spate of withdrawals – a view fully endorsed by Mrs Winchbrooke – not, I think, the best of influences.

However, Mr Topping has been most reassuring. He told the headmaster to take heart from the law of compensation. This was not a law we were familiar with but Mr Topping smiled patiently and explained that in layman's language it simply meant 'lose one, win one.' I don't think Mr Winchbrooke was any the wiser (nor I for that matter) as he just gave one of those glassy stares and asked Topping what was it exactly, given the dire circumstances, that he could expect to win. The latter observed that there is a fine line between fame and notoriety and that our little town now rested on the cusp. Thus withdrawals by sensitive parents would doubtless be offset by applications from the tougher type eager to boast a connection via their offspring. As a matter of fact, knowing some of the parents we have to deal with, I thought that was quite shrewd but I don't think

Mr Winchbrooke did. He continued to stare glassily and muttered what sounded like, 'Some fat chance, I don't think!'

Actually Topping wasn't far out, for only this morning there was a phone call from a father wanting to place his boy in our care as the child was obsessed with becoming a crime writer and wouldn't give him a moment's peace until he had been sent to board in Lewes at Erasmus. Naturally, I explained that crime writing was not our particular forte and that the school's reputation rested on its scholastic endeavour and cricketing prowess. The father said he was sure it did, but that it was the murders that mattered and he wanted the little sod to start immediately as he couldn't stand the constant carping, and would a term's fee upfront plus a donation to the cricket fund do the trick? I agreed that on the whole it would and that Erasmus House was always happy to welcome pupils with special interests. When I told Mr Winchbrooke of my modest 'coup' he looked less morose but said I should have held out for two terms' advance. Really, there is no satisfying some people!

Well, Agnes, I'll sign off for the present but be assured will write again post-haste should anything fresh come to light.

Your good friend,
Emily

CHAPTER FORTY-THREE

The Primrose Version

After the Podmore activities, I came down rather blearily to breakfast and was so intent on brewing much needed coffee that I did not at first notice the cushion on the floor. It certainly hadn't been there when I went to bed as I remembered placing it over the packet as a temporary concealment. Thus to see the thing now exposed and the cushion flung to the ground was startling. Surely not the work of some wayward poltergeist!

There was a sudden miaow, and I saw Maurice peering out from behind the stove. 'Oh really,' I exclaimed, 'what's this now? Cushion capers for a cat's insomnia, I suppose.' He gazed inquisitively as I retrieved the cushion and put the packet on the table.

Sipping my coffee and wondering what should be done with it, I noticed a mark missed earlier: a green dot stamped on the left corner. Significant? Who could tell? The essential question was my next move. Charles would not be back for three days and he had left no London telephone number.

Besides, if he was enmeshed in business affairs would he welcome a call blithely telling him his stable was being used as storage for a local drug ring? Unlikely. As to the police: that meant MacManus, and after his rather cryptic remarks about wretched Sidney Samson and the Molehill case I had no immediate desire to renew conversation with him – in or out of his bear suit. In any case were I to report what I had found then that would immediately involve Charles and thus make him central to the investigation. So acting on the principle that discretion was the better part of friendship I concluded it would be only courteous to keep quiet until we had discussed matters.

Following my escapade it seemed sensible to 'keep a low profile', as the saying goes, and to remain quietly indoors at my easel. However, as it turned out there was no choice in the matter: for unaccountably I was felled by a dose of flu – or some such beastly ague – and for three days stayed at home turgid and disconsolate. Being of a robust nature I am unused to such feebleness . . . but perhaps it was my pursuit of the toad Topping that was taking its toll. Anyway, whatever the cause, there I remained. But on the fourth day I mustered my energies, and throwing off the invalid's rug prepared to greet the world again.

And a very interesting world it proved to be: Emily rang with startling news; indeed so startling that any vestiges of malaise vanished instantly. There had been, she reported, another fatality on the downs: a murderous attack which in her opinion was 'simply disgraceful and shouldn't have been allowed', a view one could hardly dispute.

I wondered if it had been in the same place as Carstairs'

misfortune – after all one does hear of such things as 'copycat killings' which is a favourite phrase of the press these days. However, it transpired that the crime spot was some distance from the area, at the foot of Mount Caburn, that ancient hill marking Lewes's approach from the south.

This too held happy childhood memories, for occasionally our parents would visit an ailing relative in the town while leaving the pair of us to lark about in its foothills or climb to the ancient earthworks. To now learn that a man had been stabbed there – neatly in the back apparently – was shocking. It was also perplexing because Emily kept rattling on about a rabbit hole. I mean what on earth would a rabbit hole have to do with murder? When I told her to be more succinct she explained that either before or during the attack the victim's foot had got rammed down the hole and it was rumoured that it had taken the forensics people at least ten minutes to pull it out. For some reason it was this aspect of the crime that seemed to occupy her most, for when I asked her the identity of the man she said vaguely that she thought his name was Respighi, so he must have been foreign, and that he had been wearing size eleven brogues – a fact which had obviously accounted for the difficulty in disengaging the foot.

Other than the declaration that foreigners rarely wore brogues and that she had always assumed they had small feet anyway, I could get nothing further from Emily. Thus I telephoned Melinda in the hope of a more rational account.

It was Freddie who answered. 'Oh yes,' he said cheerfully, 'poor chap was found late last Tuesday night by a courting couple. It was so dark that they tripped over him. The girl had hysterics on the spot. Bad luck really – not what you would call an auspicious start to a bit of rumpy-pumpy. I gather she was taken home in a police car and her beau has been grumbling ever since.'

I have to say that the news was most disquieting. After all, one had not moved to this part of the county to be plagued by corpses. One was quite enough. However, the more I considered, the more I began to wonder if there wasn't a link between the two killings. It did seem ironic that the last known murder in Lewes had been nearly a century ago whereas now, like London buses, we had two in quick succession. Who was this foreigner, I asked myself, and what had he been doing here anyway?

As it happens, the answer, or part of it, came quickly. That morning I had to go to the chemist to collect my neuralgia rub and en route bumped into Sergeant Wilding. He was strolling up the High Street looking blithe and friendly (something MacManus has never achieved) so as I drew level I wished him good day and tut-tutted about the recent event.

'Respighi, what a curious name,' I twittered, 'sounds almost operatic.'

'Yes,' he murmured, 'you could say that. Luigi Respighi: used to be a small-time Italian actor before he took to crime. Years ago the Met had trouble with him up in Hackney; he was involved in a spate of gangland fights. But after a stretch in jug he disappeared and fell off the map. And then all of a sudden here he is resurrected – well partially that is, because now he's found knifed and with his foot stuck in a rabbit hole. Running away, I suppose. Funny old world, isn't it?'

I agreed that it most certainly was, adding that I was sure the chief superintendent had it all in hand.

'Nice to have faith,' he observed wryly, and bidding me good morning, continued on his way.

I continued on mine puzzled and intrigued. An erstwhile Italian actor turned denizen of London's gangland? Why on earth should such a one be down here in docile Lewes getting murdered? My mind was blank. And then suddenly a voice came back to me, a voice I had heard only recently. *Quick, quick*, it had said, *I need a drink. Don't mess around, just close the boot. It's bloody cold!*

The words rang in my ear. But it wasn't so much the words that I heard as the accent. It had not been English, definitely continental. I concentrated hard, trying to place the exact provenance and recalled the voices of some POWs once billeted near us at home; a charming bunch of Eyeties who had remained for some months after the war and whom mother had befriended. She had given them Francis's sweet points after he had gone off to the seminary – a charitable act exciting his rueful ire.

Yes, the more I brooded, the more I was convinced that the taller of the two men had been Italian . . . Oh my God, had Topping killed him as well as Carstairs? And if so, it must have happened shortly after I had seen them drive off from Podmore! I froze in mid-stride.

'Hello, hello!' said Freddie Balfour jovially, patting me on the shoulder, 'nice to see you vertical and not flat on your back. You made a jolly good corpse the other night. Most convincing. To the coffin born one might say. Ho! Ho!' He lumbered off in the direction of the White Hart. Idiot.

Mind gripped with thoughts of Respighi, I continued on down the hill in pursuit of fish heads for Maurice's supper.

And it was then that I made the most monstrous gaffe –
a gaffe that precipitated a train of dire events and from
which even now, sitting in the south of France, I have
barely recovered. It was all to do with that wretched
packet of cocaine (or whatever the beastly substance was).
Unsure as to what should be done and anxious to get to the
chemist before it closed for lunch, I had gathered my things
hurriedly from the kitchen table, and not trusting the cat
had thrust the packet into my shopping bag.

It was an unfortunate move, for as I emerged from the
fishmonger I was startled to see *Fräulein* Hochheimer and
Hubert Topping coming towards me. The former looked
elated, the latter did not. In fact he was looking distinctly
dazed . . . a state not uncommon with those spending any
time with that good lady.

'Ach, Madame Hooterayde,' the *Fräulein* cried. 'Ve too
hev been shopping! Cufflinks for Hoobat and hankies for
me. Zo, vell-met by moonlight, to coin an English phrase!'

'What?' I said.

'Shakespeare, I think,' she gushed; 'but, of course, also
that goot film with your *naice* Dirk Bogarde. He is most
charmink . . . isn't he, Hoobat? Ve saw ze film yesterday at
the Odeon. Wunderbar!' She clapped her hands.

'Oh,' I said vaguely, 'glad you liked it. Shouldn't have
thought it was quite up your street – I mean what with
Crete and all that . . .'

'Do not vorry, Madame Hooterayde, all that ist *long*
time ago. Ze war ist over and Jarmenee ist rising steadily
again. Ve shall all be such friends und united against ze
common enemy. Mark mein vords!'

'How nice,' I replied, failing to enquire the name of the
common enemy; and instead turned hastily to 'Hoobat'

who wore an expression of benevolent boredom.

Frankly, for one who had probably just put paid to one of his accomplices he struck me as remarkably composed. He smiled politely and it was then that I made my dreadful blunder: I dropped my shopping bag, and the whole contents spilt on to the pavement – purse, fish heads, compact, lipstick, crumpled handkerchiefs, a packet of Craven A, a bag of peanuts . . . and, of course, the damned cocaine.

There was a general flurry as the three of us stooped to scoop the things up; but, needless to say, it was Topping who retrieved the precious package. He looked at it thoughtfully, turning it over a couple of times, and then said quietly, 'And where did you get this from, Miss Oughterard?'

'From the grocer, of course,' trilled *Fräulein* Hockheimer, 'I expect it is that zo goot icing sugar Mr Boris sells. It is very special and he packs his own, is that not zo, Madame Hooterayde?'

'Oh indeed it is,' I replied, wresting it from Topping's grasp. But both he and I knew it was not.

They continued on their way, Hockheimer prattling volubly, Topping fumbling for a cigarette. I rather felt like joining Freddie Balfour for a brandy in the White Hart but thought better of it. They say desperation drives; but not to that extent. Instead I returned home to the oddly reassuring company of my cat and dog.

CHAPTER FORTY-FOUR

The Primrose Version

After lunch, I went up to the studio and continued my assault on the latest commission. I worked steadily for a good hour, grimly refusing to dwell on the morning's upset.

However, eventually I paused and assessed my handiwork: not bad on the whole, not bad at all. A touch more light over the trees wouldn't have come amiss, and had that sheep needed to look quite so moronic? I leant forward to make an adjustment but instead put the brush aside. Concentration had lapsed, for despite my resolve I couldn't stop my mind from returning to that meeting on the High Street . . . There was no doubt about it: he had known damn well what was in the packet! I recalled that silent scrutiny, the slight frown of surprise and its replacement by a flush of anger and the grim stare as I took it from his hands. Oh he had known all right. But what the hell was he going to do with that knowledge? Carstairs' head loomed before me . . . I flinched and, hastily banishing the image, grasped the brush again.

But as I did so a voice sounded from the hall:

'I say, anyone at home? Are you there, Miss Oughterard?'

I jumped, nearly upsetting the easel, and then remembered I had left the side door open when letting the dog out. So who was this arriving in the middle of the afternoon? There was certainly no tradesman scheduled and the vicar had called only the day before. Yet even as the question flashed upon me I knew the answer.

'Just a minute,' I called back to Hubert Topping, 'I'll be straight down.' I marched on to the landing half-fearful, half-fascinated. He certainly didn't hang about!

Descent was forestalled for he was already mounting the stairs – bearing a large bunch of crimson flowers – peonies to be precise.

'Please do excuse my intrusion,' he said a trifle breathlessly, 'one hesitates to disturb the artist but I have been deputed to take the headmaster's car to the garage in Eastbourne for its annual service, and as I was passing it seemed an excellent opportunity to drop these in.' He thrust the flowers into my surprised arms. 'Miss Dunhill's garden is not discernibly aesthetic but it does boast the most lavish display of peonies – roses among the thorns you could say. Such a shame to waste them and with luck they are to your taste. I know that some find them rather vulgar, but I thought that you being an artist would appreciate their delicious ebullience.'

'Er, yes,' I said, utterly wrong-footed, 'yes, yes, of course. How kind.' And then standing irresolute, cradling the peonies, I added, 'You had better come up into the studio and I'll find a vase.'

He followed me in and gazed around at the mess of painting debris and half-finished canvases. 'Ah,' he exclaimed, 'so this is where it all goes on: the vital hub of all vision and endeavour!' By this I assumed he meant that this was where I earned the dosh for jaunts to Europe and other gaieties. Leaving him pressed to the window rhapsodising about the view, I slipped next door to find a container for the flowers.

When I returned, he was inspecting one of the canvases, not the one on the easel but another stacked against the wall. It was my most recent – and as mentioned to Albert at the Masons' Arms, the only one ever to depict a stretch of water, let alone water in moonlight.

He contemplated it thoughtfully and then said casually, 'You've got the chiaroscuro awfully well, all shadow and pale shimmer; and that curve of the far bank is exactly how it is. My compliments: a most evocative rendering of Chalk Hill dew pond.' I tensed but nodded politely. And then, raising his eyes from the scene, he added softly, 'But it seems to me that there is something missing, not perhaps an especially pretty feature but one that is nevertheless authentic . . . that is to say authentic at the time when we were both last there.' The tone was suave but the amiable features had become coldly expressionless. He regarded me steadily, all bonhomie vanished.

I swallowed hard, hearing the wood pigeon's call from childhood, *Keep cool, you fool, keep cool . . .*

'Really?' I asked lightly. 'And when would that be?'

There was a pause, and then he said even more softly, 'Oh I think we both know that, don't we? As does your distasteful cur.'

That did it. 'Bouncer is not distasteful,' I cried, 'and he is certainly no cur! He is a totally pure bred mongrel. I have no idea *what* you are talking about and I think it is time you continued on your way to Eastbourne – and you can take those footling flowers with you!' I glared angrily while at the same time imagining my brother's voice, *Oh Primrose, you've put your great hoof in it now!*

With a shrug he drew out a cigarette case, wafted it vaguely in my direction and then helped himself. 'You are becoming irksome, Miss Oughterard,' he sighed, flicking his lighter. 'First you intrude on our little business at the dew pond and perchance may have witnessed who knows what. You then lurk tediously outside my house in the depths of the night and—'

'But you couldn't have known that: you weren't there!' I blurted out.

'Really? And what makes you so certain?' he enquired mildly.

'The place was obviously deserted; there wasn't a sound and no lights anywhere.'

'A hasty assumption if I may say so. Absence of light does not mean absence of occupant. As it happens, I came home about ten minutes before you arrived and was annoyed to find I had to undress in the dark. Southern Electricity in its wisdom had elected to cut the power. It was off for at least two hours. Most tiresome; I couldn't even make a cup of tea. Then as I was fumbling my way to bed I saw you drive up . . . not that I knew it was you but when someone parks their car close to the house and stays there for ages without getting out, one does become a trifle curious. So using my binoculars I ascertained the car's make and number. I watched you for some time. I also watched PC Plod drive up and, like you, sit without moving. *Un*like you he eventually got out and started to prowl around – indeed if I'm not mistaken I think he approached your vehicle.

Anyway, you suddenly revved up, rather noisily I fear, and zoomed off. Not long afterwards he went too.'

Topping gave a dry chuckle: 'I must say, what with all that toing and froing anyone would think that the quiet little lane outside my cottage was Piccadilly Circus. Quite a cabaret! Still, having two spies skulking about in one night is a bit much and my vigil was rather tiring. It was a great relief when the electricity came on again and I could make that cup of tea.'

I stared at him stonily, feeling a complete fool. To think that I had gone through all that palaver unaware that the whole procedure was being monitored by the little squirt with his binoculars. But that was irrelevant compared to what he had just brazenly acknowledged: that he had done something unspeakable to Dr Carstairs. I had been right all along!

But my sense of triumph was more than eclipsed by desperate fear. Nevertheless I remained po-faced and said bitterly, 'It's dope, isn't it, that's what it is all about; you have been using your school teaching as a convenient cover for the most dastardly—'

He nodded. 'Yes, you picked up on that all right. In fact I have to admit that when you produced that packet on the High Street this morning I was quite taken aback. You see I identified it immediately by the green spot. It marks a special grade which we store only at Podmore – or rather we *did* until tiresome Penlow came along with his grandiose conversion schemes. I couldn't think how you had got hold of it, still can't really.' He looked at me enquiringly.

'You dropped it, or your accomplice did. I was there last night and found it after you had gone,' I told him woodenly.

Topping gave a genuine laugh. 'Good lord! So you were

there stalking us, were you? Amazing. Now you really do impress me. Who'd have thought it!'

I shrugged indifferently. 'And I suppose Carstairs had been involved in your sordid drugs racket.'

He nodded. 'Yes, the fool had been trying to double-cross us, thought he could embezzle some of the takings. Once he started on that game I knew he wasn't to be trusted. As I told Respighi, he was a potential squealer. He had to be checked.'

'But you hacked his head off!' I cried. 'It was monstrous, obscene!'

'I couldn't agree more,' he said smoothly. 'Obscene: exactly my own sentiments – and totally unnecessary.'

'Why the hell do it then?'

'But my dear, Miss Oughterard, I didn't. I merely put the bullet through his heart. Although I say it myself, I am rather a deft shot; he died instantly. No, I fear it was Respighi who did the dirty work. As a youth, he had a penchant for that sort of thing when he was with us in the old Messina days. I had rather hoped he had grown out of it but, alas, I learnt otherwise.' Topping shook his head and looked rueful, while I gazed speechless.

However, recovering my tongue I said, 'So Respighi just happened to have an axe in his pocket, did he? How convenient.'

'Well not in his pocket, in the van. Naturally, had I known it was there I should have objected, though it is doubtful whether he would have taken any notice; he had always been wayward and enjoyed the ritual. It had first been enacted on Malta just after the war when our little group was being compromised by some rather dangerous ruffians from Gozo.' He paused and smiled. 'I think they called themselves the Gozo Gondoliers – can't think why, unless one of them came from Venice. Anyway, whatever their name, they were queering our pitch and had to be taught a lesson. Respighi rather took to the technique.'

I swallowed, and enquired if the technique had also entailed the careful distancing of the head from the body.

He gave a disdainful sniff. 'Respighi's idea of artistry, but then culture was never his strong point.'

'I see. So was that why you killed him too?'

'Surely, Miss Oughterard,' Topping laughed, 'you don't think me as fastidious as all that, do you? No, I killed him because the fool was a liability. He knew his drugs all right but not much else. Oddly enough, and despite his treachery, Dr Carstairs and I got on quite well; he wasn't the most magnetic of types but perfectly passable and rather surprisingly was a good amateur locksmith. Indeed it was through him that we were able to fabricate a key to the stable. Nevertheless he had to go, I am afraid: one can't allow people to step out of line . . .

But Respighi was a different kettle of fish – or *caccabus piscium* as one might instruct the third-formers.' He smirked, while I fixed him with a cold eye. Not being a third-former I could do without his beastly instruction.

'In what way "different",' I enquired, 'other than his crude artistry?'

'Ideas above his station. He thought he could supplant me and take our little business into his own grasping hands. Imagine! I mean to say, one needs finesse for this sort of operation, a cool nerve and delicate touch. Respighi had none of those; a veritable thug really.'

And you are not? I was tempted to ask but thought better of it. Wiser to indulge his vanity.

'But, as a matter of fact,' he continued, 'it was the beheading farce that really fried his bacon. It was utterly crass and turned what might have been a local nine-day wonder into a gross drama of national interest. Never underestimate the value of discretion, Miss Oughterard. I realised immediately that such theatricalities could endanger the whole scheme, upset the rather lucrative gravy-boat, and I certainly wasn't having that. Respighi was a loose cannon we could do without. Thus I squared it with our London people and took the appropriate action.'

'I see,' I murmured, 'a tiresome encumbrance whom you discarded.'

'Exactly, my dear lady, I couldn't have put it better myself.' He beamed; and then still with the smile on his face, added, 'And as I fear I shall have to do with you.'

He must have seen my muscles tighten for he said, 'Oh don't worry, I don't mean at this very instant. And besides, your disposal can hardly take place in this immediate locality which is acquiring what some might call a surfeit of stiffs. Or should that be a charnel of corpses? These old idioms are so interesting.'

'How about a basket of bastards?' I suggested acidly.

'Oh just a *trifle* crude, don't you think? I am sure someone of your creative invention could contrive a more elegant phrase.'

I said nothing and thought of Pa in his shell hole with the Boche bearing down on him. Pa had stood his ground and so would I! I also thought of my brother. Francis had been in many tight corners, and yet despite not being noticeably assertive he had somehow managed to escape. What the younger brother could do, so surely could the older sister.

However, before such resolve could be acted upon, to

my fury he had approached my easel and with his forefinger started to scrape away at the paint on the canvas. 'Not of the best quality if I may say so, texture's too thin. You should go to Lerner's in London, pricey but certainly the best,' he remarked.

'Now look here, Topping,' I said fiercely, 'take your greasy hands off that picture. What do you think you are doing?'

'Just testing,' he replied. And putting his hand into his back pocket he slid out a small penknife, clicked it open and flourished it in front of the painting. 'My dear Miss Oughterard,' he smirked, 'I am sure that neither Lewes nor the London cognoscenti will regret the loss of this particular piece. Personally, I consider that all ham art should be cut up and consigned to the dustbin.' He made a swoop with the knife but stopped in mid-air. 'Tut! One must curb such urges. Besides, this isn't the moment for indelicate horseplay, there are more pressing matters.' He gestured towards the chair where I had slung my coat: 'Now put that on, we are going for a little drive. As said, I have to deliver the headmaster's car to the Eastbourne garage. But there is still time to drop you off at Beachy Head. A bit out of the way admittedly but it shouldn't take too long.'

I stared aghast, enraged less by the imminent vandalism than by the man's disgraceful words. How dare he disparage my work in that way! But then my fury turned to stunned disbelief as the import of that last remark stuck home.

'What do you mean "drop me off at Beachy Head"?' I heard myself falter. 'I don't have any need to go there.'

'That's rather debateable,' he answered silkily. But then his face suddenly darkened and took on the same malevolent look I had seen that time in Charles's library.

And still holding the penknife in one hand, with a swift movement he produced a revolver from his pocket.

I gazed transfixed at the two weapons pointed straight at me, their closeness – the muzzle of the gun, the point of the blade – were absurdly unreal. Frozen incredulity. Was this what Pa had felt, faced by that ogre looming down at him from the rim of the bunker? But I had no retaliatory bayonet . . .

'Hurry up, would you,' Topping said softly. 'We haven't got all day,' and he gestured at me to walk ahead of him. But somehow I maintained my poise and said scathingly: 'If you imagine that dropping me over Beachy Head is going to get you anywhere, you are much mistaken. Emily Bartlett knows all about you, Topping, and I can assure you she will immediately put two and two together and go straight to the police.' I rather doubted the 'immediately' part, but in view of the circumstances it didn't hurt to boost Emily's acumen.

He gave a dismissive laugh. 'Oh I think I can run a few circles around your worthy friend. There is no proof and she is hardly the sharpest adversary I have had to deal with.'

'But she is not the only one,' I murmured, thinking of Nicholas.

'Oh you mean the upstanding Alastair MacManus. Yes, he's been dutifully sniffing around but he's not exactly Sexton Blake, is he? Besides, should he get too officious I happen to have a little something guaranteed to divert his attention. No man likes to look a fool, least of all our splendid chief superintendent. I don't think he will be a bother once he knows what I have on him.' He leered.

'Actually I wasn't thinking of him. There is someone else,

someone you once knew – rather slicker than MacManus.'

For a moment he looked puzzled, and then said, '*Ah*, presumably you refer to the Ingaza spiv; I saw him with you in Brighton only recently. It quite shocked me really – I wouldn't have expected the respectable Miss Oughterard to be consorting with that type. I remember him from Oxford: a good scholar but a touch unsavoury. Slippery, I should say.'

'My God, that's rich coming from you, Topping,' I burst out, 'Nicholas Ingaza is worth ten of you!'

He shrugged indifferently. 'Nevertheless not the most upright of citizens, wouldn't you agree? A police record and dubious business dealings: not exactly a useful ally, too much to conceal – and certainly not what the courts call a reliable witness. A good lawyer would soon root out his past.' There was some truth in that I privately admitted.

Yet despite Topping's casual dismissal of Nicholas I had the impression that my words had ruffled him. There was a silence while he appeared to reflect.

During the pause I heard a faint creaking and noticed that Bouncer had nosed his way in from the other door. His muzzle was encrusted with mud; obviously been after the rabbits again.

'Bouncer,' I commanded, 'kill!' The dog wagged his tail amiably and sat down. Typical.

Topping chuckled. 'Not the best of guard dogs, I fancy.' He moved closer, still smiling. 'Come along, my dear.'

I am a good height and taller than Topping; so I was just wondering whether in spite of the weapons I could somehow floor him by superior inches, when from the far corner came an unearthly roar – and like a lion out of hell the dog had launched himself upon the man.

There was a shot and a bullet hit the ceiling, and then the revolver and penknife went scudding across the floor.

The ensuing scene was not pretty, albeit perversely satisfying. But my initial relief quickly turned to fear – fear that the dog would go too far and that at any moment I should be faced with another decapitation. However, just when I thought the worst might occur, there was a fiendish howl from the open window and instantly the rampage ceased and the room fell quiet . . . Maurice insinuated himself over the sill and jumped lithely on to the floor.

I gazed mesmerised by the triptych before me: the man gasping and quivering on all fours, the dog scratching itself earnestly, and the cat crouched, watchful and purring. Yet given the dramatic ferocity of the attack I was surprised to see that Bouncer's victim was relatively unscathed. A colossal nose bleed most certainly, his face glistening with sweat, and shirt and jacket torn to ribbons – but other than being in a state of abject collapse, Hubert Topping seemed broadly intact. I cleared my throat and enquired if he would like a glass of water. There was no response at first and then a barely perceptible nod.

I picked up the weapons and left the room, debating my next move: a call to the police station reporting molestation by an intruder? But I hadn't been molested, and in any case Topping would doubtless make pious denials and play the injured innocent: he had come to borrow a library book, had brought flowers and then was unaccountably attacked by the demented artist and her vicious dog.

But perhaps this was the time to reveal all: to come clean and tell the police of my suspicions and my dedicated pursuit of this glib and dreadful man . . . But even if I told them everything that Topping had just told me, would I be remotely believed? After all, the authorities can be so cynical! I hovered in the pantry next to the studio, mechanically filling a glass from the tap, my mind awhirl with ifs and buts.

Such deliberations proved irrelevant. When I returned bearing the water another scene met my eyes: Topping no longer on all fours but lying on his side in rigid foetal position, eyes wide and staring with teeth bared in a rictus snarl. He was very, very still. The room was utterly silent: not a hint of breath, the cat's purring had stopped and Bouncer's scratching stilled . . . I gazed down at the heap on the floor, fascinated and appalled.

'Oh my God,' I whispered, 'he's dead.' No voice, least of all the victim's, said otherwise. I glanced at the two animals now mute and intent like statuesque pointers, their noses riveted on Topping's form. 'They *know*,' I muttered to myself and with shaking hand raised the glass of water to my own mouth.

The action must have galvanised Bouncer for the next moment he had padded over to the corpse's raised shoulder and made to lift his leg.

'Bouncer,' I squeaked, 'stop that! Show some respect!'

He had the grace to look mildly abashed and gave a sheepish wag of his tail. Maurice meanwhile had also moved back to the sill whence he had come. Seconds later, having rushed to the open window for air and to calm my spinning mind, I saw him sprawled on the flat roof sunning himself in the fading rays of a warm spot as if he hadn't a care in the world – which presumably he hadn't.

I tore my gaze away from the distant downs, now misty

from gathering rain, and surveyed the awful reality within. I closed my eyes . . . My dog had just savaged and given Hubert Topping a fatal heart attack, and on my premises! What the hell next, for God's sake?

The answer was immediate: for the silence was suddenly rent by the insistent ringing of the doorbell. Even on the second floor there is no mistaking its querulous screech. Like the Macbeths I froze, petrified by the rasping sound . . . Then hastily sidestepping the thing on the floor I returned to the window and cautiously craned my neck to get a view of the visitor.

CHAPTER FORTY-FIVE

The Primrose Version

Neither before nor since have I been so relieved to see the figure of Nicholas Ingaza – or rather the unmistakable form of his battered Citroën slouched on the gravel. I had no idea why he was here and didn't care, but rushed downstairs and threw open the front door.

'Huh,' he sniffed, 'you took your time. A chap could die of thirst standing in this porch.'

'Nicholas,' I gasped, hauling him inside, 'something ghastly has happened and I need your help!'

He looked startled, unused to seeing me so obviously perturbed, but responded with the usual nonchalance. 'Really? How flattering: always nice to be wanted. So what is it – no more deadheading I trust?'

'Not as such,' I replied grimly, 'though as good as. It's Topping – he's upstairs on the floor of the studio. Dead. He came to threaten and probably murder me at Beachy Head and the dog bit him and gave him a heart attack when I was fetching some water and then when I came back into the room, there he was dead as a doornail!' The words came out in a flood and for once Nicholas was visibly shaken.

'My God, Primrose,' he protested, 'I drop by for a cosy drink and you throw this at me. You almost put Francis in the shade!'

For some reason the reference to Francis sobered me and I regained my customary aplomb: 'He is already there, and don't be facetious,' I snapped. 'I trust you are not insinuating that *I* am in any way responsible. The man brought it entirely upon himself. You had better come and have a look.' I started to lead the way up the stairs.

'Just a minute,' he said, 'I have no intention of looking at anything, least of all Topping's corpse, unless I am armed with strong drink. Do fetch some whisky, dear girl, and not your usual grocer's stuff. This calls for the real thing.'

I was inclined to agree, and went off to fill two large glasses with Pa's ancient malt. Given the situation I don't think he would have objected.

When I returned, Ingaza was sitting on the stairs puffing a Sobranie and talking to the dog who had followed me down, alerted by the noise. 'Now see what you've done,' he grumbled, 'stupid hound. You'll give us all bloody heart attacks!'

Bouncer gave a sort of snort and placed a matey paw on Ingaza's knee. The latter took the whisky and regarded the paw. 'Oh I suppose that's his opening tactic – soften them up first and then go in for the kill.' The dog wagged its tail.

'I'll have you know,' I exclaimed indignantly, 'that that "stupid hound" has just saved my life. As I have told you, Topping was actually planning to shove me off the top of Beachy Head or something equally dastardly. If it hadn't been for Bouncer I could be floating among the breakers by now or being dashed to pieces on the lighthouse rocks.'

'Rather an ambitious challenge I should have thought,' Nicholas observed dryly.

'Ambitious or not, that was his intention and Bouncer has foiled him!'

Perhaps embarrassed by this spate of rare praise the dog removed its paw and ambled off into the kitchen from where could be heard the creaking of his basket followed by loud snores. Worn out by his exertions presumably.

We continued to sip our drink while I apprised my visitor of Topping's revelations and his killing of Respighi. 'He admitted everything. Brazen, he was!' I exclaimed.

'Hmm . . . The point is, Primrose, there will be repercussions and you're going to be in the thick of it all with a lot of explaining to do, and things could get—'

'Exactly. Things could get tricky. Do you imagine I haven't thought of that? Apart from anything else MacManus's nose is already beginning to twitch about poor Francis and the Molehill case; it would be frightful if it were re-opened – I mean, as his sister I could easily be dragged in. And my being present at Topping's shocking demise will hardly help matters. They'll pursue anything if they think it will give them a lead. And as it is that prig will insist I have Bouncer put down. So you see it is essential I have your help! We've got to think of something!' I took him by the arm and added firmly, 'Come on. The sooner seen, the better.'

Ingaza sighed and made a plea for some more whisky. Further fortified, we mounted the stairs.

Corpses in nightmares disappear on waking. And as I cautiously opened the studio door I suppose that is what

I had been hoping: to see the whole grisly scene magically transmuted back to the bland and wholesome, the room cluttered with its usual paint paraphernalia but minus anything jarring in the foreground.

Alas, no such luck. He was still there all right, just as last seen; the only difference being that the blood from his nose was beginning to congeal. But with a start I noticed something previously overlooked: a mangled pink rosebud lying by his right foot. Any stirrings of sympathy were instantly crushed. I saw its replica bobbing daintily on moonlit waters, and once more my mind was filled with the image of Carstairs' sodden torso and adjacent head. Oh yes, the hand of Nemesis indeed!

I experienced an improper sense of triumph. No doubt about it, my suspicions had been spot on and I was glad (and still am) that I had pursued this wretched man to expose his fakery and nefarious conduct . . . *Unfortunately* such pursuit had generated a number of unforeseen problems which, if I wasn't careful, could rebound embarrassingly. Failure to assist the police in their enquiries by lying about one's presence at the crime scene doesn't look good, especially if it is also revealed that one has bribed with cakes the grandson of a high court judge to extract crucial data pertaining to such crime . . . and then kept it for one's own use. Just think, I might be seen as some sort of accessory after the fact – or fore and aft if one counts Respighi. It is amazing the absurd conclusions people jump to.

As a professional artist and a single woman living on her own, I do have my reputation to consider. Thus it was essential, and remains so, that nothing should surface from the Topping pursuit to start tongues wagging . . . let alone to rekindle enquiries regarding my brother's wretched gaffe at Molehill. I remember when we were children Pa incessantly intoning, 'Keep mum and guard your rumps.' Sound if indelicate advice and which I proposed to follow.

So with that in mind I smiled plaintively at my companion shuffling on the threshold looking slightly yellow and said, 'I say, Nicholas, you really will help me, won't you?'

There was a long pause as his eyes scanned the room; its ceiling, the canvases, the corpse, the open window with its now darkening clouds, and finally me. I suspect I wore something of the look that Mother wore when trying to convince Pa that all was for the best – anxious yet adamant.

'I might,' he said slowly, eyes becoming more hooded than usual. 'But if you don't mind the enquiry, what's in it for me?'

'For you, Nicholas?' I asked in some surprise. 'Well I imagine the satisfaction of knowing you have helped an old friend out of a tight spot.'

'One that the old friend has thrown herself into. Had you been less meddlesome none of this would have happened and you wouldn't have chummy here splayed on your floor.'

'Hardly splayed,' I retorted. 'He's doubled up, the victim of sudden heart failure.'

'Brought on by your dog.'

'Brought on by his own beastliness!'

We regarded each other in silence. Me wondering how best to appeal to his better nature (there somewhere presumably); he doubtless weighing up the odds and formulating some bargain.

A faint smile creased the thin features. 'You know me,' he said mockingly, 'a right little knight errant; can never resist a lady in distress.' Like hell, I thought. 'I am sure we

297

can come to some arrangement. It's all a question of a quid pro—'

'Yes, yes,' I said impatiently, 'a quid pro quo. That's exactly what you used to say to poor Francis.'

'Indeed I did and he found the arrangement invaluable.'

'If you say so,' I muttered dryly.

I suddenly felt very tired, and at that point would have agreed to anything if only the heap on the floor could be shifted and the whole matter disposed of. Frankly, I was in a tizz – not a state I am accustomed to – and if Nicholas Ingaza could help me resolve the problem, then whatever the penalty, so be it.

'So what do you propose?' I asked.

'Initially another tot of this delicious Glenfiddich. It's not often one gets the chance and I rather think we may need it.' He presented me with his empty glass and meekly I went downstairs to bring up reinforcements.

CHAPTER FORTY-SIX

The Primrose Version

Ingaza's plan was outrageous, scandalous really. But as a means of emptying my studio of its wretched encumbrance and my life from the threat of awkward questions, it held a certain appeal. It also held a certain piquant irony which shortly will become clear.

When Nicholas finished unfolding his proposal I tentatively asked whether it might be sensible to get Eric to assist us. I can't say I was enamoured of the prospect but various telephone encounters made me think he might have the brawn useful to such a venture. However, I was quite relieved when Nicholas said firmly that his friend had no head for heights, and that in any case he was in strict training for the next darts match and it was imperative he kept his right wrist in sound nick. When I said that there was a chance in a thousand of Eric's right wrist being damaged by thrusting Topping's corpse off Beachy Head, Nicholas replied that given the efficacy of sod's law it was the thousandth chance that would be his undoing.

Yes, as might be guessed, it was the towering cliff above Eastbourne that was to secure the Latin master's downfall; a site, which in view of his choice for my own disposal, seemed eminently fitting . . . Now, like my deceased brother, I am not especially attracted by danger, but dire situations require dire remedies. There are times when needs must – and this was just such a time. Topping needed to go, and go quickly. Thus distasteful though the whole thing was I readily fell in with Ingaza's plan. The logistics were as follows.

We would put Topping into the back seat of Winchbrooke's car, and with me following at a discreet distance, Nicholas would drive this up on to the downs at Beachy Head. At one point the road runs fairly close to the edge – in places only about two hundred yards away – and at a suitable spot (not terribly easy to find) he would park and assess the surrounding terrain. If this looked empty – on such a rainy night likely to be so – he would signal to me to leave my car and together we would then drive Winchbrooke's to the point most favoured by suicides, that bit where the turf slopes downwards, facilitating desperate legs and closed eyes. Here we would drag Topping into the driving seat, engage the clutch, release the handbrake, leap out, and with a concerted shove from behind, set the vehicle in motion over the cliff. When car and man were eventually found there would, of course, be no injuries other than the effects from the fall itself. After all, it was not as if he had been murdered: his heart had failed, clearly the result of his suicidal drive over the cliff. Then with mission accomplished we would race back to my car and drive hell-for-leather down into Eastbourne and then home via the A27. From there Nicholas would regain his own car and return at a respectable pace to Brighton.

But what about Bouncer's tooth marks? I had enquired.

Ingaza shrugged. 'A risk we must take. With luck they won't be particularly noticeable, and actually from what I can make out there doesn't seem to be anything much. It was the clothes he was ripping. I rather suspect that your hound favours sound and fury over actual butchery. Fundamentally he is a pacifist.'

'For goodness' sake, don't tell him that!' I said in alarm. A thought struck me: 'But what about the jacket and shirt? They are torn to shreds. Surely a cliff fall *within* a car wouldn't do that?'

Nicholas sighed ruefully and said that had occurred to him and if I didn't mind he would remove his own, put them onto Topping and borrow Francis's old tweed coat he had seen hanging on the studio door. 'Can't think why you keep it,' he said, 'sentiment, I suppose.'

It was my turn to shrug. 'Just be careful of it, that's all . . . Oh and by the way would you mind awfully mopping up that nose bleed, those floor boards stain so easily.'

So that was the plan and that is how we proceeded. Up to a point. For like all best laid plans, events conspired to frustrate it.

The turning point came just as we had heaved Topping into the driver's seat all poised for his lumbering exit over the clifftop. With gloved hand – oh yes, we had taken that precaution – I was just reaching to release the brake when there was an anguished cry from Nicholas. 'Christ almighty, Primrose, stop! Look over there!'

I turned around, and through the now stinging sheets

of rain saw a blurred figure about three hundred yards off moving slowly in our direction. I froze. Oh my God who was it – a coastguard? An intrepid dog walker? Whoever it was I had no intention of being seen trundling Topping's hearse to its destruction. And neither had Nicholas. 'Leave it,' he cried. 'Just run!'

And run we did – like hell and in panting tandem, until sodden and gasping we gained the refuge of my car. Without a word I started the engine and off we sped.

For a while we drove in silence. And then puffing his cigarette as if about to devour it, Nicholas said faintly, 'Bleeding strewth, I'm getting too old for this caper. You can expect another heart attack at any minute.'

'Do try not,' I replied, 'one fatality on my property is quite enough.'

There was a further silence. And then he said thoughtfully, 'You know, I am not sure that being with you isn't worse than being with your brother. Fairly lethal, the pair of you.'

'Really?' I retorted, slowing to placate an oncoming police car. 'It's funny you should say "lethal" because that's what Francis used to say about you – although from what I recall he added various other terms as well.'

Out of the corner of my eye, I thought I detected a faint smile.

Wrangling gave way to earnest discourse as we set about exploring the likely repercussions. 'Well,' I observed, 'at least Winchbrooke won't have lost his precious car. He's rather fond of it, I gather. On the other hand he will still have to endure the chore of looking for another Latin master, and I don't think they've found a suitable Maths replacement yet.'

302

'Actually, dear girl,' Nicholas said, 'that little problem has somehow passed me by. More to the point is the immediate upshot as it affects *us*. I don't know who that creature was in the pelting rain or indeed whether he saw anything. But you can bet it will be he who discovers the car and reports it to the police . . . Who knows, perhaps even now the wires are buzzing and a posse of heavies are pounding up to Beachy Head.'

'Let them pound,' I said carelessly, 'we shall be back in Lewes at any moment where I shall hit the hay and you can tootle off to Brighton.'

Somehow the prospect of soft sheets and hot-water bottle seemed to take precedence over everything else. In fact it was becoming increasingly urgent. So much so that when we arrived back I omitted to offer Nicholas a nightcap (though from his looks it was doubtful if he wanted one) or even to wave as the car sped away. Instead, not taking a blind bit of notice of the hovering animals, I marched straight up to bed and the relief of four aspirin.

CHAPTER FORTY-SEVEN

The Cat's Views

'Well, really,' I exclaimed to Bouncer, 'I consider that the height of ill-manners. After all, we did to thwart the intentions of that unsavoury creature and not a hint of recognition; we might as well have been part of the furniture!'

We had been sitting in the kitchen patiently awaiting P.O.'s return after she and the Brighton Type had heaved the corpse down the stairs and into the car. Naturally, at the time of such manoeuvres our mistress was in no state to acknowledge the crucial part we had played in her enemy's downfall – well, other than some effusive nonsense about the dog to Ingaza; but you would have thought that with the lapse of hours she would have devised some *tangible* token of gratitude such as a cream junket for me and a double dose of those disgusting Chompies for Bouncer. But oh no: straight up to bed without a glance!

'You're right,' Bouncer agreed, 'I mean it sort of takes the biscuit, doesn't it – or the haddock, as I suppose you would say.'

'It takes a great deal more than that,' I replied grimly. 'Personally, I shall withdraw my favours for at least a week.' I gave a forceful miaow.

The dog looked puzzled. 'But you don't do any favours, Maurice.'

'Beside the point,' I snapped. 'These humans cannot be allowed to ride roughshod over their valiant companions.'

Bouncer burped. 'I suppose that means over their brave mates. I'm one of those, aren't I, Maurice? Cor, I didn't half duff him up!'

'Duff him up? Killed him you mean.'

'I DID NOT!' the dog shouted. 'He was all right when I'd finished – when you called time from the window sill. It was *afterwards* that he snuffed it. I hadn't laid another paw on him!' He looked indignant and rattled his bowl with his snout.

I was about to observe that there was a blurred distinction between actively securing a death and being its indirect cause. But it occurred to me that if one followed that line of thought it could also be argued that as instigator of the proceedings I too could be held responsible . . . I changed tack immediately, and agreeing with the dog said that clearly the Latin master was physically weedy and that he had expired as a victim of his own turpitude.

The dog growled something about not liking the smell of turpentine, and then said brightly 'But I was jolly good though, wasn't I!'

I sighed. 'Yes, Bouncer, you were jolly good.' Nevertheless I couldn't help adding, 'But tell me, why did you sit down before launching the assault – cutting it a bit fine, weren't you?'

I instantly regretted the question, fearing he might take

offence, and was relieved when he explained solemnly, 'I was thinking, Maurice, that's what I was doing: making an ass-ment as you would say.' He hesitated with brows furrowed, and then clearing his throat said slowly, 'Yes, making a sort of CONSIDERED CAL-CU-LAY-SHUN.' A triumphant smirk passed over the tousled face and I was duly impressed. Thus I waved a gracious paw signalling approval of such verbal felicity.

However, as indicated, I was *not* impressed by P.O.'s cavalier attitude an hour earlier. And dwelling on this I was about to lapse into a sulk but was checked. 'I say,' Bouncer suddenly growled, 'what do you think they did with the stiff?'

I shrugged. 'Threw it away, I suppose. The Brighton Type would have had some bright idea, he generally has.'

I was about to get on with my sulk but was again interrupted. 'All very well throwing things away,' the dog muttered, 'but supposing somebody digs him up. What then? Will the Prim get into trouble, and if so what about *us*?' He looked anxious.

'Not everyone has your mania for digging things up,' I mewed in exasperation. 'Now I suggest you jump into your basket and chew your bone, it will take your mind off things.'

'Right-o,' he barked, and with a leap fell upon his mess of bedding and did as advised. Alas, as I quickly realised, it was not one of my better suggestions for the sounds of grind and gurgle killed all concentration (essential for a good sulk), and thus with difficulty I settled for sleep.

CHAPTER FORTY-EIGHT

The Primrose Version

After such alarms and excursions, the next day I thought it might be politic to keep a low profile – to wit, stay in bed. This I was able to achieve until five o'clock, when boredom, hunger and Maurice's complaints brought me downstairs. Collecting the evening newspaper from the mat I went into the kitchen to make some Welsh rarebit and check that the animals hadn't caused mayhem. Luckily all seemed well, and braced with an early gin and mountains of charred bread and melted cheddar I settled at the table and glanced at the paper . . . At least it started as a glance but my eyes became quickly riveted.

WOULD-BE SUICIDE THWARTED, ran the headlines. MAN'S INTENDING DEATH-PLUNGE AVERTED BY CORPSE IN PARKED CAR

Joseph Speedwell, of no fixed address, said he had been on his way across the downs at Beachy Head to perform his final act, when through the driving rain

307

he had noticed the shape of a saloon car poised at the cliff's edge.

'I was a bit taken aback,' Mr Speedwell remarked, 'after all, it isn't what you expect to see at a time like that . . . I mean it was parked just on the spot from where I was going to take a running jump. It would have meant re-jigging my whole tactic.'

*Asked what had stopped him from re-jigging his tactic, Mr Speedwell explained that it had been partly the corpse in the driving seat and partly the word of the Good Lord. 'You see,' he said, 'seeing that poor b-gg-r staring out to sea like that gave me a bit of a jolt and I knew there and then that it was **meant**, that I had been given a sign from On High to take courage and be a man!' Prompted to explain what exactly that had entailed, he said that he had lit a cigarette and walked back down into the nearest pub. Beyond that he couldn't remember much.*

Since the incident the Eastbourne Gazette *has learnt that several local churches have approached Mr Speedwell offering him posts ranging from sexton to sidesman. He is busy making his choice and thanking God and his lucky stars for his good fortune.*

I re-read the item and then looked at the cat who for some reason was wearing an expression of more than usual disdain. 'Well, Maurice,' I murmured, 'it just goes to show, there's always a silver lining for someone.' He closed his eyes and swished an indifferent tail. I returned once more to the article and reflected.

I thought about Hubert Topping and wondered whether he would have been glad to know he had been the means to another's salvation. I rather doubted it. But personally I felt considerably bolstered by Mr Speedwell's timely delivery; somehow it seemed to cast a slightly softer light upon events. A wave of moderate relief swept over me, and undeterred by the cat's icy features I bent down and pulled him on to my lap. 'Now, Maurice,' I crooned, 'this calls for a little celebration. You shall have some fresh salmon and I another snifter. How about that?' He struggled at first but when he realised I was serious about the salmon, changed tack and even uttered a few purrs of approval. It is nice to be appreciated once in a while.

Having spent the day in bed I had had neither time nor inclination to enter my studio. But one cannot remain squeamish indefinitely and I knew that I really ought to tidy up and ensure that Nicholas had made a good job of swabbing the floor. Thus supper over and armed with mop and vacuum, I forced myself to re-visit that scene of threat and devastation.

Luckily the shambles wasn't as bad as I had expected: the easel with its pond picture tipped on to the floor, a couple of other canvases on their faces and – I was glad to see – the bouquet of peonies strewn wildly in all directions. Other than that things were moderately shipshape. I flung open the windows, shoved the flowers, plus squashed rosebud, into the wastepaper basket, plugged in the machine and hoovered up all traces of my ordeal. In a way the cleansing was like a sort of exorcism and I felt almost sprightly once it was finished. Is that how vicars feel? I once asked Francis if he had ever had to conduct one. 'No blooming fear,' he had shuddered, 'it's bad enough having to cope with Mavis Briggs without parrying demons as well.'

Job over, I switched on the landing light, and had gone halfway down when I saw what looked like a crumpled envelope, its corner caught in one of the stair rods. I hadn't noticed it earlier (no doubt blind to everything except the prospect of the task ahead) and assuming it to be a piece of litter dropped by the charlady, slipped it into my pocket and continued down to the kitchen. I was about to toss it into the bin when I saw the flap folded inwards and realised something was there. I opened it up, laid the contents on the table . . . and after a moment of blank shock, roared with laughter.

Impossible! Absurd! In front of me lay three small photographs: photos which tallied exactly with the ones Sickie-Dickie said he had seen displayed on Topping's desk. I have to say that if the episode in my studio had been a nightmare then this was a dream of pantomime proportion. I gazed in disbelief. How on earth had they got here?

There could be only one answer: from Topping's wallet. We had thoughtfully placed it in the pocket of the substituted jacket, and in the course of lugging him down the stairs it had slipped out. We had thrust it back but in our haste had obviously overlooked the fallen envelope. And so here it was, its contents ludicrous proof of the chief superintendent's fondness for playing daddy bears with whip-wielding ostriches. Small wonder that Topping thought he might be immune from the policeman's interest!

In some mirth I rang Ingaza. 'You'll never guess,' I snorted, 'something extraordinary has come to light!'

'Really,' was the dour response, 'glad something amuses you. Personally, I am expecting to be hauled off to jug at any minute. I've been under the blankets all day and have instructed Eric to open the door to no one. My nerves are in pieces and my tango steps adrift. It's a bit much, Primrose!'

'They can't possibly be adrift if you've been in bed,' I retorted, nettled by his lack of interest.

'Oh yes, they can,' he replied. 'I've been trying to recreate the rhythms in my mind and instead of which all I can think of is heaving that bloody thing down *your* stairs.'

'Frightful, isn't it,' I said sympathetically. 'But you know it's funny you should mention the stairs because that is *exactly* where I have just found . . .' And before he could interrupt I rushed on to regale him with my discovery.

When I had finished, there was a long pause. And then he said thoughtfully (and I was glad to hear less sulkily): 'If I were you I should hang on to those snaps. They may not be relevant to your friend any longer, but, who knows, they might just be useful to you one day. It's always as well to be prepared, if you see what I mean.' I did rather.

'So do you think there's going to be trouble?' I enquired anxiously.

'A bloody great brouhaha I should imagine. Personally, I would make myself scarce.'

'How scarce?'

'Very.'

Ingaza's words had unsettled me. He was quite right, of course; there was bound to be a brouhaha of some sort. But I comforted myself with the thought that even if it emerged that Topping had been running the drug syndicate and had murdered Carstairs and Respighi, there was nothing really to link me with the matter or indeed with his demise . . . unless, of course, the schoolmaster had been observed turning into my drive from the lane. Or despite the precaution of gloves we had left other traces in Winchbrooke's car, or hairs were found from Bouncer's coat or a tooth mark even. Or, inspired by his recent conversion, Mr Speedwell was struck by a mystical vision of Nicholas and me racing hell-bent across that rain-swept turf. Such things happen. One reads about them all the time in detective novels.

The more I brooded, the more windy I became. Perhaps Nicholas was right and I really should make myself scarce: a discreet withdrawal until things had died down would be the sensible course. But what about the cat and dog? Kennels? It seemed a little unfair. Perhaps Charles might take them; he was due back shortly and I could enquire when I returned Duster. Still, he would hardly want them for more than a few days and that wouldn't be nearly long enough. It was all very tricky, and in my agitation I telephoned Ingaza again.

'It's the animals, you see,' I lamented, 'there's nowhere to park them, not for any length of time there isn't. It's exceedingly difficult.'

'I shouldn't worry,' he said casually.

'But I *do* worry.'

'But you wouldn't worry if Eric took them, would you? He's very fond of you, just like he was of Francis, and more to the point he dotes on furry animals.'

'He might but you certainly don't,' I said, intrigued all the same.

'Ah, but I shan't be here. Off to Tangier for a few weeks. Given the circumstances it seems a suitable moment.'

'You mean you're bunking off as well?'

'Not bunking off, dear girl, merely taking a well-earned rest. It's the strain of aiding and abetting one's artistic colleagues. Now if you take my advice you'll do the same. Dump the animals with Eric for as long as you

312

like and take off, free as a bird. It'll do you good.'

That Ingaza should consider my welfare was touching and I willingly accepted the offer, wondering wryly how Maurice would cope with the rumbustious Eric.

'Good. Most sensible,' he said breezily. 'And when we both get back, doubtless the dust will have settled and we can swap holiday pics and settle up.'

I had been about to put the receiver down but stayed my hand. 'Er, what do you mean "settle up"?'

'Oh you know, square the old hypotenuse – a little bit of quid pro quo. Things are quite pricey in Tangier, I gather; and Eric's an excellent zoo keeper, deserves recognition. Cheery-bye.' The line went dead.

I sighed. There was one thing you could say for Nicholas Ingaza: at least he was consistent.

CHAPTER FORTY-NINE

My dear Agnes,
Well my dear, all I can say is that life here has been
quite extraordinary of late; in fact so much so that I
am beginning to wonder whether you and Charles
have made the right decision in electing to remain in
Sussex. Kensington might be far safer.

For example, Mr Topping the Latin master I have
been telling you about has been discovered dead on
the brink of Beachy Head – sitting at the wheel of a
car facing out to sea. Whose car? Mr Winchbrooke's,
if you please. Yes, our dear headmaster's! As I wrote
to Mother, three deaths in such a short space takes
some beating. Needless to say, Mother didn't think so
and launched into some interminable ramble about
the Crumbles murders in the twenties . . . Anyway,
the headmaster had delegated Mr Topping to deliver
the school car for its annual service at Caffyns',
Eastbourne's best garage. He normally takes it there

himself but since the little upset on the A27 he has become paranoid about traffic police 'skulking in hedges'. Thus the arrangement was for Mr Topping to drive the car over to Eastbourne and then take the train back to Lewes, leaving the garage to deliver it to the school the following day. Evidently Hubert had decided to take the longer scenic route across the downs, as he had driven right up to the cliff edge – presumably to admire the sea view – and then promptly had a fatal heart attack. He was discovered by some intending suicide who now says he has found God – and is making a pretty penny telling his tale at every opportunity.

It has all been very unfortunate and Mr Winchbrooke is most upset. And when I pointed out that at least his beloved Rover was safe he said that was all very well but Latin masters were like gold dust and what the hell was he supposed to do now. There was no immediate answer to that but I daresay I shall find one.

Meanwhile the town continues to enjoy the novelty of the two murders, and Chief Superintendent MacManus marches about looking stern and grimly purposeful, though whether that signifies actual progress one cannot be sure. Bertha Twigg certainly seems to think so. As I was passing the gym yesterday, she bounded forth with bursting blouse, grabbed my arm and declared, 'Be assured, Mrs Bartlett, murder will out and the law take its course!'

'Well that's nice,' I said, and moved on quickly.

Alas, such optimism is not shared by our uplifting Mr Hutchins who, true to form, repeats incessantly and with great confidence that the law and its minions is an ass, and that with two members of staff already cut off in their prime he is bound to be the third. I gather from Matron that young Harris (he with the dreadful uncle) wants to know if he can open a book on it and does she reckon ten to one on a fair price. Really!

Well, as you may deduce, things have become more than a little trying. Neither have they been helped by Fräulein Hockheimer traipsing along the corridors in floods of tears demanding that a memorial plaque be erected to Topping and sited under the school motto in the chapel. You may not recall the motto but it is semper nobilis – *ever noble. I think she sees some kind of connection between the words and the deceased. Between you and me, pleasant though Mr Topping was, I cannot help feeling the link just a trifle excessive . . . Perhaps there is something in the German psyche which persuades them to take things to unnecessary lengths. Anyway, I know that the headmaster isn't too keen as his only concern seems to be whether such a plaque would be tax deductible.*

I happened to mention the idea to Primrose who remarked caustically that she was surprised Hockheimer hadn't suggested a posthumous Iron Cross, something which in her view would be immeasurably more fitting anyway. Since Primrose has never been well disposed to our German friends – and certainly not to poor Topping – I suspect this was not intended as a compliment!

And talking of Primrose, when I told her the good news that you would be returning within the fortnight and that we must have a little 'Welcome Home' celebration, she said that she was terribly sorry but couldn't possibly attend and would send her apologies via Charles. When I asked her why on earth not, she said she was going away – for quite some time apparently. I was a little surprised as she certainly hadn't mentioned this previously. I assumed it was some painting project but she said oh no, it was to do with her <u>health</u>. 'Your health?' I exclaimed. 'Whatever's wrong with it? You look remarkably hale to me.'

She then explained that it wasn't so much physical as mental, that it was all to do with Dr Carstairs' head and she needed a rest from it. I fear I couldn't help smiling as Primrose has never stuck me as the sensitive type – far from it. And after all it's not as if she had actually seen the gory thing! In fact I was about to say as much but thought better of it. She had that steely look in her eye (you know the one) so I changed the subject and asked instead what she was going to do with the animals and surely they would miss her. 'Oh no,' she assured me airily, 'I have excellent friends who are only too eager to take charge.' Frankly, Agnes, I cannot imagine who they might be, certainly no one we know. It would take a very tough hide indeed to deal with that pair. And when I asked her where she proposed going she looked vague and muttered something about taking the waters at Baden-Baden. Considering her scepticism of all things Gothic I find that rather hard to believe. However, I didn't press the point.

Well at least there is one bright spot amidst the

gloom – *apart from your own imminent return. What a triumph that the planners have at last sanctioned Charles's orangery project at Podmore. You must be so relieved. He, of course, is cock-a-hoop, and despite what poor Mr Topping urged about waiting and then adapting the stable's original structure, talks excitedly not only about bulldozers but, if you please, employing dynamite too. It always amuses me the way our menfolk so love explosions. My own husband was just the same – couldn't keep his hands off matches and lethal fireworks. Anyway, with luck the eruption will have happened before you arrive . . . And then, when dear Primrose elects to return from her salubrious sojourn, we must hold a little inaugural ceremony in honour of the first orange pip. Meanwhile, bon voyage!*

Your good friend,
Emily